CHRYSALIS DRIVE

※

CHRYSALIS DRIVE

A NOVEL

BY

KATHRYN ELI

※

SOWELU PUBLISHING

Printed in the United States of America

First Edition: 2018

Sowelu Publishing

sowelu.publishing@gmail.com

ISBN 978-0-9992647-1-3

To you, my love.

Because of you, and your gifts of love to me, and time, along with your never-ending support, encouragement, and belief in me, you have made my dreams come true, how can I ever thank you enough?

I love you.

And such enormous thank yous to my dearest, deepest, closest family and friends, you know who you are. Not only are you the world to me, you are helpful, intelligent, insightful, and ever patient readers. I thank you for your encouragement and belief in me too. You have kept me going at times when I didn't know if I was able, how can I ever thank you enough?

I love you.

❧ Preface ❧

When he looked into my eyes, I could see every future, and every past, that our souls had ever journeyed together.

"You won't forget me, will you?"

"No… How could I?" I replied, dazed he would ask such a ridiculous question, especially now.

"Because, most people do. They get a glimpse, a taste of understanding, then give it up. They give up at the first sign of Etah. It's too much for them. So they wrap up again in their cocoon of numbness. Back to where they started from, only to try and understand all over again. Such a vicious cycle."

"I'm not most people. You know that."

"I know Lydie, but please… promise me you won't forget."

How could I? I thought to myself.

It had all been so much. There was no way I would ever lose this.

After all, I had found Heaven.

❧ 1 ❧

"Our parents are dead!" I woke with a gasp.

"I know." Ike confirmed.

I pushed my whisper over the lump in my throat, "They're not here."

"I know." He repeated.

My neck had cricked and it hurt to lift my head. It had been months since they passed. Or had it? I couldn't tell the real from what wasn't. My thoughts were muddled, and fuzzy.

I rubbed my eyes. "Where are we?" I felt confused.

"I don't know. Somewhere in the middle of nowhere. On our way to Grandma's. Remember?" My brother prodded.

"Oh. Yeah." I mumbled and propped my head against the window. My eyelids were heavy. I willed them to stay open. That was right. We were moving.

I felt confused, and *afraid*. My thoughts wouldn't line up, stuck in that place between dreams and awake, a confounding meld of disorientation.

Yes, I had felt afraid, but everything was okay I realized.

But our parents are gone! The pain of their lives being ripped from us pierced my heart again. I whimpered.

"Lyd," My brother tried to soothe. "We'll be okay. We'll make it. Besides. We're almost there."

It helped a little. I had dreamt of them. I must have, and… something more? I couldn't pull the memory from the sticky grasp of dream molasses.

I tried to clear my mind. Having nothing there was better than the hurt.

I stared through the bug splattered windshield. Cold, and lonely, the morning exhaled its first breath. The sun snuck over the horizon, as if to whisper hello, but the haze of winter hindered it.

Our parents had died.

I shook my head and tried again not to think about it. Trees surrounded us as we traveled through the Ozarks, the forest lush despite the chill of late winter. The highway stretched before us, a mere crack through the dense growth, leading the way.

We were miles from anywhere familiar, hundreds of miles. Thousands. Me, my twin brother, and our furrier family members. Princeton and Addie, our dogs, and Angelina our cat. We had been on the road for days, our most important belongings, and those of the pets, crammed into the largest U-Haul our dad's old truck could pull.

That's right. Memories infiltrated my daze and my brain worked to make sense of them.

We had left Portland, where Ike and I had grown up, to move into our grandmother's house. It had been left to mom when Grandma passed and now it was ours. The only place that was. Ike had found a logging job near our new town, and we needed to get there fast. Our parents had left us a little money, but not much. Definitely not enough to cover their mortgage, *or* the costs of living in our beautiful city. Yes! The memories crystallized. We're moving. There was no way we would have been able to afford to stay in Portland.

I was thankful we at least had somewhere to go, free and clear, even if it was in Arkansas.

I whimpered again. My dream hadn't been awful, in fact I think that was the problem. My parents were with us, and I awoke from somewhere so beautiful to my life in full tumult. Ike reached over and patted my shoulder.

Our parents were gone and there was no one left but me and him. We were leaving the world as we knew it for one we knew nothing about. I held my breath and resolved to not cry. It stressed Ike out to see me hurt. He's always been my protector, and I wanted to protect him from myself. We were all we had. Off to face the world on our own.

We had just graduated when 'The Dent' happened. 'The Dent' – That's what we called it. That horrific, unbelievable wreck. The accident that stole their lives, and put the dent in ours. They were too young to have their lives taken from them, and from us.

But it had happened, and now we were left on our own. Neither of us had moved from home yet. We had worked little side jobs, drifting in the transition between childhood and what we wanted to be when we grew up. I had hoped to have a year to myself after we graduated. Perhaps I'd find a place of my own while I decided for sure what to study, but that hadn't happened. Now, who knew when it would.

And that left me stuck with my brother.

He wasn't *that* bad. But he could be blunt, and short tempered. *Usually* not with me, but sometimes. A brother is a brother, and sometimes brothers are no cupcake. Luckily, we had always been close. That's the one thing, aside from our birthdays, that we claimed from our twin-ship. Our closeness. Our friendship ran deeper than most anyone else's. Adolescence had tried to fracture our bond, but somehow we held our ground, and then thanks to 'The Dent' the fissures were cemented back in place. We had only had each other to lean on through our mourning. There had been friends, and a few distant relatives. Ike had even had his girlfriend (although in my opinion he should have broken it off with her long ago), but it just wasn't the same. We needed each other.

As a result I think he was mortified at the idea that he could lose me too. Ike's big brother protector role has been on overdrive since. He was only two minutes older, but he always took pride in it. Since 'The Dent' though it had been extreme. I knew it was his way of trying to cope. With his own pain, in his own way, and still feel like he's taking care of me. Heck, it's no cupcake *living* when your parents are both dead, and so unexpectedly.

Thoughts of them reverberated off of every passing moment. Sometimes I would just miss them. That's when it was easy. When I just missed them. When I remembered how caring and thoughtful my mother was, or how much my dad and his crazy antics could make me laugh. I remembered the happiness we shared as a family. But sometimes…

Sometimes their deaths blistered over my soul with no end in sight.

"Hey Lydie," Ike's voice distracted me. "Put a CD in, will ya? Apparently they don't believe in a decent station out here in BFE."

My pale hair tumbled forward as I rummaged through a sea of fast food containers and candy wrappers. I hauled up the CD case and flipped it open. I knew he wanted me to put in one of his old school favorites, like Disturbed or Korn, but I had always been more partial to softer stuff, and right now I thought some Doris Day would hit the spot. She reminded me of my mom, which always cheered me up. A difficult feat as of late. My mom loved the oldies. They reminded her of her mom, and as a result they had always had a special place in both of our hearts, well, just mine now.

"Awe Lyd! You've got to be kidding me!" He whined when "It's Magic" crooned from the speakers. Princeton's oversized nose nuzzled me from the back where the animals were curled in a tangle. I flashed a smile at Ike and he submitted with an *I give up* shrug. Secretly, I don't think he minded my music at all, and only protested to maintain his machismo.

We continued to drive for what felt like ages. With each turn the GPS donged the roads shrunk, heralding ever more rural landscapes. Now and then the forest gave way to plots of land, and farms, or old houses with cats sunning themselves in the early morning, and dogs out to take themselves for a walk.

When Doris was through I found a station that played an eccentric, eclectic, collection of music. "Edelweiss" was the first song we heard and I knew I was hooked, although my brother wasn't impressed. I was captivated with my new station and the whimsical scenery and was startled when dad's GPS donged and ordered "Turn right on Chrysalis Drive, to arrive at your destination."

The bubbly ba-ba ba of Perry Como's "Magic Moments" crackled to life on the radio.

Ike turned the truck and the road dipped. Trees shot up thick and almost blocked the morning rays from following us. A sweeping curve of dirt and gravel embraced a meadow and the woods gave way.

There it was.

I knew it had to be. My mom often spoke of its sunflowered color from her childhood memories.

"Holy crap," Ike breathed. "Is that really ours?"

I grinned a smile of recognition at him.

Before us, saturated the color of toasted gold, stood a grand old farmhouse, dressed in Victorian trims and a wraparound porch. It sat atop a small knoll, with a pond that lapped it's edges below. The sun stroked the water and sent it twinkling onto a worn dock. Beyond a tire swing hung from the beautifully spiraled tree my mother always swore was full of enchantment. The little dirt road continued past it's driveway, then gave way to another meadow before it disappeared around a corner.

I twisted in my seat, taking it all in, until I came full circle to the road that leads us out of our nowhere, back into everyone else's somewhere. I was enchanted.

I loved it!

I could tell Ike did too, his tired and bored grump from days of driving gave way to a lighthearted version of himself.

We followed the driveway to the top of the hill and stopped.

"What time is it?" He asked.

I wriggled my phone from my pocket. "Man, only one bar… um, almost nine." I opened the door, hopped out and stretched my legs.

"Ethan's not supposed to be here for another hour." Ike informed me. Ethan was the attorney from the nearest town, Nepenthe. Which from what we understood, was about 15 minutes away. I liked that. I liked that we would live far enough in the country to feel a blissful secluded-ness, yet be close enough to grab a gallon of milk if the need arose.

Ike opened his door too, "Wanna explore till he gets here?"

"*Oh* yeah." I tingled with excitement. A much nicer sensation than the confusion I had awoke to. "I think we should let the babies out too." I knew they needed to stretch their legs too. The dogs had endured nothing but leash walks and hotel rooms this whole time, and our poor Angelina cat, I was afraid would hold an eternal grudge for displacing her life. If only she could realize she wasn't the only one to have her world turned upside down.

Ike scanned the yard around us. "I don't see why not, this is where they'll be living. Guess they're gonna have to get used to it sooner or later."

"Princeton! Addie! Come on guys!" I beckoned our shaggy golden retriever, and little min pin out of dad's truck. "Angelina," I peered in the back at her, "Would you like to join us too?" She stopped grooming her calico coat just long enough to acknowledge me, then went back to preening. I left the door open for her. She would find her way out in her own sweet time, she always did.

Princeton and Addie bounded through winter trampled grasses and nosed tufts of green that spoke of spring to come. Protection wasn't their strong suit, although Addie did believe she was every bit of a real Doberman. Still, I felt better with them near while I scouted and wandered, peeking into windows and outbuildings, marveling at remnants of days past, and the hidden magic of things forgotten.

Soon I found myself at the little dock. I eased on to its sun warmed boards and let the breeze tousle my hair. I smiled. Arkansas was pleasant in February. We were fortunate to be here, and so far, it felt good, which I thought would have been close to impossible after so much heartache.

A glimmer prodded the corner of my eye. *Probably a bird,* I thought. I turned and looked… Nothing. Just an old potting shed. I leaned back and closed my eyes. The sun traced my face, and for the first time in what felt like forever, I let myself relax.

The soft scent of early blooms mingled with the earthy damp of the pond. Birds merrily greeted the day, and it wasn't hard to imagine they were singing just for me, welcoming me home.

"GRRaw! Raw! Raw-raw raw! "Addie's alarm clipped my ears. Princeton contributed a solid "Rwoof! Rwoof!" Spooked, my eyes instinctively shot back to the shed, nothing out of the ordinary. I sat up to see what the crisis might be.

"Graw raw raw raw GRrrrrrrrrr Rwoof rrrrrwoof!" They bawled together in full charge, making their way down the road. I squinted to see what they were terrorizing. A rapid glint of sunlight shot from spokes- attached to wheels, attached to a bicycle, on it a masculine frame in a pair of cargo shorts and a thin T topped with a rough housed mop of golden hair. He glanced back at our dogs, then stood and pedaled faster.

"Crap! They'll scare our new neighbors." I muttered.

He looked back and smiled at them, then shouted something inaudible. *Was he teasing them?* I didn't appreciate some stranger taunting my dogs.

My heart raced. At first I thought it was simply annoyance, until I noticed the floating sensation in my stomach. He was pleasant to look at, and apparently my body agreed.

"But that doesn't give him the right to aggravate our babies." I huffed and stood. "Princeton! Addie!" I shouted. They didn't pay any attention to me.

He hadn't seen or heard me either, or if he did, he just didn't care.

Irritated with all three of them I realized I was going to have join the chase in order to bring the dogs back home. I felt a twinge of self-consciousness. There was no way after our long trip I was dressed to meet new neighbors, especially the cute kind, even if he had irked me. Parents passing, days on end in a truck, and nothing to sleep on except hotel beds were all together *not* a recipe for being well rested, or beautiful.

Reluctantly I got up from my tranquil seat by the water, and to my surprise I felt rejuvenated. My soul felt lighter, and a bit healed. Maybe it was the excitement of our new haven, or was there more to it? My heart didn't hurt nearly as much as it had the past several months, and I was certain it had nothing to do with the chaotic dogs and whomever they pursued, no matter how good looking he was.

"Ike! The dogs are chasing someone! It might be our neighbor!" I called up the hill. I half hoped he'd be willing to get them so I wouldn't have to deal with any of it.

"Here's the keys!" He shouted back as a silver tangle rained from the sky. Somehow he had maneuvered onto the roof and was hefting old branches off of it, just like dad would have done.

"I don't want to maneuver the trailer just to get the dogs!" I yelled back, but it was no use, debris was already flying from around a different corner and I was sure he couldn't hear me.

I abandoned my rare notion of vanity and jogged to the driveway. I breathed a small prayer that our babies wouldn't run into some *other* dogs, like the kind that may not care for them particularly. "And please don't let them upset our new neighbors," I concluded. I knew our dogs were harmless, but someone else wouldn't know that.

I rounded the bend in the road and there were our two mongrels, trotting merrily towards me. Mr. bike rider was nowhere to be seen. Just more trees and more road, disappearing politely around another bend.

"Bad dogs!" I scolded. They looked shocked that I was upset, they had after all, just triumphed over evil. I could see it all over their faces. "What were you two thinking?!" I added half-heartedly. "Fine." I gave in. "And me, you've triumphed over me. I'm such a sucker for you two." I leaned down and nuzzled Princeton's fur onto my face, then picked Addie up and let her wash my cheek. I followed them as they strutted toward home, my scolding a distant memory.

"We're back!" I shouted at the house, hoping Ike could hear me.

"Everything okay?" He sounded distant and muffled.

"Yeah, they were on their way home by the time I'd reached them."

"The neighbor wasn't pissed?"

"I hope not. Didn't see him." The sound of a car interrupted me. "Maybe that's him now." My cheeks flushed as the sound grew close. To my relief it came from the other direction. A man waved as he passed then turned up our drive. "I think Ethan's here!" I informed my unseen brother.

Something scraped, then fell from somewhere high, thankfully it didn't sound human. Another scrape, clank, then thud. Ike strolled around the corner dusting off his hands, a fresh rip in his jeans.

"Having fun up there?" I raised my eyebrows at him.

"Well, it needs to be done."

"You could have waited till you changed into different clothes." I poked his knee through a new hole. He shrugged, and headed over to greet our visitor, reaching down to stroke Angelina on his way. She had indeed come out from the truck, but hadn't ventured much further than its front tire.

Ike stopped and turned toward me. "Where are the other babies?" He asked.

I hadn't realized they weren't around, which was unusual when there was company. I turned to look for them, and found them sniffing that same old potting shed. Incessantly even.

"Down there." I pointed. "I didn't notice anything peculiar when we were scouting earlier."

"Dogs." My brother dismissed. "Who knows what goes through their minds. They're probably after a squirrel or something."

But it didn't look that way to me. Their inspection was much more severe. *Interesting.* I made a mental note to take another look later.

"Lydie, this is Ethan," My brother introduced me as I joined them.

"Heya Lydie, ready to not be homeless?" Ethan greeted me with a warm smile and a solid handshake.

"Definitely." I grinned. Ethan was a manicured version of handsome, and looked just a bit older than us. *Were all the men attractive here?* I wondered. But around Ethan, I still felt like myself, and didn't mind if I looked haggard from days of travel. I wondered why I had let it concern me when I went to retrieve our dogs.

"Let's go inside then. I'll have you two sign a couple of things, then pass over the keys and you can get settled."

Princeton and Addie made it half way up the hill before they burst into a raucous of recognition that a stranger was near. After their commotion we followed Ethan to the door, where he produced an old key and wiggled it into its iron lock. It took some finessing before he was able to free the door, and then he held it for me to step through first.

I inhaled, and the mustiness of a house left lonely too long tickled my senses. Goose bumps crept across my skin. It was instantly dear to me, as if I had been handed a long-lost treasure.

Ethan fumbled along the wall until he found the light switch. A kitchen flickered to life with '50's style charm that shared space with a great room where comfortable coziness danced and swirled everywhere I looked.

"Shall we sort this out here guys?" Ethan made his way to a scarred table, pulled out a chair, and gestured for me to sit. Ike settled next to me, and Ethan arranged himself across from us, his briefcase waking the fine layer of dust that appeared to cover everything. I didn't mind. It felt as good in here as it had on the dock.

Ethan made the process much easier than I had expected. He explained it well, yet kept it light, and even managed to make us laugh. After we had signed what must have been at least a hundred pages Ike and I waved good bye, and were left officially, legally, and finally all on our own.

❦ 2 ❧

That night I slept on the bed that had once been my mothers. I imagined her there with me, and even though she wasn't, somehow being in her room brought her memories closer. Instead of bringing pain, like they often did since 'The Dent', remembering her here was soothing.

Sleep came to me easy. I hadn't realized how exhausted our travels had made me. A dream slipped over me, strange, and foreign. Mom and dad were here too, visiting. They helped us unpack and settle in. Then in true dream fashion everything morphed. I was whisked to somewhere I had never been. Somewhere otherworldly. I didn't feel scared, in fact it was exquisite and beautiful there, though strange. I thought for a moment that I glimpsed him, the one I had seen earlier. I felt that same familiar tug in my stomach. I heard a voice, but not one I recognized. I couldn't see where it came from. It surrounded me, it filled me. I was alone with it. I couldn't see him anymore, but somehow, I think he might have still been there.

"Don't worry, everything is going to be amazing." The voice breathed.

"Hello? Where are we? Who's there?" I whispered.

"Not just okay, but amazing." It assured me.

Then he appeared in front of me, although I couldn't see him clearly, I knew it was him. I knew we were there together. The voice and those words reached a place deep inside of me. I knew they were meant to be true. I could feel the sincerity in them. I felt serene. I felt safe. Then I drifted back into the nothingness that dances between dreams.

When I woke the voice echoed through my thoughts and it's words lingered, "Don't worry, everything is going to be amazing." It resonated deep, and soulful throughout me. It made me feel hopeful.

And so, I began my day of unpacking, cleaning and settling in, with a cheery disposition, and a whistle on my lips.

Feeling this way reminded me of myself, the myself from before. Perhaps I would find me again, amidst the gloom that had pervaded.

Ike on the other hand, had not rested quite as peacefully. His deep-set eyes were bloodshot, his heavy brows had a cemented crease in their center, and his dark hair, which was always short, tried to spike from an apparent night of tossing and turning.

I always mused at our stark contrast in appearance. Our twinship is obviously not identical, but I figured our looks should have at least a little more in common. I was willowy compared to him. Not that he was chunky, by any means, but he had always been sturdy, healthy. As we went through adolescence he grew to be almost a full foot taller than me. I wasn't short, mind you, but I wasn't tall either. I was just me. Ike had grown into a dark, perhaps even mysterious, sharp-faced young man. Maybe that's where our commonality was, a hint of mysteriousness to both of us. At least my father always said so. My face small and soft, round in its features. The complete opposite of Ike's bold presence. "You're a little elf, aren't you? Full of hidden magic. Only truly special people are born so lucky. And I'm truly lucky to have you as my daughter." My father would tell me and tousle my near white hair. It never grew out of its baby pale, and fell in tumbled waves, too strong to wear straight without a battle, and too soft to twist without a curling iron. Mostly I just let it go. Sometimes I made it up, but those occasions were few and far between. I did, however, indulge my femininity through my wardrobe. I was different from most girls, as in, jeans were *not* my favorite. They might be fine for others, but not me. I was prone to climb trees, or jump creeks on a whim. Sometimes I would break out into a funky little dance when I was certain no one was looking. As a result, I wore sundresses, skirts, leggings, anything that allowed my legs to move. Anything that made me feel delightful.

Ike sat at Grandma's old table with a huff that stated he'd rather be back in bed.

"Oh come on. We're here. The hard part is over, and you have today and tomorrow to unwind before you start your new job." I reminded him.

He only answered with a grunt. One of his morning specialties.

I produced a box of Lucky Charms I had picked up on our way for our first breakfast in our new home and shook it in his face. "I got a surprise for us, my favorite. Okay, okay, yours too. But as we haven't been to town yet, we have to eat it without milk."

"Dry cereal? Bleck!" He made a mock disgusted face, then tapped his chin in thought. "But since it *is* Lucky Charms..." He smiled. "I don't mean to grouch Lyd." He apologized after he swallowed a crunchy mouthful with a gulp of instant coffee. "I kept thinking about my new job, and just couldn't sleep. I really hope it works out. Or I don't know what we'll do."

"Look, don't worry. We still have a little money left from mom and dad, and we don't even have to pay rent. How many people wish they were in our position? Besides, I'll try and find something too."

"Yeah." He said, and stuffed another mouthful of marshmallows and oats into his mouth.

"We're a team, and we still have each other." I said. "We're somewhere new, and while I'm pretty sure it's going to take a while to not think of home every five minutes. I'm excited to be here. It feels good to me." I smiled, hoping it would coax one out of him.

"I know, me too. I just miss mom and dad," he confided, "and I want to be sure you're safe. That nothing happens to you. That's what big brothers are supposed to do." He gave me a weak smile.

"Big brother? Ike, I hate to remind you, *again*, but you're only two minutes older."

"Yeah, but I'm still bigger." He stuck his tongue out at me, then his face sobered again. "I just want it to all work out."

"It will." I threw a marshmallow moon at him hoping it would lighten him up. "I know it will." I declared.

I'm not sure how I felt so sure about it, but I did.

It must have convinced him too. Because he finally smiled for real, then threw a whole handful of cereal back at me.

✎ 3 ✍

The two days before Ike had to start his job rushed by. We frantically unearthed our bare essentials as we unpacked the U-Haul, then headed for Nepenthe to return the trailer and scout out our new town. Country roads led us from Chrysalis Drive through an intimate dance of forests, farmlands, and budding flowers that pirouetted in the breeze. Eventually the pavement yielded to a stone sign, greened with the mosses of time, that welcomed us to Nepenthe.

A small grocer and a few boutiques shepherded us to a cobble stoned square. Trees that whispered in colorful accents of spring lined the streets, and early flora brimmed from pots and graced colorful doorways. Ike parked and we split up to explore on our own. He made a beeline for a local music shop, and I was left to peek into cozy antique stores and novelty shops. Growing up in Portland I had been able to choose between quirky mom and pop shops, or shopping malls with relative ease. That wouldn't be the case here, but I didn't mind. These little shops reminded me of the eclectic gift store I had worked for part time my senior year, then full time the last couple of months- until we moved here. So far the charm of Nepenthe was worth it to me.

I rounded a corner just off of the square and was greeted by a hint of incense. The street had the same flowering trees and the same pots boasting with flowers, but felt bare with only two entries along it. Then I discovered a third, a little red doorway, set in from the brick. An illustrated sign above it read simply, ~Unicorn Books~.

My heart skipped.

I loved books! New, used, any and all. I loved to escape to lands where anything was possible, with characters that felt as real as people I knew, and sometimes more so.

A window laced in painted vines and flowers beckoned me from the door. *What a neat piece of hidden magic,* I thought as I let myself inside.

Bells jangled over my head and it took a moment for my eyes to adjust to the delicate light that fell from windows high on a second-floor balcony. Enchanted harp and nature sounds met in a whimsical melody and I was caressed by a pleasing spice of incense, a soft aroma, unlike the abrasive tang some of the off-beat boutiques in Portland carried.

"Good day to you!" A bubbly woman with a paperback in her lap greeted me. Her smile was bright and natural, and framed perfectly by a red headed pixie cut.

"Hi!" I smiled and glanced around, this place was marvelous.

"Welcome to Unicorn Books. Don't say I've seen you in here before."

"I'm new to the area..." My eye caught movement on the counter. An oblong hump of black stretched, yawned, then rolled to expose a blaze of white toward the ceiling.

"Well then! Welcome to Nepenthe. It's a small town, but friendly. At least I like to think so." Her smile broadened, "You can pet him if you'd like. Mortimer meet..."

"Lydie, Lydie Baker." I reached toward the cat.

She squinted her eyes. "Baker?" she whispered under her breath then addressed Mortimer again. "Mortimer, meet Lydie. Baker." She looked at me again. "He's a friendly gus, I'll warn you though, once you love on him, he'll never let you stop." She chuckled.

I couldn't help but scratch his chin, he approved with a head roll, and another stretch to pull himself closer.

"So what do you make of our town so far?" The lady asked.

"I'm not sure yet. I'm *really* new." I confided. "My brother and I just moved into our Grandma's house a couple of days ago. It's not even here in town, it's out on Chrysalis Drive." I explained and ran my finger over a cluster of amethyst on a nearby shelf.

When she didn't respond I glanced back at her. Her eyes were lost in contemplation. "Ah, Chrysalis Drive." She said, her voice soft, and she focused on me again. "I know the one." Her smile returned. "Your grandmother was a friend of mine. But then, there aren't many who could say she wasn't. She was a regular to these shelves. I'm glad you're here."

"Thank you, I'm glad to be here." I realized it was the truth. I was glad to be in our new little town, in Grandma's beautiful old farm house, even in Unicorn Books.

A rich leather-bound book caught my eye and I lifted it from its place. Mortimer sat his rotund body up in sleepy protest, groomed a paw, then rubbed against my arm, hoping I might lavish more affection on him. I obliged with one hand, and traced the fine embroidery and gems that embellished the book's cover. I peeked in the cover to find the price, certain it must cost a small fortune, but there wasn't one listed. I flipped it over, still nothing. *If you have to ask you can't afford it*, I told myself. I flipped a couple pages more. Not only no price, but no writing, I gently fanned through the rest. There was no writing anywhere.

"I suppose that would make Kara your mother then? I don't think Jack ever had children, am I right?" Her question caught me off guard, but warmed me to hear my mother's name, and my uncles, although I hadn't met him. He had passed before we were born.

"That's right, did you know her too?" I looked up from the journal and noticed more curios and crystals tucked amidst the books throughout the shop.

"Of course I did." Memories crinkled the corners of her eyes. "Your mother and I were kindred spirits once upon a time. It was hard to find one of us without the other when we were growing up."

Recognition pawed at me. My mother had talked about her childhood friend, her most bosom buddy, many, many times. She always had a mischievous glint in her eye as she regaled their adventures. "Are you Ada?" I asked.

"The one and only!"

"I've heard so much about you!" I exclaimed. I thought I could feel her then, my mother, stronger than I had since she had been gone. She was here, even if only in our memories, and in our enthusiastic chatter.

I had no idea how long we had been wrapped up in our conversations, but by the time I browsed a few shelves, and made my way back to the counter the windows had tinted with dusk. I was sure Ike was waiting, wondering where I had disappeared to.

"I've found a few things." I unloaded my arms in front of Ada: a novel that would be perfect to read on Grandma's dock, a book mark made of pressed flowers, a crystal and two gemstones that came with cards of their special meanings, and a jeweled trinket box. "I didn't see a price on this..." I laid the journal on top of my collection.

"It's yours." Ada stated as she rang up the other items.

"Ada, that's too much."

"It's not. Besides, it's been sitting on that shelf waiting for the right person. You're obviously it. You're the only one it's convinced to bring it to the counter."

I bit my lip and traced the jewels on it. They were real stones, not pieces of plastic, or glass.

"But, Ada," I protested.

"No buts. Consider it a gift from both your mother and me. She would have liked you to have it. I know. And I would like you to too, but *only* if you reserve it for your most sacred dreams and wishes. It's too pretty for anything less. Wouldn't you agree?"

Speechless I bobbed my head up and down.

I paid for the rest of my treasures, hugged and thanked Ada, then turned to leave. I had one foot outside when I heard Ada again. "Lydie," she motioned me back to her, "would you perhaps like to come back and work for me?

"Really?" I questioned.

"Yes, really. I'm usually the only one here, Renea comes on Saturdays and Sundays, but if you wouldn't mind, I could really use some extra time for the business side of things. It piles up while I run the front. I usually end up spending my days off in here playing catch up." She raised her eyebrows and sighed. "I've been meaning to hire someone for ages, and just haven't had the chance. Besides, you bring Kara close again. And I like you."

"Oh, Ada! I would love to!" It was difficult to not shout it. This day had turned out far better than I had expected.

"Unfortunately I'll only be able to give you part time, but after you get settled we can see about getting you more. Could you come in Thursday at about nine? I'll bring Renea in so you can meet her, and that will free me to show you the ropes."

I told her that it sounded perfect and after another hug, and more romancing from Mortimer, I left, my heart light as air.

Ike was leaned against the front of the truck when I entered the square. He was bent over something, strumming notes to the best his novice ability.

"Lydie! Check it out!" He called and held up a guitar. He looked happy, and if his grin wasn't enough to prove it, it rang in his voice. He and dad had wanted to learn guitar for so long. A large white book was splayed on the hood behind him. "Teach Yourself to Play" it read, with manly fingers embracing an electric guitar. Dad and Ike had scheduled lessons together for this coming summer, that was before 'The Dent' of course.

"I swear Lydie," he said in a hush when I got close, "it felt like dad was there, pointing over my shoulder, saying, 'Get us that one.' Do you think I'm going crazy?"

"Only if I am too." I whispered. "You'll never believe what happened to me." I told him I thought I had felt mom with me too, and filled him in on the bookshop, Ada, and my new job. That not only was Ada the friend mom had always told us stories about, but that she said that I brought mom close to her too. "I really do think they were here, visiting with us today. Maybe we're crazy. Maybe we're not. But it felt good." I concluded.

"Yeah, it felt really good to me too." He agreed, and our lashes were laced with a silent tear as we climbed into the truck.

There was one last stop for us to make on our way out of town, to a used car dealer that Ethan had recommended. We were able to find an old powder blue Volkswagen Rabbit. It was beat up with a menagerie of scratches and dents, but I didn't mind and quickly dubbed it my Baby Blue. I finally had my very own car, and I was thankful, even if I wasn't very good at driving it. I had only driven a manual a couple of times, and that was in an empty parking lot with my friend Megan's car.

Our parents had wanted to get each of us a car for graduation, one more thing they were never able to do. To be honest their gifts wouldn't have been in much better shape than the Rabbit. I thought about my new Baby Blue and imagined it as another gift from them, one of many today. I smiled.

Without a doubt they were doing all they could, from where ever they were, to help us settle in.

❧ 4 ❧

Acceleration sporadic, and gears grinding I followed Ike home. By the time we turned onto Chrysalis Drive I started to get the hang of it.

Confident, I followed the sloping bend, shifting into third- just because I knew how- the car groaned in protest. It was a bit slow for third, but I was still proud of myself. I slid Baby Blue back to second and she purred again. I smiled. Then slammed on the brakes as something disappeared into the trees.

A figure.

Like one on two feet.

It's dark shadow slunk from view. I squinted into the smudge of tree line but saw nothing except shrubs and low branches. I half wondered if it had been the cutie our dogs had chased. Another part of me worried I might be seeing things, and somewhere deeper, I worried it *might* be someone, dark and shadowy, someone that wanted to vanish into the tree line in order to hide, and watch.

But I couldn't let myself entertain that idea. I had to be strong, especially now that we lived in the country. This was no place for little girl fears. I shook my head and was glad when I turned up our driveway. Glad to be back home, glad to be back near my brother and the babies.

Ike had let himself in and turned on the porch lights for me. Their glow was a warm contrast to the settling dusk. *It was probably the last of the daylight playing tricks on me.* I rationalized away my worry.

"See anyone on our street when you got home?" I asked and dropped my bag of goodies onto the couch.

"Nope." A hint of concern flashed across his face. "Why?"

"No reason," I shrugged, "thought I saw someone from the corner of my eye, but it was probably shadows messing with me." I tried to sound casual.

"You and your imagination." His face relaxed. "Nah, didn't see anything. Besides Ethan *did* say we have neighbors further down the way."

Neighbors. Yeah. It was probably one of them. If not the cutie, then perhaps a kid playing in the forest. If I even saw anyone, I really began to doubt that I had.

Ike didn't give me any more time to think about it. He had a hammer and was ready to hang our favorite pictures from home. I didn't protest. It was a welcome distraction and it would be nice to have pictures up of happy memories. I coaxed him to let me help so they were hung in a less haphazard way. Then we scrubbed and dusted some of Grandma's stuff that we wanted to keep, and unpacked some more of our own belongings. Princeton and Addie settled into a nap, and Angelina made an appearance, and not even just for food. The farmhouse was quickly becoming a livable home, and it finally felt like an end to the upheaval of our lives was within reach.

Monday came and Ike left for his new job.

That's when I saw him.
Not the blond him.
A different him.

He stood, looking at our bay window. Looking at *me* standing in it. He was next to the old potting shed on the other side of the pond. There he was, this strange man, who wasn't supposed to be there, but was.

I froze. What was I supposed to do?? I didn't know anyone to call, except maybe Ada, or Ethan. Did I *need* to call anyone? What if he was one of the neighbors from further out in our nowhere?

He wore a stocking cap with hair that poked from places worn too thin. His beard was the color of dirty snow, and his clothes, weighted with stains, were ragged and crumpled, exhausted from laboring harder than an article of clothing should ever have to.

Perhaps he wasn't a neighbor? I thought. What if he was some unfortunate hobo rummaging around in my sanctuary? *WHAT if he was the man from the trees?*

A crooked smile spread across his face, as if he could hear my thoughts. He turned to the shed, slowly looked over his shoulder, smiled again, this one bigger, and toothless, then opened the door, and disappeared inside.

This *definitely* wasn't right.

I watched for him to come back out.

But he didn't.

So I waited. I waited a good twenty minutes, although it felt like much, *much* longer, but there was still no sign of him. I wondered if I should confront him, investigate why this intruder was in our potting shed, but the courage to leave the house eluded me. Instead I pulled a chair to the window, grabbed my book, and waited some more.

An hour passed and I managed to read only a page or two and I still hadn't seen any sign of the man.

I wondered again if I was seeing things.

"That's it. I'll just have to see for myself." I muttered in an attempt to shoo away my apprehension. "He's just an old man anyway." I added. It worked, a smidge, but enough to get me out of my chair. Princeton and Addie padded along beside me, oblivious to my dread.

Outside our world appeared peaceful and glorious under the early spring sun. I crept down our little hill, a couple of frogs splashed in retreat as I skirted the pond, and then I was there. I peeked in the window.

Nothing.

Not one thing different than when I had peered inside when we had first arrived. Nor was there anyone that I could see.

I remembered that first day, how I thought I had seen something from the corner of my eye. I remembered Princeton and Addie's preoccupation with this little building. They were at it again, their fervent sniffing returning over and over again to the door.

Maybe I'm not seeing things, I snatched the door open to satisfy my itchy curiosity and the sanctity of my sanity. Still, I didn't see anyone. I stuck my head in and stepped inside.

Nothing.

I dropped my shoulders and rolled the tension from my neck. If there had been a man in our shed I suppose it hadn't been the wisest idea for me to investigate alone. Then worry that I really might be losing it seeped through my spine. I couldn't figure it out. It started to drive me crazy. There *must have* been someone. The dogs circled in their doggie way, noses suctioned to the ground as they paced. I ducked to search under the counter, pushing aside old pots, and bags of mulch and top soil. There was nowhere anyone could be hidden. Or anywhere for them to have snuck out.

I leaned against the wall and slid to the floor. "Everything must be taking a toll on me." I sighed and watched the dogs circle. "Whatever it is, it has you guys fooled too, doesn't it?" I reached to stroke Princeton's soft fur and his coat lifted, full of static, to meet my fingers. A brilliant flicker snapped the air between us, startling us both. He nuzzled my face and sniffed my ear. I patted and rubbed him.

His hair grew fluffier as it filled with more static. I let my head drop back to the wall, and my hands fell to the floor. The floor was warm, much too warm, no matter how high the sun was outside. Addie, as if confirming my observation raised a front paw, then switched it to lift a back one. Princeton did too. I stared at the floor boards to try and find some clue, again to no avail. The warmth radiated through my shoes.

"Princeton, Addie! Let's go!" I leapt for the door and the dogs darted out around me.

Nothing outside had changed. Everything looked the same. Felt the same. No static. No unexplained sear. I dropped to my hands and knees and inspected beneath the shed but it rested flush against the ground with nothing but bluegrass, dandelions, and happy grasshoppers chomping away around it. Still, I was spooked. Addie and Princeton on the other hand were unconcerned and chased a field mouse that promised more entertainment. I opened the door to the shed again and touched the floor. It was an ordinary blasé, barely cooler than room temperature. I stepped in and laid both of my hands flat on the floor. Completely normal. Significantly creeped out, I sprinted back to the house. Princeton and Addie raced along side of me, convinced I was continuing the game of chase that the mouse had started.

Back in the safety of Grandma's house I locked the door behind us. To look at the dogs you wouldn't think anything had been amiss. Even Angelina sat placidly in the window, grooming her precious fur coat.

I couldn't think of anything else I could do.

For the rest of the day, the image of the man haunted me along with the eeriness of the floor, and static. Even *after* Ike arrived home, they were predominant thoughts lodged in the forefront of my mind.

I debated on whether or not I should tell my brother. I knew he'd be concerned. He already hated to leave me home alone, and besides, it was all so bizarre, and I didn't have any proof.

Yes, he would worry, not only for my safety, but if I might be having a breakdown of some sort. *Was I?* I decided not to tell him yet. *If things got worse, or continue,* I told myself, *then I will tell him.* But maybe, *hopefully*, it was just my imagination.

With reluctance I checked the shed the next morning, again that afternoon and then once more the following morning. Nothing but a plain old potting shed. The next couple of days passed with no events to be had, in fact, everything was ordinary enough I was almost able to put the whole thing out of my mind. Almost.

I kept myself occupied by dusting and cleaning more of Grandmas house, and luxuriated in unpacking some of our not so essential belongings. They made everything feel safer and even more like home. Like somewhere I belonged.

In the evenings Ike clomped through the door, exhausted and dirty, but happy. He liked the crew he worked with so far, and the job itself. "Lyd! Guess what!" He charged in one night.

"What's that?" I pulled my head from Grandmas hearth and dusted ash from my hands. I was determined to have a fire to ward off the early spring chill.

"My boss said I'm ready to tag along on a work trip soon!" He exclaimed and wriggled out of his canvas work coat.

Trip? I'd be left alone. The image of the man roared in my psyche. I gulped and forced a smile. "That's great Ike." He was too excited to notice my apprehension. *Big girl time Lyd.* I coached myself. *It was your imagination. It must have been, nothing else makes sense. You've been under so much stress. That's all, you've checked the shed, over and over. Your mind was playing tricks on you.* I tried to soothe myself. Then came thoughts of the floor, and the static. I chalked them up to my imagination as well. *Too many changes, too quickly.* I reminded myself. *It's probably over exhaustion.* It helped to calm me.

I busied myself with the fire while Ike changed from his logging gear. Satisfied the meager flames were beginning to catch, I nestled onto the couch and persuaded Princeton and Addie to snuggle with me. Determined not to think about it anymore, I covered us with one of Grandma's chenille throws, then dove into my novel for a welcomed distraction. A couple of pages in and Angelina joined us. I ran my hand along her back, inhaled, and sighed. *Truly, I must have imagined it all.* I reassured myself and this time I felt certain about my rationalization. Rest and relaxation were in order, and where could be a better place to heal? Grandma's house was growing more and more comfortable each day. It felt as if we had been entrusted with our very own safe haven. Our own paradise.

"We'll be fine won't we guys?" I asked the babies. Angelina chirped a mew and Addie cocked her head. Princeton didn't bother to acknowledge me. "Yeah. We'll be fine. Even when brother has to leave for a few days. We'll be just fine." Addie laid her head back down, and Angelina circled until she found a spot to settle. Content, I let my imagination be carried away by my book.

But somewhere, in the furthest reaches of my mind, back where the boogey man still lives and noises in the night still whisper in voices, back where things that truly frighten, scratch and tap-waiting, just waiting- for a chance to sneak from the door they've been shut behind, the man grinned and raised a withered hand, and joined their incessant rapping.

ॐ 5 ॐ

Morning light bounced through my window and brought with it anticipation for my first day at work. It felt good to think of it as work. I had always longed to have a job somewhere I adored and I hoped Unicorn Books just might be that place. Waking up came easy and I dressed quickly, with no time for worry or wondering. I skipped every other step down the stairs to the kitchen and met up with Ike.

"I made a gourmet breakfast for you." My brother shoulder-pointed toward the toaster where some pop tarts waited.

"Awe gees Ike, what would I do without you?" I grabbed a paper towel and scooped them up.

"Probably starve." He gulped the last of his coffee.

"Yeah, probably." I agreed and chuckled at him. Ike bent to tell Addie goodbye while Princeton nosed my pastries. "I'm sorry boy," I patted his head with my free hand. "I don't have time to share, or you know I would." He sat and pouted. "We'll be

home again soon guys. Promise." They followed us
with sad eyes to the door, then I locked them safely
inside. I got into my baby blue then followed my
brother down our little road until we split into
different directions once we reached the
countryside.

I couldn't help but smile as I found a place to
park, and when the shop bells announced my
arrival Ada greeted me, her face full of smile. A jet
black, bob haired girl sat behind the counter, and
raised her eyes and one eyebrow. Her lips twitched
in what I hoped was an attempt at a smile, but may
have been a sneer, and with one hand she flipped
through a large coffee-table picture book while the
other slowly stroked Mortimer. Ada sidestepped
around her, then collected me in a hug larger than
her stature should have been capable of.

"Lydie! Good to see you!" She exclaimed and
pressed the air out of me. "This is Renea." She
swung her arm toward the raven-haired girl.

Renea lifted her chin and peered down her nose
at me. "Hey."

"Nice to meet you." I held my hand toward her.
I got the impression she wasn't happy I was there,
but I wasn't going to let petty foolishness stop me
from being polite. She took it, her fingers barely
grasping mine. They were dry, and cold. "I'm
happy to be here." I told them both. "I can't wait to
get started."

Renea shrugged then looked down at the book
again. I glanced at it and saw intricate artwork
covering the pages, of what exactly I couldn't be
sure. I didn't want to stare and was relieved when

Ada touched my back to usher me to the rear of the store.

There was more to Unicorn Books than I had realized. Much, *much* more. What I had assumed was the back wall of the shop was in fact not at all. It was only a wall, and tucked in the very left corner was a beautiful arch.

"Only the passionate and creative make it past this more…" Ada paused, searching for the word she wanted to use, "*commercial* room," she explained, "and are therefore offered a living, *breathing* space for their imaginations to frolic." She ducked into the entrance and pulled me through a small passage covered in brightly colored glass stones. When we stepped through to the other side she spread her arms wide. "*This* is the Unicorn room." Her smile beamed. "Because, like the Unicorn, only true believers will find the magic." Her eyes twinkled as she motioned for me to follow.

Living and breathing was right. A labyrinth of treasures welcomed us with twists and turns. Fanciful cages hung low from the ceiling and held little birds, their playful twitter harmonizing with the babble of a waterfall fountain. Nearby plants flourished and were tucked amongst books and graced the tops of shelves where skylights of inspiring colors stroked them with dreamy light.

I stumbled behind Ada admiring it all, too fascinated to pay attention to our direction. She didn't seem to mind, and held my fingers to lead the way. Finally we reached another entrance. Not quite as eloquent as the archway, but still pretty with a planked door that opened to the office.

Ada nestled into a velvet chair. "Go on, have a seat." She waved to a matching one in front of her comfortably cluttered desk.

"Thank you." My cheeks warmed as I realized I had been standing, mouth slack in awe. I loved *everything* about this store, to include behind the scenes. Even here recesses were carved into the walls that cradled trinkets and fragrant candles.

"Just need to fill out some paperwork and go over a couple of things." She nodded toward a pen embellished with a whimsical plume.

"It's real?" I couldn't help but question.

"It is, and we sell them." She leaned over the desk and whispered, "This place *is* magic you know." She grinned like a little girl divulging a secret, then passed me some papers.

I raised my eyebrows. "I'm starting to believe it!" I exhaled, Ada and her shop gave me the same feeling of belonging that Grandma's house did. Thoughts of the shed flitted through my mind. *Magic, hmph.* I smiled back at Ada. "Even Grandma's house, and Nepenthe, I think they're magic too." *Magic, or imagination,* I thought. As long as I didn't let it scare me, I didn't mind either.

Ada nodded. "Well, if you're wise enough to figure that out already, then you must be meant to be here." She passed me some forms and wooshed out regulations while I filled out the pages. Then she slowed to reveal more of her adventures with mom. "I'm so excited you'll be working with us. I truly think you'll bring a breath of fresh air to Unicorn Books." She concluded.

I felt daunted. *Me?* This place was amazing. Astounding even. Her excitement felt unwarranted, especially before she had seen me work.

I knew it was because I reminded her of mom, and brought memories of her close again.

Hopefully being myself would be enough.

"Alright sugar, I think that's it." Ada said as I signed the last form. "Why don't you go on out front, and tell Renea to take the rest of the day off. I'd like to train you myself and get to know you better. And you can get to know us, me and Mortimer, the shop too! Feel free to look around and get yourself comfy and familiarized. I'll be out to show you the specifics in a few."

"Okay," I replied, hearing my own hesitation.

"Now don't worry, I'll be right there if any customers come in. I don't expect you to know *everything* on your own, although a lot of working here will probably be pretty self-explanatory. You're a bright girl," she winked at me, "I can tell. *And* as you're Kara's daughter, I'm sure I'm right." She pointed to the corner behind me. "You can tuck your jacket in there."

Larger holes were carved into the wall, each with a pretty little hand painted sign above. One read- Ada Sinclair, another- Renea Craig, and the last- *Lydie Baker*. Warmth spread goose bumps over my arms. Ada's was full of a beaded purse and a silk scarf, Renea's held only a half-eaten bag of chips, and mine was empty, or so I thought until my jacket scraped against something. I ducked to peer inside, and found a little box with a gold bow.

"Well, go on, open it." Ada said with a knowing smile.

"Oh Ada, you didn't have to." I shook my head at her generosity. "You've already done so much."

"I wanted to. Besides I think you'll like it."

I tugged the end of the ribbon and lifted the lid to find a silver chain glitter at me with a small oval locket. I gently opened it to a picture of two young girls- hair haphazardly roughhoused and large smiles plastered across their faces. Their arms were slung over each other's shoulders. Across from the photo read an inscription, '*To the most bestestest best friend EVER, love from Kara.*'

Tears filled my eyes and blurred the words.

"Thank you, Ada." My throat was tight as I worked to push the words out. "Thank you so much- for everything."

Silent tears escaped down her cheeks as well. She didn't say anything, or couldn't, and only reached her arms toward me. I squeezed her close. It felt natural to be near her, and I realized regardless of how well we would work with one another, the truth was, we both brought mom back for one another.

It was difficult to make it back through the Unicorn room. I swiped at my eyes. There was so much to take in. I was amazed at how, though I missed my mom, I felt happy. But that wasn't all that made the trip difficult, all of the books and treasures were so tempting. Hidden cozy nooks begged for me to explore them. Somehow, I managed not to get side tracked. *There will be plenty of time to get acquainted with all of it,* I reminded myself.

Renea was zoned-out in her own little world when I neared the front.

"Hi." I startled her back to reality. "Ada said you can take off for the day."

"Thank God." She huffed.

I joined her behind the counter. "What was that you were looking at earlier?" I asked in an attempt to make small talk. "It seemed neat. I might like to take a peek." I added when she only gave me a blank stare.

"The Tale of How." She dismissed.

"Guess I'll see you tomorrow?" I asked.

She rummaged under the counter and fished out a backpack. When she stood she looked straight at me, her expression bored and vacant. "Look, just cause we're going to work together doesn't mean we're going to be friends." She swung her bag over her shoulder, turned, careful not to touch me in the small space, and made her way to the door. She called bye to Ada and left, jarring the bells in her wake.

❦ 6 ❧

I sat, stunned.

Great.

Just *freaking* great. Everything about the shop had seemed too good to be true, and now I knew it wasn't. Not if I was going to have to work with *her*. "What a… *bitch!*" I muttered under my breath. Cussing wasn't something I did often, but she called for it. How rude! She'd certainly come across as a bitch, and I don't like to prejudge people either. But her? I didn't care.

The bells over the door tinkled again, signaling a customer, or worse, Renea again. I sent up a silent wish to not be forced to work with her often, made myself smile and lifted my head.

It was him!

Not the older him. Not the scary one that disappeared before my eyes, but the younger one that disappeared thanks to my dogs. The sun stroked his hair with iridescence as he stepped inside, lending to an angelic appearance. He was

even more beautiful in front of me than when he
had been pedaling off in the morning light.

My breath hitched and I couldn't stop looking.
My eyes wouldn't be moved no matter how hard I
tried. My chest came alive as my heart rate doubled.
After a moment or two, or perhaps an eternity, I
blinked and was able to look at the counter. *I wish I
had the Tale of How out now, I wish I had any reason to
look anywhere, other than at him.* I glanced up again.
He was looking directly at me, walking straight
towards me, and smiling. A big, broad, winning
smile.

"Hey there! You must be my new neighbor!"

"Iyuh, uuhhh…" *Come on get a grip,* I told
myself. "Hi, yeah, I think I saw you the other day,
my dogs tried to eat you alive." Man I felt awkward.

"Nah. We were just havin' a good time. They
followed me all the way to the door, so I gave them
a treat. They seemed to think I was okay after that."

"You didn't have to do that! I'm sorry they
bothered you…"

"Really, it's no problem." He assured me.
"Heck, I'm sure it won't be long before you'll meet
Jake. He usually wanders where ever he wants.
Can't miss him, a big ole red hound. He's mom and
dad's dog, but he really thinks he and I belong
together. Thankfully I live with them so he doesn't
have to know any better." He smiled and my lips
reciprocated on their own accord. "I'm Ken, by the
way, but everyone calls me Craig."

Craig- it nagged at me, then clicked into place.
No. No, no no. Not Craig. Renea's little hand
painted sign pinched my memory.

"I was hoping my sister was still here." He confirmed my suspicion. "Mom wanted me to tell her she's making her favorite tonight, homemade soup." An idea lifted his brows, "In fact, I'm sure mom would love it if you came too, if you'd like. I'd like you to." He bit his lip at his own forwardness. "And you could bring your brother." He amended.

How on earth did he know so much about us already? *Oh, probably Ada,* it occurred to me, *welcome to your small town Lydie.*

"Wow, uh- yeah, that's good, I mean that would be good. That'd be great. I'll talk to Ike."

"I assume Ike is your brother? I don't suppose you have a name?" One side of his lips climbed higher than the other, revealing an enticing dimple.

"Oh," My voice came out raspy, I swallowed to clear my throat. "I'm Lydie." A moment too late I offered my hand and prayed he wouldn't notice the lace of moisture over my palm.

Our eyes locked.

"Good to meet ya, Lydie." His hand engulfed mine with a confidant ease that made me feel protected. My shoulders relaxed. His face was sure, like his grip, and his eyes seemed kind. My mind crowded with a life's worth of daydreams, possibilities, and what-ifs. He made it easy to wonder.

Then I realized he looked a little old to still live with his parents.

My musings deflated.

Now if only I could stop trying to embarrass myself.

Ada's cheerful voice rang out as she came to my rescue. "Ken Doll! Ya just missed her."

"And *that's* why I prefer Craig." He flashed a smirk and held my hand just a moment too long before he stepped back. "Ada!" He smiled as she made her way to the front of the store. "I hope you're not taking it too easy on my new neighbor." He winked at me.

"Oh, you know me, cracking the whip like always." She replied.

"Wouldn't expect anything less." He had an easy way about him and seemed friendly. Even if his sister wasn't.

A brick dropped in my gut as I realized Renea must be my neighbor too.

Mortimer, thankfully, made himself known and let me busy myself with loving him. I stroked his black silk, and afforded a peek at Ken, Craig, whichever it was. If nothing else he was scrumptious to look at.

"Really, Ada's a big pushover." He informed me, then draped an arm over Ada's shoulder. His tall self made her appear even shorter. "I *know* you let my sister get away with too much. Like getting off early. I thought she was off at five?" He chided her. "Wonder if she's home yet."

"She left right before you came in, I don't think she could have made it out to Chrysalis Drive." I offered.

"Oh, she lives here in town." Ada said. My stomach lightened in response. She wrapped an arm around Craig's waist. "I'm surprised you didn't run into her."

"This *is* Renea we're talking about, she probably made a bee-line straight to that dungeon of hers."

"Now Kenny, that's not nice." Ada scolded.

"It's not my fault she locks herself away in self-made misery."

Maybe it's not me she has a problem with, I wondered to myself, *maybe she just has a problem with life in general.*

"You know it's not easy for her. She was *so* close to your Pa." Ada squeezed his middle.

"Yeah, but she could at least help. Pitch in every once in a while, you know? It wasn't *her* in the accident." His eyes widened and he snapped his mouth shut. "Shit…" He breathed. "Lydie, I'm sorry." Sympathy softened his voice.

"It's okay." I tried to shake the unexpected pain in my chest. "Did your father pass too?" What if he was able to understand? My eyes searched his.

"Not pass… but… man… well… look, come tonight and you can meet them. They were in an accident, 'bout ten years ago. Man, I'm sorry. I didn't mean… I wasn't thinking. I didn't mean to be insensitive." He took a deep breath. Ada leaned her head against his shoulder. "Both of our parents are still alive. Mom faired the best, she's in a wheel chair, but Pop, well, he's- his mind's just not the same. His head was hit pretty hard. Out cold for weeks."

"Ken doll's such a dear. He's stayed with them ever since. He helped his mamma finish raising Renea. Best they could that is. Now Renea's wantin' to break outa this town fast as she can. All the more reason I'll be needin' you darlin'." She nodded a smile to me.

Mortimer rolled out from underneath my hand, sauntered to the edge of the counter and reached a fluffy paw toward Craig, but he was staring at the ground, his thoughts somewhere inside of himself.

"Renea was a daddy's girl." His eyes shifted back to me. "Those two were inseparable. After the accident he barely recognized her. Grief's been eating away at her since. Mild at first. We were surprised how well she was handling it. But as a teenager she harnessed that pain she had tucked away and has clung to it as the root of all the unjust she's ever had to face." His arm slid from Ada and he gave in to Mortimer's plea with a tickle under the chin. "She rented her own apartment the second she turned eighteen and she's planning to move to New York as soon as she saves enough. Mom likes to make sure she eats at home as often as possible. She's worried she'll wither away on a diet of Cheetos and Ramen." This got a chuckle from Ada, and the somber mood lifted as quickly as it had come.

My heart softened for Renea, and for Craig. Okay, maybe the fact that he lived with his parents was actually endearing. Really endearing.

The bells tinkled again, and in walked a squat man with slicked back hair the shade of ink, and a slice of mustache to match.

"Joseph Perelli! Good to see ya." Ada straitened and clasped her hands in front of her.

"Aeya Ada. Craig." He nodded then paused when he saw me behind the counter. "Hey." He squinted and pointed at me. "You must be da new goil."

Geesh were we really such news? He sounded like he was new himself, and straight out of Brooklyn.

"That's me, Lydie." I reached my hand toward Mr. Perelli, not so awkward this time. I snuck a glance under my lashes at Craig.

He nodded to Joseph with a simple, "Heya Joe."

"Lydie. Good to see yas in here. Heard lossa good things 'bout you." He winked at Ada. Her smile broadened and a hint of pink garnished her cheeks. Joe shook my hand. "Good strong shake yous got's there. She's a keeper Ada."

"I think so." She replied.

"I hope I will be."

"You will." Craig said, his voice low, meant only for me. I slipped my eyes back to him, he was watching, that dimple making an appearance again. Then he turned, and gave Mortimer one last fluff. "Alright Ada, I've got to track down that sister of mine."

"See you soon sugar."

"Tonight then, Lydie? Come 'round six?" Craig asked.

"Yeauh-esh, uh- sounds, good- I mean." Darn awkwardness. He didn't seem to notice.

"See ya Joe!" Craig made his way to the door.

"How will I know which house is yours?" I called, still awkward as ever.

"Easy," he answered over his shoulder, "it's the only other one down our road."

The bells jangled behind him, then a car door thumped outside, followed by an engine purring to life.

Maybe Craig was a little more responsible than I had given him credit for. Yeah, he seemed like he might just be an alright guy.

Butterflies tickled in my stomach.

"Guess I have plans-" I turned and stopped mid-sentence. I had been left. Ada and Joe had disappeared. All that was left was a whisper of thick accent and a giggle a shelf or two over.

I smiled, plopped onto my seat, and succumbed to Mortimer's vie for more attention. I hummed with the whimsical melody that carried throughout the shop. I felt giddy. The past week had been the best I had felt since 'The Dent'.

I couldn't wait to tell Ike we had plans for dinner. He'd have to change quickly for us to make it in time.

Thoughts of Craig lured me into my imagination. I pictured us on the dock, the sun toying with his hair while that dimple of his flashed. *Lydie*, my thoughts scolded, *you're getting ahead of yourself. He probably has someone anyway. As wonderful as he seems to be? He must. But I can dream, that's what day dreams are for.*

I wondered what Ike might think of Craig. I didn't know what his impression would be. Heck I didn't even know how *I* felt about him, they were daydreams, that's all. I drifted back to them. Thoughts of Craig were exciting. *Maybe he and I could go on a date. Maybe I could have* him *over for dinner.* That was an enticing idea, and intimidating. Intimidating because I didn't know what I would do with my brother. My brother, ever the protector. Always ready to run defense if my date ever turned out to be a creep, whether I agreed or not. Ever the protector. Always ready to come to my rescue.

Rescue- the tapping in the back of my subconscious burst into a raucous- then there *he* was.

The him that had disappeared before my eyes. My throat tightened.

If the Craig family was the only other on our road, who had disappeared inside the shed? Who had vanished into the tree line? *Maybe it had been his father?* I worked to soothe the din in the back of my mind. This made sense and seemed to help.

❧ 7 ❧

"Lydie!" Ike flung the door open that evening. He seemed as excited as I felt. He marched straight toward the back of the house, still shouting for me. "Lydie!"

"Ike! You walked right by me!"

"Oh! Good." He bounced back into the room with a smile plastered on his face.

"Well?" I coaxed. "What is it?" He flopped next to me on the couch in a rush and nearly landed on the floor.

"I get to go to back to Oregon!" As quickly as he had sat, he was up again. "I can't wait to tell Brit!" He chucked his jacket onto to the back of Grandma's old rocker.

"Oh! That's… great." I stuttered. I was genuinely happy for him- even though I had never been fond of her, the girlfriend he had left when we moved. She was spoiled and ungrateful. Yet my brother always went to such lengths to try and be the best boyfriend he could be. She just never gave much in return. I think she cared about him, to the best of her ability, I just don't think she was very able.

"Can you believe it Lyd?!" He thumped my shoulder as he paced by.

"Wow, that's um, great Ike." I repeated, then paused. I wasn't sure Brit would be as excited as he was. I shook my head and gave her the benefit of the doubt. "I'm sure she'll be thrilled, you obviously are." I teased and swatted at him as he circled by again.

"Yeah, I almost couldn't believe my ears when they told us. We had just come off our lunch break when Big Ron called us together. All he said was, 'Pack up! We're goin' to the Oregon conference!' It's next week Lyd! And I didn't even tell you the best part!" He took a deep breath and scrubbed his hands into his hair. "It's in EUGENE! I can get to Portland in just over two hours!" He blew out the rest of his breath, jumped and punched the air, then sat back down.

"Man, I need to pack." He hopped up again. "Man, I need to call Brit." He stopped and his eyes glazed over. "Lydie! What if," His focus returned and he grabbed my shoulders. *"what if I surprise her, Lyd?!"*

He let go of me and was on the move again. The dogs joined his circling, filled with exhilaration at Ikes' fine game. "Lydie, I get to see her, can you believe it?"

"Yep. Because if it wasn't true you wouldn't be acting like a five-year-old on Christmas!" I hollered, he was already in the hall closet grabbing his freshly unpacked suitcase. "Now it's my turn!"

"What's that?" His muffled voice asked.

"My turn! To talk! Come back so I don't have to shout!" But I was already headed his way. His head peaked around the closet door, his eyebrows raised in a way that said I was allotted about two seconds of his attention. I got to the point quick. "You need to change, we've been invited to dinner. We're due in fifteen minutes."

"Huh?"

"Our neighbor, the one the babies chased? He's invited us to dinner. We're supposed to be there at six."

"Agh. I wanna get packed!"

"Yeah, but you *never* turn down free food." I persuaded. "Besides, you still have a week before you leave. You can pack later. It would be nice to meet our neighbors you know."

"Yeah, alright." He conceded. "Lemme shower real quick." And with that he left down the hallway, his empty suitcase dragging behind.

The walk to the Craig's was more beautiful than I could have imagined. Chrysalis Drive stretched and yawned in a lazy twist, scooping us over an old bridge where a creek meandered past wild shrubs and graceful willows before it gave way to a peek-a-boo bit of lawn. From there our road delved into a forest, we followed it around another bend, then stopped. No sign, no warning, just no more road and a lot more trees. A little stone house sat nestled amongst a manicured version of wild, with a freshly cut lawn, and trees and shrubs left to gallivant on their own, complete with window boxes full of sprouts, awaiting springs invitation to blossom.

"Is this place for real?" Ike exhaled as we followed the path to the door. "I mean really, Grandma's house? Nepenthe? Now *this* place? It's like we've moved straight into a… a…"

"Fairytale?" I offered.

"Well, yeah, but I was going to say something… more…" He puffed his chest. "Manly, of course."

"Uh-huh, anyway, you may not think so after you meet Renea." I chuckled and knocked on the door. I had regaled my encounter with her, and my first day at Unicorn Books to my brother along our way.

"Hey, I'm just here to be polite, and hopefully get some good homemade cooking. Yours stinks. I couldn't care less about the batress from hell."

"Ike!" I elbowed him as footsteps sounded toward the door. "Shhhhh!"

It was her.

She rolled her eyes as she pulled the door open, until she saw Ike. Instantly her shoulders hoisted and her posture straightened. She didn't smile, but did lift that corner of her lip again.

"Hey, I'm Renea." She said coolly. She didn't acknowledge me.

"Ike." He said.

She opened the door wider and waited.

"Hi Renea." I said as I passed, she barely nodded.

Delicious scents invited us through the entryway into a cozy, if not cluttered, living room. Light poured from lamps on tables and shelves. The couch was adorned with a funky afghan, and a white-haired man with skin stretched over a frame that looked to have once been strong. He toyed with a Rubik's cube. I remembered that Craig had mentioned his dad's injury, and I was impressed, if this was his father. Then I realized he kept spinning the same piece over and over.

"Is that you Lydie and Ike?" A soft voice called from a room I assumed to be the kitchen.

"Who else would it be Ma?" Renea sassed.

Ike slid a disapproving glance at me.

"Oh, Renea!" The kitchen voice edged in exasperation. "Behave yourself, please? Make yourselves at home guys, dinner will be ready soon, just finishing up now."

"Sit where ever you want. Ken will be back soon." Renea sounded bored and started toward the stairwell then stopped and looked at my brother. "Want anything to drink?"

Ike sat next to the man on the couch. "Sure. What do you have?"

"Tea, Pepsi, I think Ken has a beer if you'd like."

"Really?" I heard Ike's approval of Renea increase. I squinted a stern 'No' at him. He pretended not to notice.

"Yeah. Want one?"

"Your mom won't mind?" He asked.

"Who cares if she does?"

"Oh." He tried to hide his disappointment. "I'll take a Pepsi please."

Renea muttered something under her breath that sounded a lot like "*Weak.*"

"I'll take one too." I said, but she was already out of the room.

"Ken? Who's Ken? I thought you said the guy's name was Craig." Ike whispered.

"It is. Craig is their last name, he prefers it over Ken." I told him.

"I would too. He was probably called Ken-doll a lot." My squint turned into a scowl. "What?" He feigned innocence. "I'm just saying… anyway, you were right about her. A class A- ah, thanks." He finished when she came back in the room, two drinks in hand.

"Is this your Dad?" I asked as she handed me my drink. She stopped about an inch away, my question had caught her off guard. She stared at me a moment before she finished passing the can.

"What do you think?" She said in her snotty, absent way, then spun and clomped up the stairwell.

"Lydie," Mrs. Craig's sing song voice called again, "would you mind coming in to help me a moment?"

"What's that Agnes?" The old man sat up and cocked his ear.

"Never you mind dear. Why don't you say hello to Ike?" The voice called back.

The man looked at Ike like he had appeared out of thin air, and Ike's eyes flashed 'help' at me.

"Well hello son! You must be Agnes's boy. I'm Carl."

Ike shrugged his shoulders at me, then turned his attention to Carl. "Hello sir, I'm Ike." He answered.

The voice had in fact come from the kitchen. A lady with an auburn bob, similar to her daughters but with bangs, waved me over then pointed above her.

"Lydie! So glad you're here. Would you reach into that cupboard for me? There'll be a soup tureen, a cobalt blue one. Go on and take it down will you?" Her way was easy, just like her son's, and something about her made me feel comforted. At home.

"Of course!" I obliged. The cupboard wasn't high at all, but from the wheelchair it would have been impossible. "You're Agnes? I'm guessing?"

"Oh no no baby, Agnes is Henry's aunt."

"I'm sorry, Craig hadn't told me your names, and neither had Renea…"

"That's quite alright dear, I'm Carolyn, and you obviously met Henry."

"I think so, but he said his name was Carl?"

"That'd be his brother, you'll have to excuse him. He's not been right since our accident, and I have to say I haven't either." With a good natured laugh she patted her legs. Deteriorated from years of non-use they were dwarfed in comparison to the rest of her.

"Craig mentioned your accident. I'm sorry." I said.

"He mentioned yours too dear." She shook her head. "I'm awfully sorry to hear about it. What a *terrible* thing for the two of you to have gone through." Instead of an off handed condolence, genuine concern was threaded through her remark. She reached her arms toward me in that inviting manner mothers have and I bent to meet them. I thought it might feel awkward, hugging this lady I had only just met, but the moment her arms circled me my apprehension dissolved. "I know it must have been difficult, and still is," she continued, "I know, because I know how hard ours has been for our family. And we're both still living! Best we can that is!" The mood should have felt somber, but it wasn't, thanks to Carolyn's infectious lightheartedness.

We continued to chat as Carolyn laid rolls onto a cookie sheet and I busied myself with adding carrots to the salad.

"Hey guys!" Craig greeted in the other room and I heard the front door close. "Got the whipped cream Ma!" He shouted. His voice sent a flurry of butterflies beating in my stomach. There was a mumbling of men's voices, more clomping from the stairs, and then Renea's annoyance that he hadn't picked out the low-fat kind.

"Lydie, would you be so kind to taste the soup, and add some salt if it needs? I think it might need just a touch." Carolyn asked. She was right. I sprinkled some, and jumped when a hand touched my back.

"Excuse me Lydie, just gonna pop this in the fridge." Craig's fingers remained as he leaned around me to open the fridge. Then his other hand touched me, and for one moment he stood with both of his hands rested at my sides, time stopped and everything melted away.

I swear I felt his breath along my neck.

Then he reached around me, plucked the spoon from my hand and scooped a mouthful of soup.

"My-my ladies. Mom, you've out done yourself this time. Lydie, we need to have you 'round more often." A slight squeeze to my waist sent goose bumps dancing over my skin, then the spoon was placed back in my hand and he was gone.

I heard Renea complain as she umphed against the couch, followed by shrieking and giggling. Ike's laughter rumbled and it sounded as though Henry was in on the fun.

I stood, still stunned, and stirred the soup.

"Kenny!" Carolyn startled me with a shout. "Don't you start roughhousing and break anything! You're not too old for a spanking you know!" But her smile betrayed her. "Well how is it?" She asked me.

"Mmm, well," I worked to regain my composure, "I like it, a lot. It's yummy. And Craig, I mean Ken, seemed to think it was good, too."

"You can call him Craig, dear. We're all used to hearing it. He's asked everyone to call him Craig since he was a youngin'. It didn't occur to me he'd be teased as a Barbie toy, but he sure is handsome. I can see why the name's stuck." She wheeled over and spooned a taste for herself. "Yep, tastes mighty fine to me too, and if we're no good as soup judges, what's it matter anyway? SOUPS UP!" She hollered. "Come and get it!"

We filled the tureen while bodies filed through the door, Henry first, followed by Renea, then Ike. I watched for Craig from the corner of my eye, but he didn't come.

"Excuse me again, Lydie." He said over my shoulder. How did he do that? I turned to look at him.

Those eyes! I was ensnared. Alluring, ice-over-water blue. Crystalline. His scrubs even accented them.

"You're in scrubs?" I asked, my words fluent and not so awkward this time.

"Ah. Yeah. I'm a nurse. Guess I didn't get to tell ya, did I? Guess there's a lot we need to learn about each other." He winked and opened the oven to pull the rolls out.

"Somehow Craig missed that nursing is a woman's job." His sister chastised.

"Interesting Renea, I would have pegged you to be a little more equal opportunity?" I countered her and surprised myself.

"Whatever. My brother's just gay. What more can I say?" She dismissed my comment. To my dismay her flippant remark fueled my reproach. It wasn't natural for me to be confrontational, and for some reason I found myself feeling protective over him.

What if she's not being flippant? My thoughts questioned. *No, there is no way the energy I felt between us could only be imaginary. Is there?*

"Anti-gay too, Renea? *Really*, are you that closed minded?"

She pursed her lips. "No. Obviously I didn't mean, you know what?" She squinted her eyes as her mind searched for ammunition to fire back at me. "Never mind. Just never mind." Her eyebrows knitted and she fidgeted with her nails, then spun around. "I'm not hungry."

"Oh, Renea, not now. Please?" Carolyn pleaded with her daughter but Renea darted from the room. I expected more clomping from the stairs, but instead we heard the sound of the front door again.

Shame burned my cheeks. I was mortified. "Oh my gosh, I'm sorry." I said. *Great Lydie! What were you thinking?*

Ike guppied his mouth at me before he left the room too. The front banged again.

Embarrassed, my hand flew to my mouth.

"Wow Lydie! Good on ya! It's about time someone stuck up for me around here." Craig apparently wasn't concerned with his sister's distress.

I turned to apologize to Henry and Carolyn, but Henry was busy trying to pour a napkin from one glass into another, and Carolyn had her own apology written over her face before I could say anything.

"Lydie, please excuse her. She's had it rougher than most, not saying most don't have it rough, we've all got things to deal with, but she sure has struggled with hers, that's all."

"I'm so sorry." I clambered. "I don't know what got into me. I didn't mean to make a mess of your wonderful meal."

I wanted to leave. I wanted to run. While it was true comments like Renea's bothered me, I never intended on making enemies with my coworker, and certainly not my neighbors.

"Oh no no no Lydie. You mustn't be hard on yourself. Really." Carolyn worked to soothe me. She seemed more concerned that I was upset than she was about Renea's resentment. It didn't come across as an indifference toward her daughter, but more that it was a tribulation they often endured, one she was accustomed to.

Craig laid his arm over my shoulder, and drew me toward him. "Hey Lydie trust me, trust us, Renea is mad at the world. Has been for a long time, and probably will continue to be. I'm just impressed you didn't let her walk all over you." He gave me an affectionate squeeze. "And even more impressed you had my back." He leaned his head toward mine and said in a low voice- "And I assure you, I'm not gay." He squeezed again, softer this time, then straightened, and let his arm fall away. "I enjoy nursing. To help alleviate a little bit of pain for someone, and maybe bring a smile to their face while I do? It's the best. Besides, it helps to know I can be ready for Mom and Pop if they ever need."

Carolyn nodded in agreement.

It felt nice to be near him. In fact, everything felt nice, with the exception of Renea.

Once again, the feeling of family and feelings of home, resounded inside me.

The door opened and I heard Ike's voice followed by Renea's. She almost sounded happy.

"Alright Lyd! I promised her we would call a truce! Even if only as guests." Ike winked at Renea as they walked into the room. She gave him that one sided smile of hers, with a bit of knowing tucked somewhere beneath.

Carolyn's grin wasn't nearly as elusive, and she was right back to her cheerful self. "Shall we have supper guys? I'd hate to think we cooked all this food for nothin'."

❧ 8 ❧

The evening turned out magnificent after that,
and dinner was scrumptious.

Carolyn definitely worked magic in the kitchen.

Henry chimed in sporadically through
everyone's conversations, and sometimes even
made sense. I, myself, didn't fumble over my
words, too much anyway. Craig and Ike buddied
up, discussing everything from music, to cars,
girlfriends and beyond. Ike did mention Brit,
although not nearly as much as I was accustomed to
hearing. Craig offhandedly remarked that he was
still waiting for 'the one'.

It may have been my imagination, but I swear
he nodded in my direction when he said it.

We gathered in the living room after dinner,
and while everyone laughed at something Carolyn
said, I felt a tap on my elbow.

"Lydie," Renea leaned close, so that only I
would hear. "I… I'm sorry, about, you know,
earlier."

I didn't say anything, giving her the chance to say more. She didn't. So I replied.

"I didn't mean to react the way I did. I truly wasn't trying to instigate anything, I just can't stand…" What couldn't I stand? Her picking on her brother? That's what siblings do. Her acting like I didn't exist, all day long? Or the fact that she came across as a bigot? "Narrow mindedness." I finished. I thought that was a fair conclusion.

"Me either." She quickly agreed. "Sometimes I say things… I don't know, just because. Maybe because I hear other people say them. But that's really not me."

"Then you don't have to say them." I said.

"Yeah." She sighed. "I want to be different. I *am* different. But sometimes I feel like I never fit in, *anywhere*. So, things just come out. Sometimes to prove I'm different, sometimes because I'm tired of being different, and I think it's what people want me to say. Or I try and show that I don't care what they think. And sometimes I don't, and sometimes I do…" She trailed off. I was shocked by her quiet apology and appreciated her unexpected openness. It takes a lot to admit those things, especially to someone you don't seem to care much for.

Perhaps we were growing on one another.

"Man, I forgot it would get dark early." Ike observed the waning light as we stepped out to leave.

"I know it's not far, but since I'm going that way anyway, I could drop you guys off." Renea offered.

"That'd be great." Ike was quick to accept, then they slipped into their own conversation as the rest of the Craig family followed us out. Carolyn hugged me goodbye, then Henry did too, although I don't think he understood why.

"I hope I get one?" Craig whispered over my shoulder. I turned and saw his smirk charm out his dimple. I nodded and tried to hide my smile as his arms slid naturally around my body. My head landed in the curve between his shoulder and chest, and he pulled me closer. His soft scent was clean, and male, and bore hints of forest. It traced my face and soothed a hidden part of me. I breathed deep. I could have stayed like that for hours, or a lifetime, but I let go, and pulled away. I didn't want the effect he had on me to be as obvious as it felt.

He let go of me and stepped back. His fingers stretched and flexed. I wondered what he was thinking. I wondered what it meant.

"Now, you two be sure to come over as often as you like. It was such a pleasure having you around." Carolyn invited, her arm cradling her daughters side.

"Yes. Truly." Craig agreed. His voice was low again, like he meant it just for me.

"Hey ya'll! Here for dinner? Agnes is makin' Soup!" Henry greeted us.

"No Papa, we're leaving. I love you, goof." Renea hugged her father, and smacked a kiss to his forehead.

Her tough girl bravado had more than diminished over the course of the evening, exposing a sincere, genuine side of herself.

I wasn't the only one that noticed. Ike had undeniably warmed up to her.

"Be careful what you wish for." I teased Carolyn. "You may not be able to get rid of us." Secretly I longed for us to be close with their family. No one would be able to replace our parents, and I would never want anyone to, but 'The Dent' had been devastating to my brother and I, and dinner with the Craig's had felt healing with its real sense of wholeness.

Besides there was no way around the kindle of fascination I was developing for their eldest.

"That'd be wonderful dear." Carolyn assured me. "I mean it."

I opened the door to Renea's old hatchback, yellow with accents of rust, and crawled into the backseat. Ike got in the front and with three turns of the key she was able to get it started. We waved good bye one last time, and left.

The drive that should have been short, passed in nothing flat. Next thing I knew we rounded the last bend to our house.

A glow from the potting shed caught my attention.

"Do you guys see that?!" I lurched and pointed to the shed, which looked normal again, no light to be seen.

"Geesh Lydie! What?" Ike asked, startled.

"I think I saw," Renea whispered, her eyes darted to meet mine in the rearview mirror, "a light?" She questioned, her voice finding it's way back to her. "Maybe a reflection from the sunset, *or*"

She sounded confident as she nodded to herself, "probably my headlights." She declared.

"Yeah... maybe." I acknowledged, except I knew what bothered her. It had been blue. Glowing, ultraviolet blue. The dwindling sunlight wouldn't have created such a color, nor her old headlights. And it was gone so quickly. I tried to tell myself there must be an explanation, just like she was trying to convince herself.

It wasn't Henry I saw that day. The realization dropped heavy in my gut. I'd been too distracted throughout the evening to make the connection. *Static is blue...* I remembered the heat from the floor and the charge in the room. If that had been what had caused the light, Ike and Renea would be able to feel it too, and I would know I wasn't going crazy.

And if it is happening? If it is real? What does that mean? Goosebumps crawled over my skin.

"Can we check it out guys? To make sure?" Hopefully they didn't hear the quiver in my voice.

"Awe Lyd, I'm *tired*." My brother protested.

"I know Ike, but come on, I swear I saw something." My hands trembled. "I don't think it was a reflection."

"Are you telling me I'm wrong?" Renea's snarky attitude was back. I understood it this time. She was afraid. I recognized it might very well be the driving force behind most of her bitchiness.

"Renea, you saw the color, right? It was strange. I think we should make sure there's no one in there, that's all." The waver in my voice was unmistakable. "Don't you think Ike?" I hoped this would ignite his protective streak so ingrained in him.

"Why are you worked up Lyd? I'm sure it's nothing." He hesitated and his eyebrows cinched. I had in fact struck that chord. "We'll check it for you though, okay?" He said like he was doing me a favor. He really was a good big brother, protective streak or not.

Renea pulled up our drive. "I think I'm gonna go ahead and take off." She nibbled her lip.

"You're not scared too are you? Come on- don't you want to see what the fuss is about?" My brother teased, although he seemed like he might be more worried than he let on.

"Umm... okay." She gave in.

She parked the car and Ike held the door for me while I climbed into the dusk. Renea remained in the car a moment before she eventually joined us.

"Why don't I let the babies out? Couldn't hurt could it?" I suggested. The dogs would provide an extra sense of security, even if only a false one.

"Sure, maybe they'll keep Renea safe." Ike prodded her arm. This got a smile from her, a small one, but a real one.

"I'm not a baby you know." She half-heartedly elbowed him.

I was glad their mood had lightened, but my hands still shook. It was unnerving to think that someone, or *something*, might really be in the shed.

I opened the front door and Princeton barreled onto the porch with Addie sprinting behind. She licked my ankle while Princeton nearly knocked Ike over, then he slobbered all over Renea, always pleased to make a new friend. She barely noticed. Then he slapped one more lick onto Ike, then bounded to me as I joined them. I looked back at the house over my shoulder. Angelina sat in the window, her ears pricked as she stared at the shed. Princeton seemed to notice as well, he spun and his hackles crept to attention. Addie followed suit.

"Raw-raw raw! Rwoof! Woof!" Their warning filled the air as they darted down the hill.

"Shit." Ike breathed. "I'm getting the gun."

"Oh my God!" Renea squeaked and dove behind me.

The dogs reached the shed and gave up their protest in lieu of frantic sniffing.

"Maybe we should go in the house with Ike." I suggested, and hoped I sounded braver than I felt.

"Yeah, okay." She clutched onto the back of my jacket. We only made it a couple of steps toward the house when Ike emerged, dad's pistol in hand. He jogged by us and straight down the hill.

"Think we should still go in the house?" Renea panted while we tried to keep up.

"Yeah, probably, but there is *no* way I'm letting my brother go alone." Guess I had my own protective streak.

Ike made it to the shed and motioned us behind him with a nod. He held the pistol in one hand and snatched the door open with his other.

Princeton and Addie charged in with Ike right behind.

"What the-" Ike breathed.

I was apprehensive to see whatever my brother had found, but I peeked around him anyway.

Nothing.

Once again nothing at all.

Ike knocked over stacks of old pots, and shoved bags of mulch out of his way.

"I'm going to stay out here, and, uh, stand guard." Renea called around the door frame.

I couldn't blame her, besides, maybe she would see something we weren't. I stayed close to the door, just in case.

"Not a thing." Ike huffed.

"I know I saw a light Ike, and Renea obviously did too."

"I know you *think* you saw something. She was probably right, it was probably the headlights reflecting. Or the sun. Maybe there was a raccoon in here."

A raccoon, right. I thought sarcastically, but it was no time to argue.

I felt it again, the charge in the air. It pulled at Ike's hair, standing it on end. The heat infiltrated my shoes. It was slight, Ike wouldn't recognize it, but I had felt it before.

"Feel the floor Ike!" I dropped both of my hands flat on the ground. He looked at me like I was crazy. "Trust me! Do it!" He did the same. Renea peeked her head in to see what the fuss was about. "Can you feel it? Feel how warm it is?" It began to cool beneath my touch.

"This place has been sitting in the sun all day, Lydie." Ike reasoned.

"But your hair, Ike." Renea commented.

"See Ike?! I'm *not* crazy. Renea, come feel the floor." I waved her in.

"What? What's wrong with my hair?" Ike reached and touched his head. Most of it had fallen back in place, but enough remained for his expression to morph to concern.

Renea didn't come in, but did lean down to touch the floor like we were.

It was no use though; the heat had left.

"It's kinda warm- I guess." She said, her voice was still small and nervous.

My eagerness to prove I wasn't crazy had made me forget what that proof would mean.

"But just like it would be if it had been sitting in the sun all day? Right Renea?" Ike stood and ran a self-conscious hand through his hair.

"I think so." She hesitated. "But your hair…"

"*What* about my hair?"

"It was full of static Ike! You looked like a cartoon that had just stuck his finger in a socket." I informed him.

"You're exaggerating." He argued.

"I'm not. Didn't you feel it?"

"My hair was hanging forward, that's all. I was bending down. Stop freaking out." His tone didn't promise the reassurance he proffered. "You saw the headlights reflect, and the dogs…" He watched them continue to inspect the whole of the shed, sniffing and sniffing. "I'm sure there's a raccoon, or 'possum, or *something* to blame."

Skitch ch ch chch hfffff. Hfff if hfffff.

Our eyes grew wide and we all stopped.

What was that? Scratching… and… breathing? Sniffing? It sounded like sniffing, but it wasn't our dogs. They stood frozen with their heads cocked.

Hfff if hfff. If if hfffff. HFFFFFFF.

Renea bolted inside and ducked behind Ike.

"What the heck is that?" She shrieked.

Ike brought his finger to his lips in a silent shhh. We stayed as still as possible.

Hff if hfffffff if if if hff ifhffff. *THWUMP!*

I ducked behind Ike as well. I was surprised he was able to stay upright the way we crowded against him.

Ifhfff hff iff hfff. Thwump! Hfff Thwump thwump thwump.

Princeton and Addie raced outside barking their alarm.

Then they stopped.

Just stopped.

"Shit!" Ike hissed. Heavy shuffling bumped along the wall outside, followed by more rapid breathing. "Wait here. I mean it." Ike ordered and crept toward the door.

But before he got there a huge writhing mass of hair and fur erupted into the shed, moving so quickly I barely recognized our dogs amidst the blur.

"JAKE! Jake!" Renea screeched. "Dang you dog!" Her panic wilted.

"Ha!" Ike burst out. "Haahahahaha!" He laughed at the flurry of dogs. "See Lyd! I told you not to worry!"

"Oh c'mon! You were freaked out too!" I pointed out.

"Well, maybe a *little*, but I'll never admit it again!" He flung an arm over Renea's shoulder, then reached his other to me. "Come give us a hug. We've just survived a *terrible* ordeal." He winked at Renea.

"No way! You're picking on me." I protested, but joined them anyway. Under normal circumstances my brother wasn't overly affectionate. I took this group hug as proof that he had been more upset than he had let on. Not only that, but I think he wanted an excuse to comfort Renea. She didn't seem to mind. In fact, one of her genuine smiles was back in place.

ᔰ 9 ᔰ

The dogs were excited to have found a new friend. They played, and played *hard*.

Ike and Renea were soon over the scare, but not me. Thoughts of the man haunted me. The crumpled one who had watched me. The one who had disappeared. There were too many similarities to when I had seen him the other day.

It was just Jake Lydie, give yourself a break. You didn't see a man, or a shadow disappearing into the trees. You've really been through a lot lately, you know. I tried to shake it all off.

I inhaled, held it a moment, then slowly let it out.

Renea and Ike horsed around on our way back up the hill, he even bowed as he opened the car door for her.

We waved goodbye to her as she drove away.

"Well Sis? Quite the night eh?"

I sighed. "Definitely, glad it was just Jake!" I had *almost* convinced myself it really had been the dog, but it still made me uncomfortable, so I changed the topic. "You and Renea seemed to hit it off." I chuckled.

He smirked. "What are you talking about?"

"What would Brit think?" I prodded. Although in truth, I didn't think she would notice, or care.

"Awe, it's nothing Lyd. Trust me."

"Looked like more than nothing to me. She's into you."

"Nah." Ike held the front door open for the babies then gestured me through.

Inside the house was a cozy and warm sanctuary from the uncertainty of the night.

"Man, I love it here." I said as I pulled myself from my jacket.

Ike sniffed the air. "Yeah, but this old place sure is musty."

"It's not bad." I defended Grandma's home. Our home. "And it's free. And it's ours. We can't complain. Besides, I *really* love it here." I admitted again.

He stopped and gasped with a hand over his mouth. "Even with our big, bad, wandering neighbor dog?" He mocked.

I tossed a couch pillow at him, but he dodged and I missed. "Even with. Give it a chance. It will get better in here as we clean it up and get settled in. After it remembers how to be lived in." I said.

"Yeah, yeah, I know." He picked up my ammunition and stuffed it onto Grandma's rocker. "I like it here too, but still-" He opened one of our still packed boxes and rummaged into it.

I started a bath for myself and dosed it with a generous helping of lilac scented bubbles, then left it to fill and froth while I made a cup of cocoa. Ike ventured into another room still in search of whatever it was he hadn't found and I eyed the shed one last time as I turned out the kitchen light.

A red glow floated across it's silhouette.

"IKE!" Panic struck me hard and fast.

"What now? You really need a chill pill. Geesh." He joined me to peer into the night, the unmistakable scent of fresh incense accompanied him. I turned to see a stick of it in his hand, it's reflection glowering at me in the window.

"I thought I saw a- it was a-" Embarrassed, I pointed at the reflection. "It was the incense. I'm sorry. I really am wound up, huh? On that note I'm off to soak it away!"

"Yeah I think you need it." He carried his smell good into the living room and flipped on the TV.

I gave the window one last look. Angelina hopped up next to me and her ears flashed forward. I leaned against the glass and cupped my hands around my eyes.

The outline of the shed sat dark against its backdrop of stars and late-night sky.

I was relieved to see nothing out of the ordinary. I ran a hand along Angelina's silky coat.

"It's alright, girl." I cooed. "It was just Jake, a silly old dog. You two should become friends, you know. Hopefully we'll be staying here a long time."

She hissed at the window in reply.

I cupped my hands against the glass again. "Shhh gir-"

The word ensnared in my throat as I watched a shadow form into a figure. A dark one, on two legs. It drifted toward the shed then disappeared. A brilliant, violet glow, beamed from one of the windows. The other lit in a deep orange. Then both windows darkened and colored light burst into the night.

Fear paralyzed me. My mouth gaped and my voice lost its way, unable to escape.

"*a*aaaaahhhhhhhh," I managed a ragged whisper. I tried harder, "Ahhhhhhhh." *DAMN.* I felt like I was trapped in quicksand.

The ethereal glow framed the shadowed figure into a silhouette. The colors pulled into themselves, creating two spheres. They radiated and floated in a soft, circular dance.

I tried to call out again. I wished desperately for Ike to come back. It took everything I had to muster the strength, "aaa- *AaaaaaaAAAAAhhhhhIKE!*" I cried out.

My brother moaned as he hoisted himself from the couch.

The lights flew toward one another, then met and hovered inches apart at the center of the figure. His face lit, displaying a haphazard grin.

It was him!

The one with the dirty snow colored hair. The one who had watched me from that same spot before. Grinning that crooked smile- and staring directly at me.

Checkerboard sparkles tunneled my vision.

I heard Ike's voice behind me- "Lydie? Are you okay?!"

My whole body swayed and I couldn't answer.

Then black swept over it all, leaving me in a nothingness.

❧ 10 ❧

"Hello Lydie." A voice greeted, calm and soothing. Familiar. I remembered it, but couldn't remember from where. "Don't worry, everything is going to be amazing..." It whispered.

My dream. It was the voice I had dreamt of when we had first moved here.

Everything was still dark and I couldn't see anything.

"Hello...?" I whispered.

"You're safe. You know that, don't you? You've found your way. We're so happy for you."

"Huh?"

"Shhhhhhh, everything is alright. Don't worry. We'll meet again, when it's time. Right now it's important to rest."

"But, where am I?" My head filled with questions. "Why can't I see anything?"

"Open your eyes. You could see if you would only open your eyes." The voice paused. "It sometimes helps to visualize your human eyes, imagine opening them." It encouraged. "But truly, for only a moment Lydie, you mustn't stay very long now."

I didn't quite understand, but I tried as it suggested.

An array of color bled into sight, beautiful and breathtaking. It didn't make sense though, as if I looked to a rainbow-colored sun from beneath water.

"What is this?" I asked. "Where am I?"

"You're here. You've made it. But it's time for you to go back. We'll meet again. Shhhhhhhh. Close your eyes, let yourself rest." The voice was extraordinarily relaxing and my eyes slipped closed.

"You've found truth Lydie. You've discovered happiness is a choice, a decision." The voice continued as I drifted. "A state of consciousness. You've realized this, despite the pain you've had. You've found what many refer to as heaven. Not many choose to believe it though. They choose to believe it's a destination." The tenderness of its voice tinged with a hint of regret. "It's easier to believe that it's a far-off place."

I was confused. "Heaven?" I opened my eyes again. The colors increased their vibrations and swirled in front of me. If I had found heaven... "Does that mean Mom is here? Dad!?" Excitement surged through me.

"Mom and Dad *are* here with you, they always have been, and always will be." The voice paused. "We all are, we're part of a whole. We're all one. Humans use a manifestation of their energy to hold ideas that make things easier to understand." The colorful array engulfed and surrounded me, just as the voice was. "When we choose to engage into our human experience, it's easier for the living body of our experience, our "self" if you will, to see things as separate and tangible while we learn what the human experience has to teach us. A lot of us forget the lessons we came for though, and instead become obsessed with the imagery. Some begin to believe the manifestations *are* the existence. But every once in a while, we break through. We remember. We understand that we started this journey with an intention. For its essence. With the hope of understanding the truth of the whole thing. We're all one. We're just different threads of the quilted fabric of our whole. Of existence. Of the universe. We never leave, Lydie. We just change. Our focus moves to our next lesson. Our next state of being. Throughout our entire universal lives, and I don't mean only our human one, we continually change focus, but it's all here, it's always been here. You're finally beginning to understand. That's why you're able to hear me now."

"Who are you?" I interrupted. Although the confusion was monumental, uncertainty and fear were oddly absent. I felt more peace than I had ever experienced. The colors brightened, then softened and pulsed. I watched them, I experienced them, I absorbed them.

Oneness.

"I'm your Llewrenni." The voice resonated. "You'll see me again, soon enough."

"Again? But I haven't seen you yet?"

"Oh, but you have. And will." The colors shifted to form a delicate image. I recognized our dock in the early morning. The sun snuck through the trees to trace the face of a young lady, leaned back on weathered planks as the wind played in her hair. "I'm there when you quiet yourself Lydie. When you listen as the wind speaks to you. I'm there when you pause to feel the sun press its lips to your cheek. I'm with you each time you realize there is more to life than we can see, or understand. I'm with you... Always. I'm your guide. Your guardian. We've been together a long time."

The voice faded, but I didn't feel alone, I was immersed in tranquility.

"You know," it whispered after a time, "Sometimes you lead me, sometimes you're *my* guardian, my guide." It said quiet, hesitant. I almost didn't hear it. Still, it sounded so familiar. I opened my eyes wide to see where it came from, but the concept of 'around me' didn't exist. I was engulfed in color, engulfed in peace. "It's time Lydie. Time to go back. Time to wake." It lulled and I closed my eyes. Everything was soothing. "Don't worry, everything's going to be amazing." It whispered one last time.

Then everything melted to black.

❧ 11 ❧

Cold.

Sterile.

Foreign.

My senses were bombarded with a slap of tangible harshness.

Then came beeping, and the voices.

Scents and sounds alerted my body, though all was still dark. I remembered the voice, *Open your eyes. You could see if you would only open your eyes.* I tried.

They were heavy, so damn heavy. Or I was weak. Perhaps both. I tried again.

Light.

Blinding and fuzzy.

I squinted them closed. The voices whirred. I couldn't make out their words. Determined, I tried again.

It worked this time. Light swamped my eyes, and *burned*. Piercing and stabbing, but slowly, and with the aid of a lot of squinting and blinking, my eyes focused.

The voices vanished and I was left staring at an unfamiliar pocked ceiling. My brothers face popped into view above me.

"Lydie? Can you hear me?" He asked.

"a-aaaahh-h h -hh." No… not again.

Ike's head disappeared, and was replaced by one of an angel. He looked familiar. I blinked to focus better.

"Lydie." He coaxed. "Lydie? Can you hear us?" He squeezed my shoulder and sent little shimmering waves through my body.

"Aahh-an – an ah-Angel? This is - Heaven?" I questioned weakly.

A big, glorious smile spread across his face.

"Awe, that's my girl! Still has my back. Lydie, it's me- Craig."

"Craig?" I remembered my brothers face. "Ike? Wh- Where am I? What's going on?"

Ike's smile joined Craig's above me. "I'm here. You're okay, you're in the hospital. You fainted and landed all wrong. You've been out for days." Recognition nibbled at my disorientation.

"Not too much, too fast. Let her catch up." Craig coached my brother, but his eyes never left mine.

"Hi Lydie, I'm here too." Renea joined the field of vision and flashed one of her rare, genuine smiles.

"Hospital? I thought I was in Heaven… that's what it said." I wriggled, and tried to sit up.

"That's what who said?" Ike asked.

"Hey, not too fast. Here, I'll lift the bed a little." Craig ducked out of sight. I managed to turn my head and find him.

"Craig? You're still in scrubs?" I mumbled through my haze. "Hospital? Oh. Oh my gosh! I'm so embarrassed."

"It's all right Lydie, we're here and we're not going anywhere. Besides-" He winked. "Don't be embarrassed. It's not every day someone calls me an Angel." He leaned over me and reached toward the controller for my bed. When his face neared mine that dimple of his flashed. "Don't worry, everything's going to be amazing." He whispered.

"What'd you say?" My brows arched in disbelief.

He stood, controls in hand, and elevated me to a semi up position. "I said don't worry." An idea brightened his face. "Hey! Bet you're thirsty. Probably *really* thirsty. Let me get you something, what sounds good? Sprite? Juice? I'll be right back." He left the room before I could answer.

"Wow Lyd. Haven't seen my brother carried away like that in a long time."

"He's a nurse, he's supposed to take care of his patients." Ike quipped.

"Yeah, and he's good at it too, but he seems *really* eager to take care of your sister." Renea bumped her shoulder into Ike, in a familiar, comfortable way.

Had I really been out for days?

It had only felt like seconds, and yet, like a whole life time. In a whole other world.

Maybe I really am going crazy. I thought.

The eerie grin flashed across my mind, followed by a train of disturbing images. I remembered the shadow, and the lights. I remembered the isolating dark that had snuck over me. How could any of this be? Were those memories, and the place I had just left, nothing more than a bumped head? *But they must be real.* I reasoned with myself. To believe it may have all been my imagination, the product of bruised thoughts from a fall, felt ludicrous.

AM I GOING CRAZY? I wanted to scream but my throat betrayed me with a dry wail.

Ike and Renea's banter stopped and they stared at me.

"Lyd?" My brother questioned, his eyes weighted in concern. "Are you okay? Do I need to call Craig?" He started for the door.

"I remember!" I gusted a rasp, desperate to distinguish something, anything. "The lights! Our shed!"

"Oh no, not *this* again." He stopped and sighed. "We checked it out, remember?" He turned back to me. "It was Renea's old dog. Right Renea?" He nodded to her for reinforcement, but she didn't say anything. "Renea?" She stiffened.

"Yeah - Jake. It was Jake." She paled.

"Renea?" I questioned.

"Are you okay?" Ike braced her elbow.

"Yeah, it's nothing." She shrugged and shook her head. "It was just Jake."

"Renea! Did you see something?? Did you see the lights?!" I asked, eager for clarity.

"I need some water." She ducked from Ike's hand and nearly tripped over her brother as she darted from the room.

"What got into her?" Craig pushed in a cart filled with every drink the cafeteria had in stock, and under them a shelf packed with sandwiches, cakes, and even one token bowl of red Jell-O. He parked it beside my bed.

"I don't know, guess she needed water." Ike dismissed and swiped a meaty sandwich and a bottle of Gatorade. "Geesh Ken-doll, leave any food for the rest of the hospital?"

"Not sure Mike and Ike, maybe you'd like to offer them some of your fruitiness?" Craig ribbed back.

"She could have got a drink from here." I nodded to the cart.

"Ah, you think you're funny Kendra." Ike said through a mouth full of sandwich. Obviously they hadn't heard me, or made the connection themselves.

I cleared my throat. "I saw something in the shed."

Ike rolled his eyes, "Lyd, we *just* went over this. It was Jake."

"No. I saw something else, Ike. I think Renea may have too. She didn't have to leave to get a drink, she could have got one from the cart. She was spooked." I reached for the closest bottle on the cart, but my effort was futile, in part because I felt weak, but mostly because Craig got to it first.

"Ah, the shed, I heard about the haunting of Jake. Sorry about that Lyd, I should have mentioned him to you guys." He passed me the drink, and pulled up a chair between the cart and myself.

"Yeah, I guess she did look upset. Maybe I'll check on her." Ike acknowledged and left to find her, Gatorade in one hand, and his sandwich in the other.

"He seems eager to take care of her." Craig noted as he watched Ike search the hallway.

"The same was said about you a moment ago." I pointed out.

He looked around, eyes wide, "Who me? What could they be talking about, things like this?" He scooped a bite of ice cream and rested it on my lips. I tried not to laugh as I accepted the mouthful. "Perhaps they said it because it's true." He admitted.

"Oh, is that so?" His flattery heated my cheeks.

"Yes, it is." He had another spoon full ready, but I held my hand up to take a sip to wash the last down. "There's something… Something about you. I feel, I know- we don't know each other well, *yet*, but, I, uh, just- feel…" He stumbled over his words and let them fall silent with lack of explanation.

But he didn't need one. I felt it too. Oh, how I felt it, and I didn't know how to express it either, so instead I diverted. "Aren't you worried about your sister?" I tried to shift myself, suddenly aware of how uncomfortable being stuck in one spot could be.

"She's a big girl. What your brother hasn't learned is Renea can be a bit dramatic at best and extremely so most of the time. But she's a good person somewhere deep down. Heck you guys got quite a glimpse the other night, she normally doesn't let most people see her real side."

"We're not most people, you know. I-Uh, I-uh. Dizzy." My head fell back. The excitement of waking, trying to sit, and my involuntary gravitation toward Craig, had taken its toll.

"Awe, I let you do too much too quickly. What was I thinking? Your strength will come back. You just woke up, give yourself time, eh?" He reached to adjust my pillows and the closeness of him grazed the contours of my senses.

"How does that feel, is it okay?" His eyes tugged at me as they studied mine.

It took me a second to register that I had been asked a question. I blinked.

"Ahh, yes, better. You're gonna spoil me."

"Good." His smirk teased his dimple from hiding. "I want to."

A fresh heat braised my cheeks, but thankfully he was back to maneuvering bed controls and Craig raised me high enough that I sat effortlessly.

"There, now just settle back and let the bed do some of that work, k? And me, let me too. It's going to take at least a day, maybe two before we can break you outta here. At the *very* earliest tomorrow. In the meantime, you're stuck with me."

"And I hope it's sooner rather than later, no offense sis, but I've got that trip to Oregon." Ike said as he ushered Renea into the room, his hand on her back.

"I didn't mean to upset you Renea. I don't know what happened. It's probably all from my fall. I feel like I'm going crazy." I groaned.

"It's okay." She relented a small smile. "Do you guys mind if I talk to Lydie?" She took a deep breath. "Alone?"

"Uh, sure." Craig sounded reluctant. "Remember though, she just woke up, take it easy on her."

"And don't hog her to yourself for too long." Ada's cheerful voice surprised me from the doorway. "I haven't got to see her awake eyes in a while."

"Ada!" I lifted my head and smiled at her.

"Eyas, Lydie!" Joe's thick accent rolled in behind her. "Glad to see yous feelin' better."

"Why Lydie dear, I'm so thankful you're awake! We've been missing you. We've come to see you since you've been here, but you wouldn't remember, of course." Ada gestured to Craig and Ike. "All right boys, let's let the ladies have that chat, shall we?"

They shuffled out and I laid my head back.

"I wanted to tell you," Renea began in a hush, "but it has to stay between you and me only. Okay?" She watched me a moment, debating whether or not she could be sure to trust me.

"Promise." I nodded.

"Everyone already thinks I'm different. And it's because I want them to. But if they knew... I don't want anyone to think I've lost it, for real." She chewed a nail.

"I already feel like I've lost it. I would be more than happy to have company, even if I had to keep it to myself."

"I saw something too." She paused and watched me again.

"I said I promise." I assured her. "What was it? The lights? The man?" I prodded.

"I saw the glow in the shed again. Only for a second. Just like the night we checked it. Yesterday evening I stopped by with some Chinese to check on Ike and see how he was holding up. Ike had sat with you for nearly two days straight and finally went home to get some rest. He's been pretty shaken up over this, you know. Anyway, we talked and ate, and didn't stop, talking that is. We just kept right on going. I've never been able to open up with anyone the way I can with him." A subconscious smile tugged her lips, and she caught herself before she chewed another nail. "But that isn't what I wanted to tell you." She stood straight and cleared her throat. "When I left I saw the glow." Her hand flew to her mouth and she continued to talk around her nail biting. "In the shed. Definitely *in* the shed. But that's not the strangest thing." Her eyes flashed around the room before they landed on me.

I nodded for her to go on. I needed to hear more. Part of me hoped she had seen the same things. Though, if she did what would *that* mean?

"When I started home from your house, I saw *another* light in the rearview." Her voice dropped low. "And, and… It followed my car. It was purple, such a beautiful deep glowing purple…" She gulped. "I started to drive faster, but it sped up too, and then it…." Her voice faded.

"I saw them too." I whispered.

"I was hoping it was my imagination." Her eyes pleaded with mine. "Lydie, it caught up to me, and circled my car. I drove faster, and it kept up. So I stopped. I was so scared, but I couldn't take my eyes off of it. And even though every part of me was shaking, it was so... beautiful. It just... sorta.... Danced." She looked to me for reassurance.

"I don't think you're crazy."

"Do you believe me?"

"I- I uh," I felt the same insecurity she had felt about telling me, and understood why she didn't want anyone else to hear. "I saw it dance too, actually *them*. I saw two of them. Glowing and floating in their delicate dance. It was hypnotizing. I saw them, then called for Ike, that's when I fainted." Thankfully, she looked relieved and not full of ridicule. "I also saw a man. A strange, older man. Twice now. You're the only person I've told. He disappeared inside the shed the first time. I had watched from the house, and he never came back out. When I finally went to see what was going on, the shed had the same static, and the floor was hot, like when we were all there."

"You should have told us! What if he was in there? What if he would have hurt us?!" Her accusatory tone was reminiscent of her bitchy side.

"I didn't tell you because I was afraid you guys would think I was crazy. All of it sounds crazy and you know it!" I defended myself. I knew she was scared. Her face softened as she realized I was right. "The second time was by the shed again, the night I saw the lights." I continued. "It was like he was maneuvering them, orchestrating. They seemed focused on him, or had *something* to do with him, then I passed out."

"I wish you had told me! But I know I wouldn't have wanted to hear it, even less, believe you." Although she still sounded nervous she showed a tinge of relief over our shared confidence. "Mine swooped and circled my car, a couple of times, as if it was playing, with me, with the car. I couldn't stop watching. It was so beautiful. Then it flew lightning fast away. After it was gone, I got spooked, I mean *really* scared about what I had just seen. I hoped it was all a dream. That maybe I nodded off for a second, or even just my imagination tricking me. That's how I've rationalized it. Until you woke up."

"You two about done in here?" Ike cracked the door and poked his head in.

"Y'all can come in." Renea said before I had a chance to tell him to wait. I didn't want her to close up again, but the quick drop of her tensed shoulders, and the gentle way she tucked her hair behind her ear, told me not only that she liked my brother, but that she needed him near.

"Good, it's 'bout time. You guys have been gabbing for*ever*."

"Have not." She smirked at Ike.

"Just be glad you weren't here for all of our girly talk." I deflected the onslaught of questions written in his eyes, and Craig's for that matter. Even Ada looked curious. Joe on the other hand was laid back, as if he was accustomed to women needing girl time.

"I was gonna ask what the deal was, but if it was girly… Ick." My brother squished up his face and stuck out his tongue. "Doesn't everyone know girls have cooties?"

"You better watch it, son." Ada played along with Ike. "The three of us may gang up on you once your sister is feeling better. I really hope that's soon darlin'." She came over and smoothed the hair from my forehead.

"Speaking of getting better, visiting hours will be over in not too long, then we've got to let her rest." Craig insisted while he replaced my drink with a full one.

"That's right. Get your rest and you'll be outta here in no time." Ada confirmed, "Although having this hunk of a Ken-doll here to take care of you can't be half bad." She winked at me.

"Ey!" Joe protested.

I blushed.

"Oh, don't you worry, you're more than enough for me, you devil." Ada pinched Joe's cheek.

"Now, Miss Ada, if you ever need me you know I'll take care of you too, ma'am." Craig said in a sugary, sing song.

"Nope. Won't share her." Joe said and kissed Ada on her cheek.

"Oh, you two, you can quarrel over me later." She dismissed them both. "Let's visit with Lyd before Craig gives us all the boot."

"Alright Lydie, guess you get my full attention then." Craig gestured to the cart. "So, what will we start with? Time to spoil you rotten." He adjusted it so I could see everything on it.

The excitement of everyone, and the reality that I had been out for days, began to wear on me. I lifted my head less, and traded talking for listening and smiling. They seemed to understand. No one spoke of mysterious topics. But then aside from Renea and I, no one else had a need to.

Craig left to tend to other patients, but always came back between them. After an hour or so he addressed my company, and ushered them politely, but sternly, out for the night.

12

We were alone.

It dawned on me that I hadn't showered in days, or brushed my teeth for that matter. I cringed at the thought of the washed out, pale mess my face must be. Then with shock I realized Craig may have seen more of me than I wanted him to. When patients are unable to shower, didn't they give them sponge baths?!

"How are you feeling, beautiful?" He grabbed a clipboard from the foot of the bed and took some notes from my beeping machinery.

"Not beautiful at all. Has it really been three days that I've been in here?" A predatory unease began to eat at me. "I haven't showered in all that time! I must look awful, and smell worse!" My voice hitched.

"Yeah right! You? Awful? As if that were possible." He crowed.

"My face is naked, I've probably got breath that would rival a dragon, and you…" I could feel my skin turn scarlet, "Have you given me a sponge bath?!" The question came out frantic. I wished I had sounded brave, or perhaps nonchalant.

"Nah, I've been waiting 'til we were a little better acquainted." He chuckled and continued his note taking.

I felt so stupid. "I'm serious Craig! I'm embarrassed!" I blurted.

"I'm serious too!" He said playfully. He thought he was flirting. He didn't realize how disastrous I really felt.

My throat tensed, then closed, and as quickly as I tried to stop them tears refused to be controlled and poured down my cheeks.

"Lydie?" He turned when I gasped on a sob. He tossed his clip board to a side table and swooped over me. "Oh, hey! Oh Lydie... I'm sorry, so sorry. I was only joking. I'm sorry I went overboard." He wrapped himself tight around me.

"Y-y-you," I struggled to speak as my body racked.

"Shhhhh, it's alright Lydie. Don't worry." He stroked my hair, then stopped rigid around me. "Shit!" He exclaimed under his breath. "I'm so insensitive! Do you want me out?!" He dropped his arms away and started to stand.

"N-n-n-no!" I stammered, and leaned toward him. He understood my silent request and pulled me to his chest. "I-" hiccup, "I'm so embarrassed!" I hiccupped again, then couldn't help but laugh at myself. The rumble of his own chuckle was warm and soothing against my ear.

"Lydie," He tilted my chin toward his. "You have nothing to be embarrassed about. I already told you, it's not every day someone calls me an angel." He teased, but his smile was so genuine I couldn't help but feel lovely in his arms.

"See! I have every reason to feel embarrassed." My breath hitched one last time and my tears eased.

"You are beautiful." He smoothed a hair from my face. "Honestly, I haven't been here for your *personal* care." He cracked a smile. "I promise to let you get showered and find a toothbrush for you, as soon as I'm sure you won't beat yourself up anymore." He winked and coaxed an unexpected smile from me.

"I am feeling better, thank you." I breathed. "I guess everything just caught up to me."

"I know it did, and you should be resting anyway. I should have known better than to let everyone stay so long. They wore you out."

He leaned his head forward, and rested it against my hair. I felt him breath a long, inhaling breath, and hold it. And then, so soft, it could have been the wings of a butterfly, his lips brushed my forehead.

I didn't move.

I didn't want him to ever stop.

"Toothbrush." Craig eased away from me.

"Hmmm?" I was entranced.

"Toothbrush, toothbrush, toothbrush." He chanted and paced the room a bit dazed himself.

"So, my breath does stink, eh?" I tried not to feel insecure.

"What? Oh! No. I just want to make you feel better." He pulled open a drawer.

"Trust me, you are." I admitted and felt shy again.

He turned to look straight at me. "I will do everything I can to make you a happy lady, Lydie." He smiled and turned back to search through a cupboard

I blushed. I couldn't be sure if he was serious or mocking me. What was happening? Did he really feel drawn to me, like I felt toward him? Is what I felt just euphoria from my dream? Or was this real? My head started to spin, and not only from the uncertainty.

"Craig?"

"Mmm?" His voice was muffled.

"I'm still starving, would you pass me a piece of cake? If I'm going to eat, it should probably be before I brush my teeth."

"Sure!" He whipped his head out and almost slammed into his chair as he darted to the cart.

"I'm not going anywhere. No need to rush and hurt yourself." I grinned.

"All in the name of comfort!" He regained his composure and pointed to the sugary spread until I nodded at one that looked like birthday cake.

Half of it was gone before I paused long enough to thank him. "This is the best thing I've ever tasted." I scooped in some more. "I really have been out for days, haven't I?"

"You know you have if you say that about hospital food." He unearthed a plain white toothbrush, and mini tube of paste.

"You take such good care of me." I grinned again. My vanity had been so thoroughly pummeled that I didn't care how goofy I looked anymore. Besides, Craig, and the cake, both had me feeling much better.

"It's my job!" He handed them to me. "But I'd still do it, even if it wasn't."

"Your job…" I swallowed the last bite. "That's right. You'll be leaving soon? Certainly you haven't stayed here three days straight."

"Done in an hour."

"Oh." I tried to disguise my disappointment.

"I don't have to leave, you know."

"I don't expect you to stay! Especially not after you've worked all day." But as exhausted as my body felt, I wasn't tired. I couldn't believe I had missed three days of my life. I didn't want to sleep.

"And I don't expect you to want me to, but if you don't mind, I would like to." He sat on the edge of my bed, his casual demeanor back intact.

"I would like that, if you really don't mind, I'm tired of sleeping, and would love the company." I shrugged my shoulders and gave a sheepish smile. "And besides, I want you to."

"Well," He leaned toward me and wiped frosting from my cheek. "That makes two of us, and I don't think anyone else would be able to offer you this much cake. I know, because I cleaned them out." He handed me another piece. German chocolate this time.

"I love that you're spoiling me. But I still can't help but be embarrassed. I've been such a baby and now I'm being a pig. I guess you're getting the best of me." Finally I was able to chew more slowly.

"Pig? Pshh. I thought you were done beating yourself up. Besides, you haven't seen anything yet." He picked up another piece and stuffed most of it in his mouth before he stuck his pinky toward me. "I'm loving every minute of it. Pinky promise."

Pinky promise? Who still does that? I knew I liked him. I set down my fork and my pinky joined his. Next thing we knew, our faces and stomachs hurt from laughter.

Craig finished his rounds, then joined me with some warm mush the cafeteria called stew. He scooted next to me on the bed, keeping our distance cordial and friendly. Maybe too much so. I wanted to feel his lips again, even if only on my forehead. He did however link my arm through his after we ate. Conversation came to us easily and freely. He ran the back of his fingers along my arm as we chatted about anything and everything. Before I knew it we had talked for hours.

I leaned my head upon his shoulder, and closed my eyes as he whispered my name.

"Lydie… Lydie, beautiful…" I was too sleepy to respond, and listening to him whisper was divine.

"God Lydie," he breathed, "You are incredible. I want to make you happy, if you'll let me." His voice stirred against my hair. "I want to make you happy, if you'll let me, and protect you, and keep you safe. Will you let me?"

My heart clattered, and my breath jumped, still I didn't let him know I was awake.

"I'll be yours, if you let me. Don't worry, everything will be amazing."

❧ 13 ❧

"Lydie…"

"Hmmm?" I nuzzled his shoulder.

"Good morning beautiful." He did it then, laid his lips upon my forehead. My blood excited to feel his kiss again.

"Morning?" My voice was thick with sleep.

"It is. We slaughtered the night and now the morning is here to take over."

I cautiously opened my eyes, invigorating light poured through the windows.

"Already? But I've only just,"

"Fallen asleep? No, we've both been asleep for hours, although you drifted off before I did."

"I fell asleep?!" I squeaked, then groaned. "Did I drool all over you? Oh, no! I probably snored, didn't I?"

"You did. Both." He laughed and ran his hand over my hair. "That makes me happy, that you were comfortable enough to sleep like a rock. I listened to you as long as I could stay awake."

I smiled as his words settled deep inside me.

"What time is it?" I stretched my arms. "Do you have to work??"

"Nah, I'm off, *and* if I have my way, we're gonna break you outta here."

A realization struck me, and to differ the significance I felt from it, I made a haphazard attempt at an accent to lighten my observation.

"Oh! Craig," I stifled a giggle as I elongated his name so it sounded like cray-egg.

"What is it Miss purdy Lydie." He answered in an even more exaggerated drawl, perhaps straight out of Texas.

"Why, Ken-doll, I do declare, do you realize we've just spent our first night together, all... *alone*..." I broke character and laughed at myself. "In a Nepenthe Hospital bed! The epitome of romantic."

He on the other hand, continued the jest, and tipped an imaginary hat. "Why Miss purdy," he cleared his throat, "I mean Miss Lydie, ma'am, you just wait little lady, I'ma gonna break you on outta this joint, and we'll do romantic right." His slow drawl over the word "right" made it sound a lot like the word 'riot'.

"Why Kenny, I do say, is that an invitation for our first date?" Somehow playing a fresh debutante made the question less awkward.

"It shore is Miss Lydie, if you'll be havin' me, that is."

"Not until I get showered, and into something other than a hospital gown!" I laughed.

"Right! Let's get you on your way then." He shifted effortlessly to his laid back, confident self, and set off to start my discharge.

It was still early when everything was finished and we were ready to go. Craig suggested we surprise Ike and show up at the house unannounced. I thought it was a fantastic idea, and was secretly ecstatic about the extra time we'd have together.

"But, only if you'll let me push you in a wheel chair." Craig insisted. I opened my mouth to protest, but he interjected. "*Only* because I'm still spoiling you, as long as I can get away with it. Not because I think you're unable to walk."

It made me feel special.

I got cleaned up, then climbed into the wheel chair he had waiting, which in reality made me feel kind of foolish. "Really, I think I'm capable of walking."

"I think you are too." He agreed. "But trust me. It will be great!"

His convincing worked, and I shrieked when he took off at a sprint down the hallway.

"Kenny! You know better!" A large woman called after him, which encouraged him to zoom me faster through the rest of the hospital, then down a long ramp outside, where he stopped just short of crashing into an earthy green Wrangler.

"Great Jeep." I admired.

"It is." He opened the door and held my hand as I got in. "I enjoy it. A lot. Just wait 'til the temperature warms up and I can take the top off. Boy will you have fun!"

Little prickles snuck across my arms to hear him mention me in his future. It reminded me of his words as I fell asleep.

Our natural ease and ready laughter permeated our trip out of town. By the time we reached Chrysalis Drive it felt like we had arrived too soon.

"Home sweet home." Craig announced as we turned on our road. The morning sun danced on early spring seeds in the air, and a quiet breeze sent frenzied glints across the water. I sighed and felt Craig's hand slide over mine in response.

"It's so surreal here." I said and traced his knuckle with my finger.

"I know, and we get to live here. Pretty great huh?" His thumb reached to graze mine. "Dad used to say there was something special about this place, that's why he and mom stayed. He said once they arrived they never wanted to be anywhere else. Said he could never put his finger on it, but it must be for good reason."

"Do you want to leave Nepenthe?" I asked.

"No." He glanced at me. "I don't." Seriousness tugged the corners of his mouth. "I know our town is small. Nothing like Portland. I would understand if you felt like you wanted to leave one day. I shouldn't assume you'd want to stay, too."

"Oh! No, I think I do. I mean, I know we haven't been here long, but, you're right. It feels like home to me, it really does. Like my own little heaven. That might sound silly... It's just, ever since we've been here it's been very-" I bit my lip while I thought how to put into words the way I felt about Grandma's home, and Nepenthe. "healing for me. I really love it here. I'm almost ashamed to admit it, but I never felt this at home in Portland. I just wish my parents were here. But I suppose they're in their own Heaven."

"I'm sure they are. Hmmm, Heaven..." That luscious dimple of his winked. "Does that mean I get to be your angel?"

"Always have to pick on me, eh?"

He responded with a brush of his lips along the back of my hand followed with a playful nip.

"Ow! You might be too naughty to be my angel." My hair fell over his arm as I brought our hands to my chin to play the picture of innocence.

"Who, me?" He rebutted, but his smirk gave him away.

I kissed his hand, and let it linger a moment longer than I should have.

"Lydie," He breathed and slowed the jeep to a crawl. "Why are we so close to home?" He rolled his head and stretched his neck.

"Because I'm not sure the hospital shower counts as a real one?" I laid our hands back in my lap, and smiled because he didn't want our time to be over either.

"Oh, but if you only knew how beautiful you are, even hospital showered and dragon breathed." His smile was almost as large as mine.

"Not fair!" I scowled.

"I love having fun with you." His smile was replaced by creased brows. "Seriously though," he brought the jeep to a standstill, "Most people around here can't wait to leave. They run off to bigger and better places. I've traveled, and plan to more, but Nepenthe is *home* for me. Especially Chrysalis Drive."

"You don't plan to move from your parents' house?" There was after all, only theirs and ours on the whole of our road.

Sunlight caught in the edges of his hair and framed him in a celestial glow. It was difficult to keep from staring. "I don't want to leave my parents, Lyd. I want to be there for them for as long as they need." His expression brewed. "Past girlfriends haven't understood." His eyes, those liquid pools were full of question.

Girlfriend? I struggled to keep my cool. I swallowed and tried to steady myself. "I think that's honorable Craig. I would like to think I would have done the same for mine if they had ever needed it. Besides, your parents are wonderful."

Hope softened his expression.

"I have to admit," I continued, "since I feel like I can tell you anything already, your family eased some of the pain of my parents not being here. Our parents can never be replaced, I would never want to try, but being with your family, it somehow felt like we all... *fit*."

He let out a breath. "You have no idea how good it is to hear that." He grinned again. "It felt like that to me too, and still does. Even Renea opened up, she never does that with outsiders. Not that I've seen anyway." He took my hand and laced our fingers together. "Promise me this."

"Yes?" I asked.

"Something about you and I feels important. I know it's cliché but it just feels..."

"Like we know each other?" My eyes searched his. Perhaps he would have said 'right', or 'love at first sight' or perhaps he would have said something else entirely, but it felt deeper than that to me. "And have, for a long time?" My nerves jumped at my openness. What if I'd read him wrong, what if he *didn't* feel the same?

"Precisely." He agreed. "And I want to. I want to know you, the real you, *all* of you, for a long time, if you'll let me." He let go of my hand and slid his arm across my shoulders. "Let's promise each other that whatever happens, or doesn't," His other hand raised my chin until our lips were a breath apart. "Let's promise to never let it get weird."

"I think I can handle that." Relief flooded through me as his eyes drank me in.

"I don't want to lose you, even if it means we're just friends."

"*Just* friends?" I raised my eyebrows.

"Hopefully," he leaned toward me, "so much more." The weight of his breath brushed over my skin and his jaw muscles flexed. My heart quickened through my veins and the air warmed between us. His arm tightened and brought his lips to rest upon mine. With their touch my eyes slipped closed, and I melted.

✦ 14 ✦

Our first kiss.

We had shared our first kiss.

Heat flared through the depths of me. I wondered if he felt that way too. I didn't want it to ever stop, but the seats of the jeep weren't the most accommodating of affection. After a reluctant part, Craig revved the engine, slipped the jeep into gear, and we started home again.

The pond sparkled in the morning light. It might have been elation I felt, or maybe because I had been away for days, but it's gleam as the sun played on the water, shown with more brilliance than I remembered. The shed crouched at its edge with Angelina atop its gable, grooming a paw in the morning glow. If it wasn't for the conversation Renea and I had, it would probably go unnoticed. The image of the lights and the man plucked at my psyche. I should have felt uneasy. Perhaps it was the spring morning, or the exaltation from our first kiss, *or* merely because Craig was with me, but for whatever reason, I didn't.

What did catch me off guard though, was Renea's car parked between my baby blue, and our dad's truck.

"Your parents, you stay, so your sister doesn't have to worry. Don't you?" I acknowledged Craig's quiet motive.

"For her, for them. For me. It just happens to work out that way. We're happy, she's happy, as much as she can be I guess." He noticed her car too.

"Interesting." His voice piqued.

"Very..." To see her car this early in the morning confused me. My brother was always loyal to Brit, even if she didn't notice, or care. Perhaps, if I was lucky, they had broken up while I was out.

Craig parked and helped me from the jeep, assuring me once more that it wasn't because he believed I couldn't. "It just gives me one more chance to be close to you." He whispered in my ear as I stepped down, then he brushed his lips across my cheek before we turned toward the house.

Our brows hoisted when Renea's giggle carried to us on a breeze, but before we could comment on it Princeton barreled into my thigh, and Addie barked her warning to Craig.

"Hey girl." He scooped her up like a baby and she relaxed in his arms.

"You're a brave man to take on our guard dog. She rarely tolerates anyone aside from Ike and I."

"Women can't help but love me." He beamed at Addie and scratched her belly.

"Ah, so you're just a big flirt? And I thought I was special." I chided.

He winked at me, then offered a hand. "I promise, you are." He said as I took it.

We stepped onto the porch, and heard Renea's giggle again followed by a chuckle from my brother.

"Knock, knock, everyone decent?" Craig rapped on the door then cracked it open.

"Shyeah. Why wouldn't we be?" Renea answered with a laugh.

"I'm not sure you could call me decent." Ike sounded muffled.

"Can we come in?" I asked, it took more effort than I had expected to raise my voice.

"Oh my God Renea! I can't believe I let you do this to me!" Ike crowed and Renea squealed. Craig and I exchanged a wondering glance.

"No, Ike!" Renea shrieked "You lost the bet!"

"I've gotta check this out before it's too late." Craig flung himself inside. "Ha! HA! HA HA HA! Lyd! Quick! You have *got* to see this!

I was almost nervous to enter, but intrigue compelled me.

The room was a mess.

Renea was splayed on the ground, fully clothed thank goodness, and my brother hovered over her, roving his fingers along her ribs.

"Ike! No! You-" Renea burst, "lost the," she took a big breath, "bet, fair and squa-eeeee!" She lost control and cackled uncontrollably. A grin spread on Ike's face, accompanied by his own chortling. He was mighty pleased with himself.

That's when I saw his makeup.

Lipstick that could rival a 1920's call girl, along with pink circles of blush, gaudy eye shadow, and gobs of mascara. I erupted in laughter.

"Ike! You should have told me!" Craig blurted mid crack up.

"Oh, Ken-doll, don't think you're not next."

"No way man. I know better than to make a bet with my sister if there's the *slightest* chance of losing."

"Speaking of sisters, glad to see ya Lyd!" Ike continued his torture on Renea.

"Ike! You'd better stop! I'm going to pee, I'm NOT joking!" She screeched.

"Alright, alright." He dug his fingers in one last time, then let her up.

She darted to me and gave me a quick, unexpected hug. "So glad you're home!" Then she dashed down the hall to the bathroom.

"What on *Earth* did you make the mistake of losing a bet to her over?" Craig chuckled.

"That Lyd would buy the bunch of bull she fed her yesterday."

"What?" Confusion sobered me.

"I can't believe you bought all that Lyd. I know you fell and hit your head, but, really?" He licked his hand and swiped at his face.

I stared in disbelief. I couldn't answer. My stomach knotted, and filled with nausea. The toilet flushed and Renea rounded the corner, shaking a bottle of nail polish. Disappointment pinched my throat. "Renea? You lied?" Rage stirred deep inside of me. Not only did she lie, but she took advantage of me at a time when I was weak. "GET OUT OF MY HOUSE!" Strength I didn't know I had coursed through me. A low rumble shook in my ears and quickly grew louder.

"What are you talking about?!" She stopped and stared at me. Her brown eyes iced over. Her glare shifted to Ike. "Ike? You didn't believe me?"

There was hurt in her voice. She whipped back to me. "You know I wasn't lying to you, you saw the same things I did." Bewilderment fringed her iciness. "Didn't you?" She was hesitant and, her bewilderment was replaced with worry. The rushing roll of sound subsided as her self-assuredness crumbled.

"You weren't lying?" Unsure who he should defend, Ike fidgeted beside us. He looked at me, confusion distorting his smear of makeup. "She told me, before she told you. I didn't want to believe her. She bet me you would understand."

The sting of tears threatened my remaining composure.

"Lyd, hey." Ike hugged me.

I was so sick of crying. *When was it ever going to stop.*

"Do you believe me, Lydie? I *need* you to believe me. You're the only one who knows." Renea slipped into our hug.

Craig slid a confident arm over my shoulder, bringing with it instant repose.

"I told her I thought she made it all up." Ike stepped back and shrugged. "Until I saw the way you reacted, I still thought she had. I didn't think there was any way you would believe such bull. I thought she was trying to pull a fast one on me. So, we made our bet. I had no idea you had a similar experience, Lyd. If you didn't blow Renea off when she told you yesterday, she won, and would get to use me as her human Barbie, her idea, not mine. As far as I could tell she just told you her plan, and you were in on it. If you hadn't believed her, or didn't go along with it, then she had to cook me dinner for a week." Ike smiled at his own idea.

"Trust me Mike and Ike, you got the better end of that deal." Craig ran his hand up and down my back. "Now would someone please tell me what you're talking about?" His voice rose with frustration. "What happened to you guys? Why didn't you tell me, Ike?"

Renea swung her hair and squared her hands on my shoulders. "I have no reason to lie to you Lyd. I didn't want to let you know I had told Ike, until I was sure you wouldn't think I was crazy. He promised he would keep it secret."

"Seriously! What's going on here!" Craig began to pace, his protective streak making a debut.

"You might wanna have a seat, man. If these girls truly aren't yanking our chain, something crazy is going on. I mean *really* crazy." Ike flopped onto grandma's loveseat, still reluctant to believe any of it.

"He's right, you should sit. I think I need to, too." I curled into a corner of the couch, pulling my knees up with me.

"Would someone just tell me? Anything? Now? I need to know!" Craig raked his fingers through his hair, standing it on end.

"Ken, don't freak out." Renea attempted to soothe him. "You're not going to want to hear this, but, Lydie and I, we saw a- we saw uh- well, I don't know how to say it. I guess you could say we saw a light."

Craig's shoulders relaxed. "A light?"

"A light, and I saw a man." I said.

"WHAT?!" Ike shot up, waking a poof of dust.

Craig stiffened. "My God! did he hurt you?!"

"No, no.... I'm okay. I saw him, that's why I fainted."

"What are you talking about Lyd?! Renea you didn't tell me this!" Ike clamored.

"It wasn't my business." She slipped into her frigidness. "*None* of us understands what's going on here."

"Damn *right* I don't. This is insane!" Ike scampered to the door and locked it. Then he darted from room to room, checking the windows.

"So he had what, a flash light? A search light? What was he wearing?" Craig pulled his phone from his pocket and poised to dial.

"You can't call anyone, Ken." Renea put her hand on his arm to stop him. "This isn't anything... explainable. It wasn't a flash light. It was floating, like an... an... orb? I only saw one, but she saw two, and the man."

"This isn't time for drama Renea. I need details." Craig dismissed.

"She's telling the truth." I said in her defense.

His hand went limp and the phone slid dangerously towards falling.

"There'd better *not* be anyone living in our shed!" Ike shouted as he charged to the back of the house. I heard a drawer open, then the metal on metal of dad's gun echoed through the hall.

"Ike?" I called. The slamming of the backdoor was all I heard in response.

"Where's he going? What the *hell* is going on?" Craig demanded.

"The shed." Renea and I answered in unison.

"Shit. Stay here. I mean it!" Craig raced out the door and down the hill towards Ike.

Renea watched from the window while Princeton and Addie whined at the door, distraught they were left behind. "They're not going to find anything… are they?" She tugged at the sleeves of her hoodie, bringing her hands inside, then sat on the couch next to me.

"I don't think so. Maybe some static." I couldn't help but chuckle at the insanity of it all. I probably sounded like a mad woman. Perhaps I was. Things *were* crazy, but somehow, now that everyone knew, I felt a little better.

Renea didn't seem to notice, too preoccupied to pay attention. I leaned my head back on the couch and took a deep breath. We sat, listening, waiting. She tapped her foot in an anxious tick, and I struggled not to bite my nails.

"We should call 911." She suggested.

"What will we tell them? We've seen flying balls of light and our brothers are hunting static?"

She smiled, albeit a small one. "I suppose you're right. They'd probably lock us in the loony bin." Her face sobered again. "I don't know what to do. I don't know what this is. *Do we* need to be committed?" Her eyebrows knitted. She looked at me for answers, ones that I, of course, didn't have.

"I don't think we're crazy." Actually, I wasn't so sure. "I'm sure the guys won't find anything." I wasn't sure about that, either. In fact, I had no idea what they would find, but I knew it was important to keep her calm, which would help keep me calm.

"You're probably right." The iciness she had slipped into continued to melt. "Look, I'm sorry you thought I lied. I promise I didn't. I saw the light too, whatever it was. It scares the heck out of me that I don't know what it is." Her gaze drifted to her memories. "But the light... was... so... beautiful, Lydie. *It* didn't scare me at all."

"The ones I saw were beautiful too." I validated. "It was the man that caught me off guard. He emerged from the shadows, almost as if he had been *part* of them. He seemed to control the lights. They were enchanting, hypnotic. Then he pulled them together towards him. His face lit up in the darkness. He was grinning." I shuddered. "He was grinning wide, and looked right at me. *Directly* at me, Renea. That's why I fainted."

Renea jumped as Craig let himself in the door, followed by Ike, who shook his head and stared at the floor.

"Well?" I asked.

"Nothing." Craig sat on the arm of the couch.

"I don't get it." Ike slipped dads gun into his back pocket. "You swear you guys didn't make any of that up??" He sounded distracted and still wouldn't look at us.

"Ike!" I huffed. "You know better than to ask me that."

"I swear Ike." Renea was solemn.

He raised his baffled face and scrutinized each of us, hoping we'd tell him it was a big hoax. "There was no one there." He kicked absently. "Nothing there. No lights." None of us said anything. "I felt the static though. It was gone by the time Craig came down." He thought for a moment then continued. "The floor was warm." He kicked again, concentrating. "The floor was warm, and it's too early to blame the sun."

❧ 15 ❧

"What should we do?" Renea scooted deeper into the couch, pulling her legs to her chest.

"What can we do?" Ike replied. "We have nothing to go on. Nothing except static that only comes when it *damn* well pleases, and a warm floor. Oh, and let's not forget the screwy story you ladies told us." He thumped the side of the couch. "SHIT!"

"Alright, let's keep it calm, okay?" Craig said evenly, despite the absurdity of the situation. "Maybe it *was* the sun, Ike. I know it's cool outside, but the windows could have created a greenhouse effect." Although Craig had mentioned just before how he had felt the floor too, on Ike's command. He had agreed it was probably a little too warm. "I know it felt strange, but nothing else makes sense." He concluded.

"I guess you're right." Ike sat between Renea and I. "I'm sorry." He said then jumped right back up. Princeton sauntered over to see what the fuss was about. "Damn! I need to get ready for work! I forgot!"

"You look ready with that face of yours." Craig tried to lighten the mood. "Even if we had found someone, you wouldn't have needed the gun, your garish looks would have knocked them off their feet."

"You think you're funny, eh Ken-doll?" Ike cracked a lopsided, lipstick smile. "Alright, let me shower this off. Renea, could you stay with Lyd today?"

"Sur.. Oh, no!" She screeched. "Ugh, I forgot I have to work too! Man, what time is it? I need to go!"

"You do? But it's Monday, isn't it?" I asked.

"Yeah, but Joe has a surprise trip planned for Ada. I promised I would cover for her when he came to pick her up today."

"She doesn't know?"

"Nope. Oh, and she said to tell you to take it easy until you feel well enough to come back. Since she won't be there, guess I'll be training you. That should get interesting." She grabbed her bag from the side table, eager to leave. She slung an arm over Ike's shoulder, "Ike, ole pal, it was fun. You guys let me know if you see any strange floating lights. I'm outta here." She fluffed Princeton's hair, called bye to Addie, then was gone.

I was relieved that it seemed Renea wasn't going to be quite the monster at work I had thought she might be. I was also glad the topic switched from all of our uncertainty, until I realized I'd be left home alone. Being alone was never something that bothered me before, but today felt different. Aside from the ominous state of affairs, I was still weak.

All together it made for an uneasy writhing through my interior.

Ike didn't approve either. "Man Lyd. I don't want to leave you, but I *have* to go. There is *no way* I can call in today, especially with our trip coming up." His face dropped. "You'll be alone *then* too."

"I can stay, today at the least." Craig offered.

"No lives to save Ken-doll?" Ike asked.

"Nah, I'm off. Besides, it will make me feel better too." Craig looked at me. "I *know* you're not back to a hundred percent, yet."

"Geesh guys, you make me feel like a baby!" But I was grateful, and, even more so, excited to spend the day with Craig. "I guess I have to admit, I do feel kinda weak still, although there *will* be a time when I'll have to fend for myself, gentlemen."

Ike's expression grew serious. "You *did* just get out of the hospital. I'd really appreciate it if Craig stayed, if neither of you mind. Tonight I'll go over Dad's gun with you, Lyd. It's probably a good idea to learn how to use it since we live out in the middle of nowhere, anyway."

"Dad's gun? Don't you think that's a bit overboard?" As soon as I asked the grin, that sly, all knowing, mischievous grin in its disjointed glow, leered in my memory. My opinion changed as quickly as the words left my mouth. "You know, you're probably right, I should learn how to use it, just in case."

"My thoughts exactly." Ike busied himself with a washcloth and rubbed his face, but only really managed to make more of mess than it had been.

"Hopefully, I'll never need it. I'm thankful we have good neighbors-" I said and bumped myself against Craig's shoulder, "including you, nearby. If I ever do need help, and you're not here, I can go to them, I hope?" I added, not wanting to assume.

"Of course you can." Craig bumped me back.

"You two have sure buddied up since I saw you last." Ike commented through his wash cloth.

"You know, there is this magic solution they invented to take that stuff off. I can share some of mine if you'd like." I brushed away his observation.

"And while you two do that, I'm gonna go home, shower and change. I'll be right back." Craig said.

"I've got about half an hour 'til I leave." Ike headed to my bathroom, then stopped midstride. "Hey, wait a minute- Craig? You're still in scrubs? Did you two spend the night together? In the hospital?" He shook his head and started down the hall again.

"Hey! At least we're both unattached, which is more than I can say for you!" I called after him and hoped he would tell me he and Brit had visited splitsville.

"Not fai-" The rest of his complaint was drowned out by the bathroom faucet.

"I'll be right back. Promise." Craig circled himself around me. "I'll be here before he's gone."

"You really don't mind?"

"Of course not. How could I? Truth be told, I'm actually excited to have an excuse to spend the day with you."

I tried to control my smile, not wanting to give my elation away so readily. "Me too."

"K, I'm off to clean up. See you soon."

"Think I'll do the same." I followed him to the door, and watched as Princeton and Addie ushered his Jeep down the driveway and around the bend. I waved until I couldn't see him anymore.

The view from where I stood was nothing but a picture of peace and serenity. I studied the shed. How could a little wooden building create such an upheaval? In the morning sun it wasn't the least menacing or threatening. Angelina had moved from its gable, and was draped over a windowsill where she watched the world in her silent, kitty way. A willow reached with the breeze, and daffodils spotted happiness over the grass. If the shed hadn't been the source of so much confusion I would be observing one of the most exquisite mornings I had ever seen. Even *with* the discord it was remarkably beautiful.

A glint shimmered from one of the shed windows and my heart jumped. My breath caught in my throat as I watched.

There it was again.

Sunlight dappled through a large tree, freckling the dock with bliss, and every once in a while, the shed too.

I dropped my shoulders, and rolled my neck.

I wished for my parents. Or my grandmother. I wished for my mom's hug. The hug that only mothers know how to give, the kind that can melt all fear. The one that leaves you feeling like everything is right with the world. Always has been, always will be. The kind that makes it impossible for trouble to catch you.

If only they were alive.

But they weren't.

I shooed Ike from my bathroom, makeup remover in hand, then plugged the drain in the magnificent old claw foot bath and opened the tap full. I reached to the wicker shelf Grandma had filled with indulgent goodies. I sprinkled in some rose scented salts, then poured in a generous dose of bubbles, with a dollop for extra spoiling. I undressed, dipped a toe, stepped in, and let myself sink, deep. All the way to my chin, then my nose.

I closed my eyes and rested my head, the cool iron soothing my neck. I was worlds away when the boy's voices carried down the hall to me.

Craig had made it back. He had assured me he would, but I swear not more than ten minutes had passed.

"Barbie! Your Ken is here!" My brother called. "I've got to go. I'll see you tonight!"

"K, make yourself at home Craig!" I laid my head back again, *just one more minute.* "Love you Ike!" I shouted to be sure he heard. My brother and I were old enough for 'I love you' to not be awkward, but we had still been reluctant, until 'The Dent'. They were easy to slide across our tongues these days.

"Love you sis. See ya soon." I heard their muffled voices a moment more, then all was quiet.

My warm sanctuary had already worked wonders, but I was reluctant to leave. Only the prospect of spending the day with Craig persuaded me. I drained the tub, wrapped a towel around my mess of hair, and swaddled in terry shut the door to my room. I climbed into my favorite lounge gear, leggings, and an oversized tee that had been my dad's. Both broken in to beyond comfortable.

Comfy. I wanted to be comfy. I hoped Craig didn't mind comfy. I was desperately in need of a lazy day.

"Feel better?" Craig asked when I joined him in the living room, the towel still around my head.

"Worlds. Like I might actually be human again."

"Come, sit. Why don't we relax? Maybe watch a couple of movies. How does that sound?" He was always so easy going. He stood with a throw blanket held open, ready for me to crawl under.

"Marvelous, like you read my mind."

"And I'd really like to hear your side of the story, all of it. I want to know what happened to you. I know you're probably tired of all of this, but hearing your words, in an unhurried, calm environment, may help put me at ease."

"I don't know that it will. You might think I've lost it for real." And for some reason it didn't bother me. When I was around Craig I felt protected. And if he *did* think I was crazy? Well, I'm not entirely sure he wouldn't be right.

"Try me. I don't *ever* want anything to happen to you Lyd. Regardless of what goes on between us, or doesn't. You're much too precious for that." He took my hand in his and pulled me to him. I leaned into his chest as he wrapped an arm around me. My body eased and I inhaled the vital, male scent I was beginning to recognize as his.

"Alright, but I warned you." I said. My head cradled between his shoulder and neck. "Let's see, it started one day when I was here, alone...." My words spilled, irretrievable before I had a chance to edit them. Next thing I knew I had told him *everything.* He didn't push me away. He didn't judge, he just listened. He ran his fingers over my arm, gently back and forth, and every once in a while, he would rest his lips against my hair.

When I finished, he didn't move, but only continued to hold me, his cheek pressed to the top of my head.

"Craig?"

He breathed deep. "I don't know what to do."

"I don't know that there is anything you can do? Or need to do?"

"I will never let anything harm you." He said with a hushed intensity. "Lydie, by God, if it's in my power, I will protect you." He tilted my chin up, his eyes fixed on mine. "I swear." He brought his lips within a breaths distance from my own. He lowered them softly, as if to keep from crushing me. This time when his lips touched mine, he was gentle, and steady, and underneath it all, I felt an urgency. A reassurance.

❧ 16 ❧

We stayed like that for a while. Time evaporated and passed in what felt like minutes. We held each other close, and when we did part, it was only long enough to start a movie or grab a snack. By the time my brother came home Craig and I had run three movies, but watched only one and a half, or maybe just one. They had played through, but we continuously gave way to our natural chitchat, and also to my delight, more of our kisses. Each filled with such tenderness they whisked me away, into our own little world, where nothing else mattered except the two of us.

Craig's tiny catch of breath informed me that he had nodded off. I relished it. He had accepted the things I had shared with him. I couldn't believe it, and I was thankful. I was also thankful he had accepted me, without makeup, without fancy clothes, and my hair in a messy bun on top of my head. He felt comfortable enough to drift while I laid in his arms. He never pressured me. Even though our kisses were filled with an integral attraction, they remained only kisses. It seemed to be enough for him just to have me near. It comforted me. I nestled under his arm, and fell asleep as well.

I woke to the sound of my brother talking with someone outside the door. My head was heavy, like it had filled with sand. I blinked and lifted myself to see the window. It was still daylight, but didn't look like it would be for long. Craig's polite hitched breath had turned into a rusty snore.

"Craig?" I rocked his shoulder. "Craig. Ike's home."

"Hmm? Wha-?" He squinted and looked around, then focused those glorious eyes on me. "It wasn't a dream?" He let loose a slow smile that freed his dimple.

"You're glad to be here?" It was incredible to lay against him. I couldn't bring myself to sit up, even if it meant inviting Ike's ridicule. I was too elated to care.

"Wouldn't want to be anywhere else." Craig said, still smiling. "How are you feeling?" He wrapped his arms around me, and pulled me deep into his chest.

"Better than I have in the longest. You seem to do that for me."

"Nah, you're marvelous, all on your own. I'm just lucky enough to witness it."

The front door opened and Renea's voice traipsed into the room with my brother's close behind. They were debating whether or not dunking fries into a milkshake was a good idea. She thought it was. He didn't. I agreed with him. But before I could add my two cents, she discovered us on the couch.

"I see you two have had quite a day. Feeling better Lyd?" Renea's arms were loaded with fast food bags. She tossed one on top of us then made herself at home on the loveseat. "I slaved over dinner, enjoy."

Craig and I rearranged ourselves until we sat together in a dazed, upright position.

"Geesh Ken-doll, I asked you to stay with her, not molest her." Ike glowered at Craig as he doled out drinks.

"He would never." I said, confident in Craig's defense.

"She's right, I'd never do anything to harm her."

"Good. Keep it that way, eh?" Ike flopped next to Renea, fished into a bag and stuffed a mouthful of french-fries into his face. "No crazy business with strangers, or lights today?" He asked in a potato filled mumble.

"Nothing at all. I convinced Lyd to watch movies and take it easy today, so she could rest."

"I feel worlds better, I think laying around was good for me." It was the truth. I felt like I had energy again, finally. I mused at the idea that Craig must have a healing effect. Milkshakes seemed to help too.

"Good. After we eat, I want to show you ladies how to use a gun. We're going to shoot." Ike patted Renea's hand.

"We are? Where?" Even though I felt alive again, I wasn't sure if I was awake enough for that.

"Here. Out back. Renea and I scouted a nice gully, where any stray bullets won't have a chance to wander. I'll feel better if you know how to shoot Lyd. Especially since I'm leaving soon."

"I've always wanted to learn, too. Dad was going to teach me, but then..." Renea trailed off.

"I know." Craig said. "And after their accident you never wanted me to show you. Glad Ike can inspire you again." He threw a fry at her.

We finished eating, and gathered outside. The short spring daylight was fading, threatening to make it's exit soon.

The boys very carefully went over gun basics with us on our way to the gully. We turned out to be decent pupils, and to our credit, not bad shots either. We actually enjoyed ourselves. I luxuriated in Craig's arms around me, guiding my first shots. Ike seemed to equally enjoy doing the same for Renea. I had to wonder if he and Brit actually stood a chance. I secretly hoped not.

After we finished we started back to the house. Craig's eyes shifted to the shed and mine followed. He squeezed my hand. I saw it too, the faintest glow from one of the windows. It was gone almost as quickly as we saw it. He raised his brows at me and I nodded a recognition.

"So, Mike and Ike, think we oughta check the shed out before we take off?" Craig suggested, I appreciated his couth.

"Yeah, that's probably a good idea. Lyd, this has already been a lot for you today, why don't you ladies wait here?" Ike agreed.

"Be prepared to call for help, just in case. Mom too." Craig said low, so that only I could hear. I squeezed his hand in understanding.

Renea chattered about how great it had been to shoot a gun, and tossed around the idea of getting her own. She was unaware Craig and I had seen anything, and I didn't want to tell her. I half listened, enough to nod in response, but mostly I kept my eyes on the guys. I had seen it again, the same orange I had seen the night I fainted. Craig saw it too, and glanced back to me. I nodded acknowledgement again. Renea thought I nodded to her. Ike had been racing Princeton, and hadn't seen anything.

It hadn't been more than a flicker.

Ike pulled a flashlight from his pocket, and fiddled with the handle of the shed. Craig crossed his arms, then uncrossed them, popped his hands into his pockets then brought them right back out and raked one through his hair.

Dusk settled, rendering the shed windows black in the dim light. No bizarre lights to be seen, or bizarre man for that matter.

"*Lyd?* Are you listening!?" Renea sounded annoyed.

"Hmm?"

"I just asked you a serious question, and you're not even paying attention?" Renea's self-conscious cover chilled her, I had hurt her feelings.

"Wha-? Uh, I'm sorry. I'm feeling a little light headed, that's all. But I'll be fine. What were you asking?"

"I had asked how serious Ike was about his girlfriend." She shrugged, her iciness melted a little. "Now I feel embarrassed."

"Don't be!" I answered, eager to keep her at ease, her focus on me. "He likes her a lot. She, well, I guess she likes him, in her own way, but I don't care for her much."

"You? Not like somebody?" She pushed a smile at me. I think in part because she approved of my disapproval, and in part because she wanted to gain it.

"Doesn't happen often, but she's a little *too* spoiled for me. She has Ike pretty much wrapped around her finger, though." I watched our brothers emerge. Ike shook his head. Craig had his hands in his pockets again, and wouldn't take his eyes off of me.

"Oh." Renea was unable to hide her disappointment.

"Boys are out. Let's go down, shall we?" I suggested.

"Is he still?" She asked.

"What?" I was half listening again. Craig's face had paled.

"Do you think he's still wrapped around her finger? Geesh Lydie, maybe you should stay home tomorrow."

"Um, hard to say, I really can't tell. I think he's into you though." Her disappointment vanished. "I'll be fine, Renea. My head's just a little light. Forgive me? A good night's sleep tonight, and I should be ok. Don't want to make you work all day by yourself. Besides, it'll be good for me to get out of the house."

"Yeah, I don't know if I would want to stay alone here right now either. Even though the light was so…" She dropped off, captivated by her memory.

"Yeah, it was." I answered her unsaid observations.

"The freaking floor was warm again." Ike exclaimed as we met up. Frustration was natural for him anytime he couldn't understand something.

"I felt the static this time." Craig directed his comment at me.

"I'm calling the power company tomorrow. Maybe something's going on with the wiring. Maybe the lights you two claim to have seen are some sort of static discharge, faulty wiring or something." Ike eased at his own explanation. "And the guy, maybe he works for them. Maybe he was checking it out, working on it." He scratched his brow, then said under his breath, "Although I think they would have informed us?"

"I don't think he was a power guy, Ike." *He appeared from the shadows, and maneuvered lights.* I thought to myself, the memories played in my mind. *I won't ever forget that grin. He was* watching *me.* "It was too late for him to be out." I said.

Ike dismissed it. "If it's a power problem Lyd, it doesn't matter what time it is, they could have been working on it. I need to call them and tell them whatever it was, it's still not fixed." He chose to believe his own story. I didn't blame him, it was definitely easier.

I even tried to tell myself that maybe he was right.

We headed back up the hill. Renea didn't follow us into the house, and instead asked Ike to walk her to her car. They talked a moment before she sped off down our road. I got the impression she didn't want to leave him, but the shed made her uncomfortable. With good reason I suppose.

Craig, however, did come in. He walked me to my room, and closed the door behind us.

"I felt the static Lydie, and I saw the orange glow. I don't think it has anything to do with the power company." He sat on the foot of my bed.

"I know, I don't either." I stroked his hair, soothing myself as well as him. "Maybe I was wrong though. What if my memories are messed up due to my fall?? What if that's all it is? What if it *is* just a power line?"

"Static isn't orange like that, or any electric charge. Not one that I know of anyway."

"Yeah. I thought about that too."

"I don't want you here alone Lyd. Not while your brother's gone. Do you think we should tell him what we saw?"

"And have him miss his trip? No." As much as I didn't care for Brit, I knew he was excited to see her. "Maybe I can stay with Ada, or Renea could stay here, although she seems kinda spooked about the place."

"Or I could." He suggested. My jaw dropped a little. I didn't know what to say. Of course I wanted him to, but I didn't want to give him a wrong impression, nor did I want to be a burden.

"I could sleep on the couch. I only want to protect you Lydie. I don't want you to think I'm trying to take advantage of you."

"That might be a good idea." But I still didn't feel sure. "I can't have a baby sitter forever, and more importantly, Craig, I don't want to inconvenience you." I added.

He took my hands into his, and leaned back. He brought them to his lips then looked up at me. "You will never be an inconvenience to me Lydie. Please, don't ever think such nonsense again."

❧ 17 ❧

Ike called the power company the next day. Yes, they said, they were aware of some disturbances near our end of the county. But, they said, they were so small they shouldn't have affected any of their customers. Also, they hadn't sent anyone to our home. Ike, on the other hand, figured the person he talked to just hadn't been informed. He still thought that yes, they had sent someone out to our home. It was overly obvious to him. He hung up the phone and headed to his room to pack. He had it all worked out. I don't think it crossed his mind again.

The next few days were overly uneventful. I almost began to believe Ike's version of it all. No one brought it up anymore. Renea and Ike grew increasingly friendly, and to Renea's approval, more affectionate as well. Craig and I were very much more than friendly, and it was glorious.

Shortly after I was home from the hospital I was recovered enough to return to work. I welcomed it. Unicorn Books was a magical haven of distraction from the unknown.

Renea was nicer than I had thought she would be at work, and we got along remarkably well together. Perhaps it was because of our shared experience, or because I was the sister to her object of desire, or maybe both. I even wondered if maybe, a big maybe, she might like me for me. We extended an effort to enjoy each other's company. Luckily, it seemed to work, and I was even beginning to like her for her.

Her bitchiness only surfaced once or twice, and thankfully not toward me. I witnessed her vengeance first hand when she got after a pair of boys that had a history of pulling pranks on her. She found a toad on her lunchbox, not very original of the boys, but still effective. Next thing I knew they ran screeching from the shop, Renea in chase with a pair of scissors in hand yelling 'I'm gonna kill you!' A bit over the top, but, she informed me, it was just another day at the office. Her next target was a customer who wanted to return a book she had bought earlier that week. Renea challenged her and asked why she bought it in the first place. Then accused her of reading it and bringing it right back. I don't think Ada would have approved of the interrogation, but she wasn't there to intervene, and Renea only blew me off when I nudged her under the counter.

Other than that, she was efficient, did her job, and did it well. She was cordial with most everyone else that came through our enchanting shop, and once in a while she was even friendly. Especially to Mrs. Cumberland. An aged little lady, frail and worn from her battle with time, but still sharp as could be. Renea and Mrs. Cumberland were both witty, and shared a special, mutual affection for one another.

Renea showed me the various shop duties and daily routines: Feeding the birds and dumping their litter trays. Checking the water in the fountain and cleaning the filter if needed. Once weekly we were in charge of watering the plants, which took about an hour and a half I was informed, *without* the interruption of customers. She said it was usually done on a day when there were two of us. She taught me how to enter shipments in the computer, and find the right place to put books away. We had a table of complimentary coffee, and cookies we looked after, along with other mundane responsibilities.

Well, mundane if it was anywhere else, but at Unicorn Books every detail held an element of enchantment. I felt honored to be a part of such a marvelous and mysterious place. It was magic. From the melodies of the birds, to the treasures tucked in nooks and crannies, to Mortimer, in his sweetly seductive ways. Simply walking past the fountain was a refreshment to the soul. Somehow, despite the shops considerable size, it embodied an intimacy, personal, and close to the soul, like home. This realization made me miss Ada. She brought my mom close to me again, I couldn't wait for her to get back.

I restocked a vase full of peacock plumes for sale, then busied myself with setting out more sugar cubes when the bells jingled over the door. My brother walked in, with Renea's brother too. My face lit up to see them both.

"Hey sis." Ike nodded at me.

"Ike! Craig! What are you two up to?" I greeted.

"Leaving in half an hour." My brother announced. "Wanted to say bye. Ken-doll here said he would take me to the airport."

"Already? But you're not supposed to leave 'til the morning?" Renea sounded disappointed as she came from the back with a fresh pot of coffee.

"That's what I thought, too." I wiped some crumbs from the table, and felt Craig's breath tickle my neck, igniting goose bumps.

"You are so beautiful." He whispered.

"Well hello to you too!" I turned and kissed his cheek.

"I decided to leave early and surprise Brit. You don't mind do you, Lyd? The power to the shed seems alright now." Ike's casual observation woke an unease in me. I wondered if Craig would stay over. Part of me detested that I wanted anyone to stay, the quiet independent part. Sometimes that independence struck not at the most opportune times, *but* since it was Craig, I didn't mind too much, and even felt excited.

Renea, on the other hand, wilted at Ike's news. "Lucky gal." She muttered. Then lifted her head and straightened her shoulders. "Have a great trip!" She snapped and whipped out of the room with the empty tray.

"What got into her?" Ike looked startled.

"Are you *really* so oblivious?" I shooed Mortimer from the snack table, and straightened some napkins.

"What? What are you talking about?" He folded his arms.

"She likes you. More than likes you." I informed him. It shocked me that my brother hadn't caught on to any of this. "And from the looks of it, I don't blame her. You *have* been giving her extra attention, you know."

"It's true." Craig added through a mouthful of cookie. "On bof counts." He raised his hand to block crumbs from spilling.

"What? You're kidding. She's like the kid sister we never had." Maybe my brother really was stupid.

"No way. She *is* my kid sister, and I can see she's really into you." Craig picked up another cookie. His mood sobered. He pointed it at Ike. "I thought you knew. You need to be careful. I can't have you hurting my sister with some bullshit carelessness."

"I really didn't know. That's all." Ike looked a little disappointed. "Man."

"So, are you excited to see Brit?" I asked. My brother and I were starkly different people, but if there was one advantage to being his twin it was the ability to read him, and his emotions. He *did* like Renea, and had been too hardheaded to make the connection.

"Brit? Yeah. Shit. I was going to propose."

"You were WHAT?!" I couldn't hide my shock. I knew my brother acted like an excited little puppy around Brit, and that he was eager to visit, but I had seen the way he and Renea had been with each other. I was certain his feelings had changed. I wouldn't have been surprised if he was going to break up with her, with that one last chance to see her, end it face to face.

"Yeah. I mean I am. I mean…" He grabbed at his hair. "SHIT."

"Alright. Take it easy a minute." Craig said. He seemed to have a way of calming Ike. He peeked over his shoulder to check for Renea, then turned back to my brother. "You don't have to leave tonight. You could change your ticket to go with the rest of your crew."

"Craig's right." I said. "Why don't you have tonight to yourself. Really think about it Ike. This is serious. If you marry Brit, she'll be part of our family." I tried to coach my brother. *Family.* This made me feel particularly certain about what I thought his decision should be. But it wasn't up to me. It was his life. He needed to do what was best for himself. Although, if it was someone he loved so much, and wanted to make their relationship permanent, shouldn't she already feel like family? Heck, I was closer to Renea, and that was saying something.

"No. I'm going to go. I'll think on the way. Ken, you still don't mind giving me that ride? I swear I never meant to mislead your sister."

"Yeah, I'll take you. Just think it all through man, I don't think you're only misleading my sister, but yourself as well." Craig said, then turned and gave me a hearty squeeze and whispered in my ear. "I can stay tonight, if you'd like, or you can come over, either way. Mull it over, I'll call you on my way back."

"I will." I whispered, then addressed them both. "K guys, keep safe." I gave my brother a hug, then pushed him just far enough to look him in the eyes. "You're my brother. And I love you."

"I love you too sis." He was distracted, preoccupied. I didn't blame him. I wanted to make sure he heard me though. I jostled his shoulders, and brought his attention back to me.

"Really think about this, Ike. Really think about what it is *you* need, for you. Not for me, or anyone else. To include Brit, *or* Renea for that matter."

He nodded. I hoped he absorbed at least part of what I said.

"Mom and Dad would want to make sure you were doing what made you happy. You know that, don't you? And not just happy for the moment. Truly happy, Ike."

He nodded again.

"Listen to your heart. Listen to your gut. Whichever is right for you, will make you feel more at ease, at peace." He didn't normally care for my 'in touch' side, as he called it, but he respected it enough to not make fun of me. This time I hoped he would really take it into consideration. "I'm serious Ike." I squeezed his shoulders. "Your body will tell you the right answer for you. Just give yourself time to listen."

"I will. Thanks." He pulled me close and hugged me. "I wish Mom and Dad were here." He said quietly.

"I know."

"I've gotta go. Flight leaves in two hours, and it takes an hour to get there." He let go of me and swiped a hand across his eyes.

"Alright. Love you, brother of mine."

"Love you too, sis." He opened the door, and stopped midstride over the threshold.

"See you soon." Craig hugged me again, then swung around and bumped into Ike.

"Tell Renea, tell Renea…" Ike's face was drawn, "Tell Renea, I'll see her soon."

"I will."

He left. Craig caught the door from nearly shutting in his face, looked back at me, shrugged, then was gone too.

A sniffle came from behind a bookshelf.

"Renea?" I asked and listened for where she hid.

"Renea?" I called louder.

"Don't *ever* tell him I was crying." She tried to sound gruff, but her crying grew stronger.

"Oh… Renea…" I grabbed some napkins and offered them around the closest shelf.

"I don't need those. I don't even care." This, of course, was a flat out lie. One which racked her body with the heavy intakes of true distress.

❧ 18 ❧

As much as she could be sullen, and even rude, Renea really wasn't all that bad. She was reluctant to follow, but I managed to pull her to our stools behind the counter, and I tried to console her. She iced over a couple of times, but ended up leaning into me, bleeding tears over my shoulder.

"He really does love her. Doesn't he?" Her face crumpled. "He's going… to get… marrieeeeeeeeeeeeeeeeed?" She ended on a wail, her shoulders shaking.

"I don't know Renea, no one does. Not even him."

"I thought he was," she paused for a stuttering intake of breath, "the *one*! Awuaaaaaha-huaa!" She cried on her exhale.

She shocked me. I knew she liked him, but had no idea she felt *this* invested in my brother. I couldn't help but wonder if it was nothing more than an infatuation. Left over teenage angst. *But they really have grown close, and in such a short amount of time.* I thought of Craig. I thought of how we've

known each other for even less time, and how, it
was true- I realized, I *did* wonder if he was 'the one'.

She held her breath a moment, sat up straight
and let it slowly out. Her face hardened, then froze
in a scowl. "Screw him." Anger flexed her lungs and
her eyes narrowed. "Screw men. I'm getting the hell
out of this town anyway." She glared at the counter.
Mortimer tried to entice her into petting him, only
to be batted away.

"Renea." I rubbed small circles on her shoulder,
hoping it would help to calm her. I didn't know
what to say. I understood she was upset, but I
couldn't side with her on the 'men suck' routine.
The flush from her tears vanished and her face
swept in white.

"Do you hear that?" She said in a frantic
whisper.

I listened, but didn't hear anything.

"It's getting," She leaned forward,
concentrating. "CLOSER!" Her eyes darted around
the shop. She dropped to the floor and crouched
behind the counter.

"I don't hear anythi…." But then I did.

The rumble, the one I heard in the house when I
had felt so hurt and betrayed by Renea. It was much
more distant than it had been that day though. I was
surprised she could hear anything at all.

"Maybe it's the pipes? I don't think it's
anything to be scared of." I reached for an
explanation.

She obviously didn't agree, she shook from
head to toe, and her face was nearly green it was so
pale.

"The pipes? The PIPES?!" She yelled. "THAT IS NOT SOME FREAKING PIPE! GOD!" She threw her hands over her ears, "It's so loud!" She started sobbing again. "I wish... I wish... Ike was here!" Her shoulders shook again, then stopped. She slowly raised her head. "Gone?" Her eyes opened wide, and her mouth was left hanging. She peered around the counter, then looked back to me. "What the *hell* was that Lydie?"

I stared at her. I had thought *I* was losing it because I had seen the man, and dancing lights, but maybe I wasn't the only one. She had seen lights too, and heard a sound that I could barely make out, certainly nothing that would have sent me cowering in terror.

"Renea..." I sat on the floor beside her. "I didn't hear much, this time..."

"This time?" She inched toward me, and didn't stop till she was practically in my lap.

"Remember the other morning, when I thought you lied to me?"

"Yeah?"

"I heard it then. *Really loud.* But I was too mad to pay attention to what it was. Then it went away. It went away..." Something clicked in my thoughts. "It went away when I realized you had been telling the truth."

"Mine went away," Renea's face brightened, "right after I said I needed Ike!"

"You're right!" *But what did it mean?? A connection?*

The bells jangled over the door.

"I'll see to them, stay here." I whispered. She nodded.

"Hi, welcome to Unicorn books." I greeted and stood, acting as if I had been straightening something under the counter, but it didn't matter, the customers were already browsing shelves.

I nudged a box of tissue to the floor and then signaled to Renea when they rounded a shelf. She dashed to the back of the store and returned a few minutes later in a fresh coat of makeup, with only the red rims of her eyes to give any hint she had been upset.

"I really do wish Ike was here." She huffed as she sat next to me again.

"You do, don't you?" They *had* seriously bonded, I could see it, and I could relate. It's not every day someone comes into your life, and crawls into that sacred place in your heart. The part you thought might be there, but didn't know if anyone could ever reach it. I believe she had found that in my brother, and by some strange twist of fate, I had found it in hers.

"Just so you know," I didn't want to get her hopes up, but I did want to let her know I didn't approve of Brit either. "I hope he doesn't marry her, too."

She relaxed her shoulders, and sighed.

In between shop duties we chatted, and pondered the strangeness of what had been happening to us. Why did they happen at different times? Why didn't anyone else hear the rumbles? Or see the mesmerizing lights? How could our experiences be so similar, yet so very out of the ordinary? We questioned everything from our sanity, to the universe as we know it, to the possibility that our water might be contaminated.

Of course, we couldn't figure out the lights in the shed either, not that we had figured out anything else for that matter. It boggled us that we had such very personal experiences seeing the lights, but she and I had also seen a light in the shed together that first night. And Craig had seen the orange glow the other night with me.

I hadn't told her about that yet. It wasn't my decision to make alone. I felt like it was something that Craig and I should share together, if we were to share it at all.

Before long, the shops stained glass windows dulled with evening. We hadn't realized how much time had passed, and hurried to start the closing duties. The bells announced one last customer, and Renea signaled her displeasure with a roll of her eyes as she tidied a shelf.

"Just wanted to see how two of my favorite ladies are doing?"

"Craig!" I bounced around the counter, then stopped myself before I could knock him over, and still rescue some of my dignity.

He squeezed me, then whispered against my neck. "How can I have missed you so much already?" He always put me right at ease.

"I was wondered the same thing. We really have to stop this you know, this reading minds business."

"Why?" He chuckled at me.

"If you only knew." My cheeks warmed.

"You don't want me to know what's going on in there? Interesting." He covered his face with his hands and peeked through his fingers. "You're not some secret evil monster are you?"

"Course not!" But I played along and snatched up the scissors Renea had left out, and waved them at Craig. "But you better be careful, you know, just in case." I added an exaggerated cackle and stuck them in the drawer.

"Oh, I'm very frightened." He laughed.

"So, did you hold Ike's hand all the way to the plane?" Renea flipped her hair over her shoulder, un-amused with our banter. I assumed her sarcasm was an attempt to hold back fresh tears. She and I had done pretty well at avoiding the topic of my brother.

"Yep." Craig picked up Mortimer and hoisted him over his shoulder. "Didn't seem as eager to go by the time we got to the airport as he was when he first asked me to take him." Craig shrugged, disturbing Mortimer's cuddle.

Renea brightened. "Good." She spun and continued straightening.

"Mom's making dinner tonight. You ladies comin'?"

"Count me in." I turned the sign on the door and locked the deadbolt, then started counting the drawer.

"Renea?" Craig asked, when she didn't answer.

"It's not like I've got anything better to do." She called from behind another shelf.

"I see my sister is in one of her sweet moods tonight?" Craig sidled behind me, then kissed the place where my shoulders met.

My breath caught, and my eyes slipped closed. Distracted, it took me a moment to answer. "She had a bit of a rough day. Apparently, she *really* likes my brother."

"Yeah, I've never seen her this into a guy." He released me and began to wipe down the counter for us. "My sister can be a pain in the ass sometimes, but I don't want her to get hurt."

"He doesn't want to hurt anyone. I may not know what he wants, but I'm sure he would never want to hurt her. I just hope he figures it out before he makes a mistake."

"I know what I want." He paused long enough to flash a smile at me.

"Is that so?" I tried to sound nonchalant, and pull my eyes away, but it was no use. My heart skipped as his liquid blues searched my own.

"Yep." He said matter of fact, then turned away, and continued to help us with closing.

We convoyed home when we were done. Jake was waiting at the top of Chrysalis drive to greet us. I stopped by our house long enough to let Princeton and Addie out, then after Craig's suggestion, let them leap into his jeep, along with me, and we brought them along.

Carolyn was overjoyed to have us all there, even Henry lit up when we walked through the door. Truth be told, he lit up when he saw Renea, and even called her by name. This lifted her mood and enabled everyone to have a wonderful time.

Though there was a disconcerting moment when we discussed the man with Carolyn and Henry. The mysterious one. The one only I had seen. I told them how I thought I had seen someone disappear into the forest once, and after that I had seen a strange man near our shed, the night I fainted. We didn't mention the lights, or the static. It would have been futile to. Besides, the man alone was enough to have Carolyn extremely concerned. But soon we changed the subject back to lighter matters, and left it at that.

After dinner we filed out of the kitchen with a fresh batch of popcorn to settle in for a show. Craig tugged my shirt and held me back.

"Lydie. Promise me you won't feel pressured to let me stay with you. I just want you to be safe. If you'd rather, you can sleep here. If you'd be more comfortable." His seriousness surprised me. "I'll take the couch, you can have my bed, or Renea's old room even."

"No, I wouldn't want to make you sleep on the couch. I'm sure I'll be okay, if you don't want to come." Then I thought of the man, freshly remembered from the conversation, and the lights too. The thought of being home alone felt a tad too intimidating. I secretly wished he would join me.

"Don't want to come? You sure have some silly ideas." He pulled me close. "Please, at least let me take you home, and if you honestly don't mind, I would feel better if you want me to stay. I just don't want anything to happen to you, that's all."

"That's all?"

"Well, I can't lie, your couch seems like prime real-estate for sleeping." He flinched as I knocked him on the arm. "Okay, okay, the closer I am to you, the better I'll sleep." He amended.

"I'd appreciate it actually, you can even have Ike's bed."

"Good, then it's settled."

He held my hand as we joined his family. They had an old rerun of one of my Dad's all-time favorites playing, the Twilight Zone. Of course it reminded me of him, a cherry on top of a wonderful evening with the Craig's. They really did make me feel welcome in their home.

As it got late, Craig told them he planned to stay with me while Ike was out of town.

"Oh, that's good dear." Carolyn commented. "I'd be worried about her with that strange man about!" She patted my hand. "I'm glad you'll let him stay, I'd hate to think of you left alone in that big house with some vagrant lurking. I just wonder who might be way out here." She took both of our hands in hers. "Now you two promise me, if you see him again, you'll call the police!" She popped a bright, earnest look at me, "And don't worry none. I promise he's a good boy, Lydie."

I smiled.

"Same goes for you, mom! I know dad would protect you, even if he didn't understand why, but call me anyway, if *anything* peculiar happens. I'll be just down the road."

"That's my boy Ken! You take good care of that purdy wife of yours." Henry bellowed. My cheeks lit at his mistake, but no one seemed to care. Carolyn only smiled and kissed him on his cheek.

"I sure will Pops, I'll take care of mine, and you take care of yours." Craig beamed, and didn't make any attempt to correct his father. "I know you'd still stick up for mom, and take care of her, and protect her."

"Always do son. You're a good boy. Taught you well." Henry's attention faltered, and he went back to swirling his fingers through his popcorn.

Craig squeezed his mother. "I mean it, the second you might need me, call and I'll be here."

"You know I will if I do. I'm just glad you can stay with her." Carolyn sighed, but her smile grew. "True love is an incredible thing. It's not always easy. Especially when he's not all the way here with us, but when he is… he always reminds me of why I married him, and why I'm still here today. I love that man. Always have, always will." She wrapped an arm over my shoulder. "I have a feelin' you two might be just as lucky."

I felt that lucky, and also felt sure that my face was on fire.

Renea huffed and excused herself to the restroom. When she came back she sat on the other side of Carolyn and rested her head on her shoulder. Carolyn let go of me, and hugged her daughter and petted her hair. Renea revealed that she had decided to stay the night. She told her mom she was too tired to drive back to her apartment, but I knew better. She didn't appear to be upset anymore, but I was sure she still felt more anxiety than she let on.

I didn't blame her for wanting to be near her Mom, and Henry too. I know how many times I've wished for the same.

She did perk up when Ike called to tell me he had arrived safely. I could see her from the corner of my eye, hanging on every word I said, though she quickly looked away and pretended to not care when I hung up.

CHRYSALIS DRIVE

The evening came to a close and we said our goodbye's. Craig opened the door to his Jeep, letting Princeton in first, then myself with Addie cradled in my arms. Jake jumped in just before he shut the door. Craig laughed, and let him stay. We left, tucked amongst a sea of furry babies, and drove back to my house.

❧ 19 ❧

He did intend to sleep on the couch, but it didn't quite happen that way.

I crawled into bed, he tucked the blankets around me, then laid on top of them. We chatted, and laughed. He held me close and covered me with soft kisses between our words. He would lay his lips over my eyes, and my forehead. He stroked my hair and my arms. I watched his beautiful eyes follow his hand while he traced the contours of my face. My eyelids grew heavy. I tried to keep them open, but I began to drift. He pulled away, which led me to hold him tighter.

"You need your rest, Lydie. I won't be far."

"Noo…" I mumbled through my haze of near sleep.

"Shhhh. I'll be here, sweet dreams, beautiful… My beautiful." He let a kiss linger against me, with his lips rested upon mine, until I was asleep.

"Isn't it amazing?" The soothing voice whispered.

"You're here?" I was warm, home.

"Always."

"Always?"

"I'm here, always, as I've told you. Isn't it amazing?"

Once more I couldn't see who the voice belonged to, or where it came from. And as much as it was still foreign, the place it resonated inside of me was familiar, like a piece of my very being. I remembered it's words from before, 'You could see if you would only open your eyes.' I tried.

It was different this time. Dark, and intangible. I blinked the fuzziness away. I was in a room. Moonlight trickled through a sheer curtained window. It was *my* room, I was awake. I scanned the darkness for the owner of the voice but saw nothing. Nothing except the hazy outline of my own belongings, in the newness of Grandmother's home. Our home, my home. No one else was here.

I remembered Craig.

"Hello?" I called to the emptiness, half expecting the disembodied voice to answer.

Nothing.

"Craig!?" I hoped he could hear me on the couch. The voice had been so close, certainly it hadn't only been a dream?

I remembered the man from the shed, and pulled my sheets to my chin.

A muffled scramble slipped across the floor beside my bed.

"Craig!?" I shouted.

The thing grew louder in its scurried haste, then clunked hard against my bed, jarring it in the dark.

"CRAIG?!" Panic seeped from my pores.

"Lydie?" Craig's voice sounded as confused as I felt. "What is it? Is everything okay?"

The something grasped the edge of my bed. I could only see a misshapen dark mass in the thick of the night.

"Craig! Hurry! It's coming!"

But it was too late, the hulk rushed onto my bed. It's heaviness weighed down the mattress around me. It's large body pulled the blankets tight against my skin, trapping me inside.

"CRAIG!" I screamed.

"Lydie!" He was close. I frantically weaved my head, looking for him. But all I could see was this unnamed thing mounded on top of me. It slowed, crawling, inching toward my face, closer, and closer!

Where is he?! Why doesn't he get this creature off of me?!

"It's me, Lydie! I'm here, with you, on your bed. Can't you see me Lydie? It's me!"

I blinked and tried to focus. Moonlight caught in the iridescence of his hair. His face was distorted, void of the calm that was his normal, but it was his none the less. He was distraught, that's all. It had been him, all along.

Not some unseen monster.

Not the man from the shed.

I reached my arms around his neck and pulled him to me. My heart slowed to a heavy thunk-a-thunk against his chest.

"It's alright Lydie, I never left. I've been here."

"You didn't leave me?" Relief poured its way through me. I inhaled his familiar scent and felt the firmness of his body wrapped around me.

"No." He kissed me on my nose. "I couldn't bring myself to." He kissed my cheek, then whispered into my ear, "I hope you don't mind?" He almost sounded apologetic.

"You know I don't, silly." I hugged him tighter. "You weren't here in bed though? You were on the floor?"

"I didn't want to crowd you." He leaned on his elbow, and examined me in the moonlight. I noticed his dimple and realized he was smiling. "If I had known you would be so insisting I never would have left." He kissed me before he pulled back and chuckled. "You thought I was a monster? Not your angel tonight then, eh? Wonder if you'll ever think I'm human."

"Are you?" I studied his crystal pool eyes. I wondered if he could feel how much I loved him already. I reached and circled my hands along the back of his neck, grazing my fingers into his hair.

We fell asleep like that, wrapped close to one another.

On occasion I would awake to a kiss, ethereal and divine. They were heaven to me. Not only did I feel safer than I had in a long time, but it might be fair to say, I felt safer than I ever had.

Soon the moon relinquished its reign to the sun, and announced the arrival of morning. My eyelids fluttered and I luxuriated in the comfort of Craig's arm draped around me, accompanied by the catch of his deep-sleep breath.

How lucky was I? To lay in the arms of such an amazing man? And not only that, but he wanted me in them.

If there hadn't been 'The Dent', or the recent unexplained strangeness, I might consider that I really had made it into heaven.

Thinking of heaven, and 'The Dent', issued a fresh stab of missing my parents. A tear danced in the corner of my eye, twirled a last bow, and fell across my cheek.

I believed they would have been happy here too. Who knew, perhaps they *were* near in spirit. I turned toward Craig and nuzzled his chest. I smiled. I was happy. More than happy, I was ecstatic. I missed them, yes, but I liked to think they were able to know how good, how healing, this place was for me.

"Good morning, beautiful." Craig breathed and kissed the top of my head.

"Good morning." I smiled, tipped my chin, and let him kiss my nose. "Are you ready to rise and shine? I know you've had quite the night," I squinted a grimace, "keeping all the evil monsters at bay."

"Oh, it was *such* hard work." He pecked quick kisses over my face, slowing only when he got to my lips. "In fact, I think it was good for me. I think I should do it every night." He attempted to sound matter of fact, but his dimple wouldn't be kept at bay.

"Is that so?"

"It's so."

"We'll see." I said, my own smile refusing to be anywhere other than my face.

We lingered like that, enjoying each other's company, and a much needed respite from the world.

It wasn't long until my phone rang, disturbing our new found refuge. *Must be Ike* I thought.

"Lydie! We're home!" Ada's cheerful voice exclaimed at the other end of the line. She informed me that they had a most wonderful time, and wanted to let me know that she had closed the shop for the day.

"It's just such a beautiful spring day, and I'm not in the mood! And I think it's only fair that you girls get to enjoy it too." She explained. I knew Craig didn't have to work until the afternoon, so I invited her, and Joe, for lunch. She thought it was a grand idea.

Craig left just long enough to shower and grab a pair of scrubs. I asked him to please invite his family as well. He hurried his jeep down the driveway calling, "I'll be right back Lyd!" Then stopped, leaned out the window and yelled, "Don't let any monsters get you!" then honked as he drove away.

I shut the door and smiled. "Gah! I feel incredible!" I shouted, and laughed at myself. Addie darted to me and licked my ankle. I picked her up and rubbed between her ears. "What do you think Addie girl? Doesn't this beautiful spring morning call for some Doris?" She licked my cheek, I assumed in agreement, and I flipped the stereo on to a nice ear-full level. I lifted her high and waltzed into the kitchen, singing along- "Day by day, I'm falling more in love with you…" I set her down. She curled up on the braided rug beside my feet and I chopped an onion and added it to one of Grandma's pretty yellow frying pans.

Princeton nosed my hand. "Need to go out handsome boy?" I leaned down to kiss his nose, but he pulled away and nosed my hand again. "Alright, alright." I wiped my fingers and let him lead me to the door. I glanced out the window, reached for the handle, and froze.

It was him.

Again.

The him from the shed.

The him that disappeared with no trace to be found.

The him responsible for the lights. Those beautiful, haunting, hypnotizing lights.

He stood, facing the shed, and, as if he had somehow felt me watch him, turned and looked directly at the bay window, directly at me. His wide toothless smile opened across his face. He winked, turned, nudged the door, and let himself in.

My hand trembled on the knob. *Not again! Why when I'm ALONE? Always!* Anger ate at my fear and I stomped my foot. I'd be damned if I was going to wonder if I was losing my mind any longer. If this man was real- or not- I was going to find out. The day's light leant me a boost of courage. I opened the door. "I *will* get some answers." I said in a harsh whisper. I threw back my shoulders, in hopes to appear more confident than I actually felt, then stepped outside.

The wooden clunk at the shed startled me. He stepped out as well.

But he didn't look at me.

Instead, he shuffled around the corner, and disappeared behind it. *He's gone, again?! No! Am I losing it?!* But he came right back, his arms loaded with shabby items. He pushed the door with his hip, and slipped inside. I watched a moment longer. When he appeared again, the items did not.

I remembered the first time I saw him, how I thought he might be nothing more than some unfortunate hobo, rummaging in my sanctuary, but then there was the static… Then I remembered how he drifted from the shadows, and orchestrated that glorious, eerie dance of lights.

Who is this guy? Am I delusional?? And if not, WHAT is he doing? Moving in?! My bravery faltered. He disappeared around the back again, only to appear once more with another arm full of obscure things. Again, he ducked inside; when he emerged, they were nowhere to be seen.

I cracked our door and whistled low for Princeton and Addie to join me. As much as they wouldn't *really* take on an intruder, I wanted them near, if for nothing more than moral support, and to prove to this unnamed wanderer I wasn't completely alone. They barreled toward me and darted out the door, Princeton galloped happily while Addie barked her warning the moment she shot from the house.

The man looked up and let a slow, cockeyed, half grin spread across his face.

Then there *they* were. Two mongrels of his own. I couldn't say if they had appeared out of thin air, or if I just hadn't noticed them, but they were *there*, running full force towards my dogs. A black rotund dog with a scruffy face opened wide and her tongue dangling in the breeze. The other was a very, very small brown dog, even smaller than Addie, and just as adept at barking. They clamored to a halt the moment they reached my strongholds, and they all began to greet each other in true doggie fashion.

The false sense of security the dogs had provided, proved to be exactly that. Princeton and Addie were exhilarated with their new company, and not at all concerned with protecting me from the intruder.

I took a deep breath, lifted my chin, and started down our hill.

The stranger, still grinning, hobbled toward me.

My throat squeezed around my breath as I realized how foolish I had been. *AM I FREAKING INSANE? I should have waited for Craig! Or at least grabbed the gun!* I clenched my hands, dimly registering my fingernails as they bit into my palms.

He was halfway to me. I breathed a prayer of thanks that he hobbled in his crooked manner, and didn't move fast and strong. Still, my bravery left me. I felt defenseless, and alone in our nowhere, with someone on- and IN our property.

Next thing I knew he was inches from me. Only then did he stop.

"'Ello." He said, ragged and gruff, his voice raspy with age. He continued to smile, though his eyes bore into mine. They were dark, and pressing. So dark, I couldn't tell if they held any color.

"Uh-ahum," I cleared my throat, searching for my voice. "Hi." I struggled to keep it from shaking. I cleared it again and tried to sound sure of myself.

"Excuse me, you appear to be helping yourself to our shed?" I couldn't really accuse him of taking anything, I had only seen things go *in*. And now, standing in the broad daylight, he looked very obviously like nothing more than another human, it seemed silly to bring up the lights, or static, or anything else out of the ordinary.

He fidgeted with threadbare gloves that left his soiled fingers exposed at the ends. "Ah, your shed, eh?" He said, abrasive, and questioning, but still he smiled. Always smiling. "I'm 'fraid you've been misinformed ma'am. This shed." He cleared his own throat. "This shed 'ers, mine." He stated.

I panicked. That was the last thing I expected him to say, but then, I had no idea what I had expected.

A thought occurred to me.

What if he doesn't know we moved in? A chord of relief slowed my pulse. Maybe he was one of Grandma's long-lost friends. If so, I hoped the news of her passing wouldn't upset him too badly. I also hoped it wouldn't upset him further to find out the home was ours. It might. Especially if his mind was a little off, and it certainly seemed to be.

Any drop of relief evaporated when my original questions surfaced again. *What if he didn't know Grandma at all? What if he never did. What if he's crazy? What if he's a crazy, insane, deranged, drifter?*

At least he isn't attacking me- yet.

I decided to tell him about Grandma's home, and why we were there. It could very well be the simplest solution.

"I'm sorry, sir, you may not be aware, but-" I gulped and tried to steady myself, and my voice, all it did though was make my next words come out in a large *woosh*, "My brother and I live here now. We own this property. It was left to us by our Grandmother. She passed last year. I'm sorry for any confusion." There. I said it. That wasn't so hard.

He paused a moment. His smile still in place, I swear it might have even broadened. "Oh, no Ma'am. I assure you, like I said, this er' *shed,* as ya call it, is mine. Dis circle o' land 'round it too." He pointed in a low sweeping motion behind him.

I saw it then. The grass grew differently around the shed. The difference so slight, I hadn't noticed before. But as I looked, the morning sun caught the dew on its blades. It magnified a definitive blue. A hue that when I looked around, I realized our own lush green grass didn't hold.

Dread pulled the blood from my face and weakened my knees.

This other grass, this blue imposter, was indeed, planted in a circle.

❧ 20 ❧

I stared in disbelief. I was at a complete loss for words. The man's eyes grew wide, and for the first time since I had started down our little hill, his smile faded. He looked away. The dogs stopped their play, turned and perked their ears, then I heard it too.

Craig's Jeep rounded the corner, and sprayed gravel as he swung into our driveway. The gears shifted to accelerate, then came to a loud scrunch as he slammed the brakes. His door flung wide and he leaped out, and into a sprint. His usual ease had vanished and was replaced by something much, much more severe. I had never seen him so fierce. His eyebrows met in a dangerous angle and his jaw flexed and set. He didn't slow, and only stopped once he was between us.

"What's going on? Is everything alright?" He asked me, yet never looked away from the stranger.

"Uh- I'm not sure…" I was thankful he was back. I wanted to collapse against him, but managed to maintain my composure. "We seem to have a mix up, this man believes he owns a bit of our property. And our shed." I added. The man's larger dog galloped toward us, sat, and leaned against me. I was surprised I remained upright.

The man scrutinized Craig. With reluctance he reached a hand toward him. "Obidias."

"I haven't seen you around before." Craig's words sounded like an accusation as he grasped Obidias's hand and gave it one, firm shake, then dropped it. Straightforward. I was glad. The sooner we could sort this out the better.

"Nah, you 'ouldn't have," Obidias replied, "Last time I came 'round these parts would 'ave been before yer time. But I'm back. Been 'way for some time, but now it's time for me to be back, so 'ere I am."

"As you've been away you need to know some things have changed." Craig's voice was stern as he gestured toward me. "Lydie, and her brother inherited this property. They live here now. Rightfully."

"Lydie and I talked 'bout that already." Obidias's wrinkles morphed from an eerie stranger to something sinister as his crooked mouth drooped into a frown. The gathered and weathered lines reminded me of an ancient tree, long tested by the ravages of time. One that will never give up. "I told her, as I'ma gon' tell you, this land 'ere," His voice grew haggard and he pointed to the round patch of grass, "and that building on it, well, them there's mine." He locked eyes with me again, and refused to drop his stare, even when I looked away. Almost as if he were trying to lay claim to me as well. He reached into the front of his vest, and pulled out a piece of paper. "Ifin you be needin' proof, here it is. Right 'ere. See?" He waved the paper in our faces. It flopped open, yellowed and worn, the corners were bent or missing. Wrinkles and stains were as commonplace on it as they were on him. He smoothed it with both hands, then held it firmly in front of him so we could see.

The antiquated ink looked to be a plat, with a distant resemblance to the one my brother and I held safely at the bank. There, where the edge of the pond was drawn, was a red circle.

"Go'n. Take a closer look, you'll see what I been tryin' to tell yers."

What does this mean? Certainly he can't be right? Craig reached for my hand and pulled me close to him. I leaned my body against his back and looked over his shoulder.

There, beside the red circle, was handwriting. Then I realized everything on the parchment was scribed in hand. It all looked so aged, and perhaps even authentic, for its time. Which was obviously long ago.

Obidias croaked the words out loud, as if reading it for ourselves wasn't enough.

"As long as
 The blue grass grows,
 And this pool
 O' fortune flows,
 As long as the
 Spiral hugs the tree
 The circle here
 Round ye be,
 Yer home as long as

Your time shall last,
Future, present, and the past."

My breath caught, trapped against the beating
of my heart.

"Thar. Ya see?" Obidias said once he finished.
"Mine. 'Tis rightfully. Says right there."

"I see." My voice quaked. "But, Obidias, to
be honest, this looks like it might be outdated, and it
doesn't really make a lot of sense."

"Whatchoo mean? Says so, plain 's day!" He
countered.

"It's written in riddle, Obidias." Craig said,
firm, but cautious. "I've never seen a legal
document written that way."

"Why would we be told this property was
ours? That it had been left to us by our
grandmother, if it didn't belong to her?"

"Oh, the rest 'ere belongs to you, no doubt."
He smiled like he had conquered a small battle.
"But dis ere, dis circle o' blue grass," He made his
broad sweep again. "Dis be mine. I assure you, ifin
you look at your own deed, you'll see. Says so on
yers too. And 'bout the manner in which it was writ.
Just 'cause you don't understand a thing- don't
mean it ain't so."

I cleared my throat, hoping to make room
for my voice. "I'm sure you won't mind if I double
check then. I would hate to be mistaken about
something this serious."

"Oh, no ma'am." He replied politely enough.
"By all means. Ifin we're 'bout to be neighbors, I
want to be sure to start out on the right foots." He

sounded pleased, and perhaps even cheerful. Then he turned, and hobble hopped back to the shed.

Craig spun and grabbed my arms. "Lydie, call the dogs, and walk them back to the house like none of this is a big deal." His voice was hushed, so that only I could hear. "This guy's insane. We don't want to provoke him." I winced when his grip subconsciously tightened, harder than he had realized. He loosened his hands, and rubbed my arms, then wrapped me close to him. "Shit! I'm so sorry." He breathed, then continued. "When you get inside, call 911, as soon as you can. Maybe they've had reports of this man. Tell them we need someone out here, asap."

"But his deed?" I questioned for my own reassurance. "Do you think he could be right?"

"No. There is *no way* that it's real."

"I remember!" I grinned then. "We have a copy in our safe!"

"Good. You should get it, but first, call 911." He pulled me close and kissed me on the forehead. "I can't believe I hurt you, I …" He stood quiet a moment, "I'm sorry, I never meant, I just can't let anything happen to you."

"Craig, I know you didn't do it on purpose." I peeked over his shoulder. Obidias waddled from around the corner with an oversized terracotta pot with a dwarfed, bitty plant inside. He eyed us the entire way.

"I'll meet you in the house. I'm going to stay here and make sure you've made it safely inside first." Craig said

I was amazed at how sure and confident he was. I was surprised when I found a tear at his eye.

"Craig?" I wiped it away.

"I'm fine." He didn't waiver. "I can't imagine losing you. That's all."

He gently nudged me toward the house. I turned and called Princeton and Addie. They didn't want to leave their new-found friends, but with the bribe of a treat they soon followed. I heard the Jeep door open, then a song carried on the wind as Obidias began to whistle.

It took everything I had to steady my fingers while I dialed those three little numbers. They should have been the easiest in the world, but it felt like an eternity before a nasally woman answered, smacking her gum.

"Nine wan wan, how may I assist choo?"

"Someone is in my property." Would my voice ever stop quivering? And my throat! It was so dry! I was impressed I managed words at all.

"Okay, we'll get someone right owt. Is any-wan hurt? Do you know if the person is still there?" Did she not hear me the first time? She sounded bored, which stilled my voice then packed it with anger and frustration. I clenched the phone to keep from yelling.

"No one's hurt. And yes! He's here now! He's *in* my property. I think he might be crazy." I didn't hesitate to add, hoping it would jump-start her. "He shouldn't be here. Please, send someone, quick."

"Oh! He's there *nooww*??" Finally a sense of urgency. "I'll get someone owt right awaay, I just need your address, sweedie."

I concentrated to make sure I didn't jumble it. Next she asked for my phone number.

"Someone should be out shoitly." Her nose informed me, then click, she was gone.

The Jeeps door slammed, then in an impossibly short amount of time Craig flew through the door, with his hands over his ears.

"Lydie!" He ran to me, his eyebrows tangled and his mouth hanging. "You're okay! My God! What the *heck* was that?!" He all but tackled me onto the couch, patting me down, inspecting me.

"Did Obidias hurt you?!" I asked and inspected him too, convinced the bizarre little man must have done something. But aside from alarm, I couldn't find anything wrong with Craig.

Then recognition replaced my worry.

"Craig. Look at me." I stopped his hands. "Nothing happened in here, except a frustrating lady on 911." His eyes were wide. "Someone should be on their way." I added.

"You didn't hear it?"

"I didn't hear anything, except her strong accent." I brought his hands into my lap and absently stroked them. "Other than that, I promise, nothing happened." Disbelief swamped his face. "But I think I've heard it before." I was quick to finish.

"What the hell was it?! It was so loud! I was certain that creep had done something to hurt you!"

"No, not at all…" He really had been scared. I touched his cheek while he searched my eyes. "Was it an ear-splitting rumble? That made the Earth feel like it was falling apart?" I asked.

"Exactly!" Panic shot through him. "You did hear it! Did he hurt you?!"

"No, and I didn't hear it, this time, but I've heard it before."

"What do you mean? How could you have not heard it? When did you hear it before?! Where?!" His eyebrows worked as he tried to make sense of what neither of us understood.

"Here, the day I came home from the hospital. Renea has heard it as well. The day Ike left- at the shop."

"You never told me!"

"I didn't know *what* to tell you, or how. I thought I was going crazy. You were right beside me when it happened. I had barely heard a thing when it happened to Renea, and I was sitting next to her!"

"That doesn't make sense. How is it so loud, and no one else hears it?"

"I don't know any more about it than you, Craig."

"I know." He dropped his head, then circled his arms around me, bringing me close. "This is insane." He whispered. "Lydie, I know you don't know what's going on, just as much as I don't." He looked at me again, his expression creased in seriousness. "What I feel for you… is real." The lines softened. "Whatever this is between us, whatever this is that we have, doesn't come along every day. Or for just anyone." He touched his forehead to mine. "Please Lydie, don't ever be afraid to tell me anything. I mean *anything*. I'm only human too. I'll try to never judge." His eyebrows arched. "I hope you will offer me the same? To never judge? Allow me to be open? One hundred percent myself? And honest? Allow me to tell you… anything?"

I had only dreamed of such a connection. I had always hoped, and believed that true love was exactly that. I was so grateful, for him, for us.

"Deal." The corners of my lips lifted. Warmth spread and resonated inside of me. His aqua eyes pulled me from the uncertainty outside.

Then I saw it from the corner of my eye. The same glow we had seen the night we had come home from the Craig's.

He saw it too. "Holy…" His voice was hushed. He tapped my arm. "Do you see it?"

"Ye…" But I ended there. I did see it. And it was getting closer. The color shifted, it's light growing more prominent. An orange sphere flooded a window in the back of the room, then a red sphere hovered beside it. Each filled the pane with radiating light.

Before we were able to comprehend what was happening, they liquidated to sheer color, then formed again on the other side. They floated like bubbles, entrancing, till they were directly in front of us. Then it was too late, there was no time to dive behind the couch, no time to run from the house. Only time to draw each other near, and hold on.

Hold on for dear life.

☙ 21 ❧

Neither of us said anything. We held fast, our cheeks pressed together.

The orbs slowed, then stilled. They pulsed as they hovered in the air. Their colors softening, then growing brighter. Shrinking then expanding, almost as if they were breathing.

In a bright blaze they rearranged. Craig's grip tightened around me. They had switched places. The orange sphere slid towards me, it neared my face. My breath hitched, and I didn't dare try to start it again. It drifted along one side of me, then down the other, then swirled around my feet.

Is it inspecting me?

It was like it could *see* me, and wondered what I was. The red one maneuvered around Craig in a similar manner. Then they left our sides, swooped and dipped, over and around each other, then rushed together in front of us and didn't stop until their centers touched. Their light intensified and radiated. A shimmering wave of warmth washed toward us. Their pulses stretched to fill the room, above, then below- even behind us.

"Craig-" I croaked.

He answered with another squeeze.

"Craig, are they..." I stretched an arm out beside me. "Mimicking us?" The red one sent a ray in the same direction. I raised my arm above my head. The ray fanned toward the ceiling. We sat in bewilderment. We should have felt frightened, and perhaps somewhere deep inside we did, but they were so astounding, we only had time for awe and amazement before their light wavered, then shot blindingly bright. They shrank and pulled their color into themselves. Then they zipped and twisted, then raced to the back of the room and shot through the windows they had come in.

"Wha-"

BANG BANG BANG!

"Police! Everyone okay?" A woman's voice called through the door.

"Was that real? Did that just hap...?" More knocking cut my words off.

BANG BANG BANG!

"Police! Helloooooooo... If we don't get an answer..." A squeaky man's voice said.

"Did I faint again?" I asked. What I had seen, what *we* had seen, was so unbelievable, the police and Obidias were of little concern.

"Unless I fainted too, it happened." Craig started for the door.

Two officers stood on the other side. A man, and a woman, both in uniform and blasé expressions.

"Hey," Craig gestured to the living room, "come in." His eyes stretched in disbelief. We had experienced something extraordinary, but they were apparently clueless about any of it. If they weren't, they wouldn't appear so indifferent.

"We were told you needed someone removed from the premises. Ma'am, is *Ken* causing a problem?" The woman sounded doubtful. She wore her hair feathered and looked like she was earnestly trying to not purchase the next size up in her uniform.

Her partner was a solid meat head, complete with his pink face and blond crew cut. I couldn't tell if he was older than her or not. His broad shoulders were bulked from frequent workouts and accompanied by a waistline that was probably in shape at one point, but had since been neglected. He inched close to Craig and puffed his chest.

"Ma'am?" The woman questioned me again. I realized I had been staring at them both, my mouth slack.

"No! Not Craig." I shook my head, it felt impossible to try and make sense of anything, but these were real people. Real life people that apparently knew Craig. I chalked it up to small town privilege, or perhaps the hospital. The man let out his breath, took a step back, then clapped Craig on the shoulder.

"Good to see you Ken."

"Did you see the lights?" I blurted, then immediately wished I hadn't.

The woman's eyes swept the room before she returned them to me. "Lights?" She swung her hair and turned to her cohort. He shrugged. "We didn't see any lights." She raised an eyebrow at Craig. "Ken? This some kind of joke? We'd expect this outta your sister, not you."

"You know I'd never." Craig defended himself.

"Where is the guy?" Meaty asked.

"The man's in the shed. He says he owns it, and part of our property." I remembered I needed to get to our files, especially if Obidias was about to show them his worn parchment. "I've got a copy of our plat, I'll get it out." I said.

The woman's name badge flashed when she turned. Luttel. "Right. We'll go talk to the guy."

"You got it boss." Meaty said. I saw his too, O'Brady.

He looked like an O'Brady.

"You comin' Ken-doll?" Officer Luttel asked.

"I'll wait with Lydie. We'll be right out."

She slid a scrutinizing look my way. "And ain't you quite the little Barbie." She stuck her chin toward Craig. "Have it your way." She shouldered a nod toward the door. "Let's go Brady bunch."

"What was that about?" I asked the moment they were out. I watched the two strut down the hill from the bay window. *What was any of this about?* Life had taken a more than mysterious turn. I had no idea what was next.

Craig exhaled. "It's a long story." He paced near the door, and for the first time since I had met him he felt distant. "Everything is so crazy. I don't understand." He bit his lip and looked at me. "Do you need help finding the plat?"

"No, I'll get it." I hoped what I sensed was just unease from the day's events, and nothing more.

He turned to watch out the window.

I looked out again as well. Obidias was nowhere to be seen. Officer Luttel knocked on the shed with the butt of her baton, then O'Brady peeked his head inside. Reluctantly I pulled myself away and headed to Grandma's office.

I foraged through our papers.

I'm sure I'm just imagining Craig's distance. I told myself. *Think about all that is going on. We'll get this straightened out. The cops are here, Craig is here. Everything will be okay. Finally.*

My shoulders eased from my ears as my self-assurances settled in. I hadn't realized how tense I was.

A knock sounded on the back door. "That was quick." I muttered out loud, and rushed my search.

"Eh." The unmistakable voice of Obidias carried down the hall. "I was comin' to say it was good to meet yers, and Miss Lydie. I gots to be goin' now. I'll be back when it's time."

My heart jumped.

"Why don't you stick around a minute." I heard Craig coax.

I stood, giving up for the moment, when I saw its corner poking amidst the papers. I shoved it in my pocket and rushed toward the kitchen.

"Obidias-" I called and slowed as I got closer.

"Yes'm ma'am, I just wanted ta say I was pleased to meet yers, I've got to git goin' now."

Craig stepped to my side.

"Are you sure? We have a couple of people that would like to meet you. Won't you stay a moment longer?" I tried to sound casual.

"Oh no ma'am, I've got to be goin' as of yet. But I'll see yers again. I'll be back when it's time." He turned and hobbled out the back door. I didn't know what to do. I wanted him gone, but he needed to know he wasn't welcome *back*. I darted to the bay window. He wasn't out there, just the two officers heading back up the hill. They were... laughing? I ran back to the kitchen window, but he wasn't there either. Craig was already shouting to Luttel and O'Brady from the front door.

My heart raced. This insanity was too much! I couldn't take one ounce more of craziness. "He said he'd be back." My voice faltered and the world blurred on the other side of tears.

Craig gathered me in his arms. "We'll sort it out." He soothed, but I knew he felt just as confused.

At least he seemed like himself again.

I hugged him close and rested my cheek against his neck. We leaned into each other, allowing ourselves a second of respite.

I jumped when I remembered my pocket. "I found it!" I pulled out the paper and smoothed it on the counter.

Now I had proof that Obidias didn't belong in my world.

I looked to Craig, excited to have some assurance this would soon be over. The blood drained from his face, I followed his stare to the counter.

"Oh no." I breathed. "Oh no... No. No, no."
The muscles in my legs gave out and I grasped at the counter.

There, next to the diagram of grandmother's home, our home, my dream home, was a circle.

Inside, in very small print, it read- 'This land is not to be transferred, it belongs to another deed holder.'

❧ 22 ❧

"We couldn't find the guy." O'Brady announced as he barged through the door. "There was no sign of him in the shed. Just a bunch of old potting junk."

"None of his stuff was there? He carried in tons." I swiped at my face, embarrassed and upset. What if there wasn't reason for them to be out here at all?

"Not unless he owns some old pots, and a spade." Luttel said.

"I found this though. No clue what it is." Meaty held what looked like a crumpled piece of tarnished gold paper. "Didn't think much of it, till I picked it up, and realized I couldn't unfold it, crunch it, or-anything."

Craig reached his hand out and O'Brady dropped it inside. Craig opened the foil, smoothed it, then flexed it back and forth. The tarnish seemed to fade, or perhaps it just wasn't there in the first place.

"O'Brady, you're an idiot." Luttel said.

"What?! I couldn't."

"Anyway, since there is no one here, there's nothing we can do." Luttel ran a hand through her feathered mane. You know the number if there's a problem." The edge on her voice made me think she didn't believe there had been one at all.

I dreaded to tell her about the plat. Luckily, I didn't have to. Craig did it for me.

"Lydie found her survey, it was a property line mix up anyway. We're sorry for the confusion." I liked hearing Craig say 'we' when he easily could have let it all fall on me. Heck, I just liked hearing him say 'we'.

"You're slipping Ken-Doll. Maybe Jen was right about you." She eyed me again, then knocked Craig on the shoulder with a loose fist. "Don't make yourself too much of a stranger. Hope everything works out with you and the kid." She glanced my way when she said kid. She swung her hair and spun toward the door. As feminine as she kept swinging those locks of hers, her gait was squared and anything but. "Let's hit the road Brady bunch. We gotta domestic de-sturb-ance we need to see to. A real one I bet." She clomped onto the porch.

"See ya Ken. Tell your family I said hi." Meaty said, then he was gone too, following Luttel like a puppy.

"Sorry about that." Craig reached to hug me, but I stepped back. He had seemed reluctant to tell me what was going on, but I needed to hear it, whatever *it* was. With all of this confusion, something had to give. Soon.

"What's going on? What's her problem with me? Who's Jen?" I knew with flying lights, and a strange man living in my, ahem, *his* shed- there were bigger things to worry about, but at least this was something I could hopefully get my head around.

"I suppose I needed to tell you sooner or later. It just hadn't felt like the right time, yet."

"*What* is it? You may as well tell me, while the rest of my world is upside down." A vague rumbling opened in the far distance.

"I'm engaged."

"You're WHAT?!" My voice climbed high. The rumbling swarmed into the room in great vibrations, rocking everything around me. Disturbing the depths of my insides. Rattling my soul. But, as if I was under some sort of hypnosis, I couldn't discern what was happening, or the pain it inflicted on me, and inside of me.

"I *was*, I was. Then she left. She took off and never came back. That was a year and half ago."

"What are you talking about, Craig?" The raucous faded to a background whir, but still, I was too ensnared to analyze it.

"I was engaged, Lydie. Her name was Jen. Officer Luttel is her older sister…" He moved toward me. I stepped back again.

Colored splotches crept through my vision. *NO FAINTING!* I screamed inside of my head. *You're not that girl Lydie. Deal with this. All of this.* I wasn't weak. I knew I wasn't. There were just too many drastically screwed up things going on.

Where's mom? My thoughts whimpered. I needed her. Badly.

"Lydie," He pleaded. "That was then, this is now. What Jen and I shared…" His eyes lowered and he kicked an old floorboard. When he brought them back to mine they were filled with urgency. "We never shared what you and I have, and have from the moment we met. The connection you and I have together, naturally." He stepped forward again, hesitantly. I didn't move away. "You have to understand Lydie, we were high school sweethearts, growing up in a small town. I don't think we were so much in love as were just doing what you're supposed to do." He stepped forward again, leaving only inches between us. "Don't get me wrong, we were fond of each other, and got along well, sometimes anyways." He chanced a smirk. "Other times I think we just… tolerated one another." He moved his hand toward my face, but I pulled back.

Why am I reacting like this? This isn't like me. I thought.

"Jen and I were kinda like having oatmeal for breakfast every morning. It does the job, but it's not what you'd prefer." He cracked a smile, and my foreign determination gave a little.

From somewhere in the depths of my subconscious, the reality of the soul smashing noise trickled into my awareness, it confused me. I felt influenced by it. I breathed deep, and forced myself to relax. The residual noise dissipated.

The sound of my mother's voice breathed through my thoughts like a memory. *Relax, my love. Everything will be amazing. Listen. Listen to what he's telling you.* Then my father's echoed hers. *Everything will be amazing Lydie, just wait and see.* Thinking of them made them feel close, and like I could somehow deal with all of this.

Well what Craig was telling me at least. He had never given me a reason to not trust him. He deserved to be heard.

I lifted my hand to his, and let him smooth a stray wisp of hair from my face. "Then there was you." He said, and brought his lips to mine. Slowly, carefully. Deliberately.

When they met he pulled me closer, his hands spanned over my back. I gave in. We melted together with each shift of touch. Our kisses saturated with tenderness. Caring. Passion even, and as early as it was to admit, each kiss was filled with so much *love.* So much that I just didn't care whether he was honest about her no longer being in his life.

But he was. I knew it. I don't know how, but I did. Maybe blindly so, but I trusted my instinct, I trusted him. I trusted me.

Then a vision of the lights blazed through my mind, promptly followed by the memory of Obidias. Reluctant, I pulled away from Craig, and nodded to him, eager for more explanation. Any clarification for any part of my life welcomed.

Then my stomach growled, and reminded me we had company well on the way, too.

Craig sighed and continued. "I'm ashamed to say it Lydie, but she knew we were over before I did, probably long before."

I was surprised at how this simple sentence sliced at me. He must have cared about her *a lot* to not realize they were done.

I beckoned him to follow me to the kitchen as I listened.

He set O'Brady's foil on the counter and continued. "Maybe I knew it too, but didn't want to admit it."

The hurt was bandaged, and I set myself to work on PB&Js. Quick and easy, my plans for anything fancier long abandoned. As perplexed as I felt, the task was a return to something real, and a distraction from the overwhelming. I hoped having everyone over would help as well.

"I held on to the idea that we could be a possibility for a long time." Craig said and slathered jelly while I tackled peanut butter. "I had never known anything else, and thought I was happy enough, so, I didn't think there should be anything else." He stopped talking. I looked over at him, he had stopped spreading jelly as well.

"Craig?"

He shook his head. "None of it matters now. I think I'm rambling first and foremost, because I want everything on the table between us, now, and always." He stilled my peanut butter smeared hand, and brought my chin up to look at him. "But also, because, I don't know what is going on right now, or what to do about any of it."

"Me too." I set the knife down and faced him. "We really did see those lights, right?" Now that they're gone, I honestly wasn't sure if we had or not. They had been too extravagant to be real.

"Yeah, I think so."

"And Obidias is *supposed* to be here?" My heart quickened with frustration. "Ike is gonna flip. I wish he was here."

"I know." He pulled my sticky fingers into his hand, and wrapped my arm around his waist. "He'll be home soon. Until then you can't get rid of me, even if you try." He chuckled, then sobered again. "One thing I do know, and feel completely confident about, is that Jen and I are long over Lydie. Promise." He squeezed me and brought his face closer to mine. "And the way I feel about you…" He was cut off by banging at the door. Our guests had arrived.

"Should we tell them??" I asked

"About Obidias? Yes. But *not* the lights, not yet."

"I completely agree." My eyebrows knitted. "Although, I don't know why." But I did know. As frightening as it was not knowing what they were, something about them felt… *sacred*.

He pressed a quick kiss against me, at least I thought it was quick, until I heard Renea protest from the other side of the door.

"Hell-oooooo." She called. "Quit sucking face already and let us in why don't you?"

"Re-*nea*." Ada's sweet voice chastised. "Lydie? Everything okay?"

"Hey guys, come in." I invited as I opened the door. They were all there. "Hope PB&J is alright, I was planning something more, but Craig and I have had quite the adventure since we talked to you last.

"That was only an hour ago. How much adventure could you…. Oh! *Yuck.* I can't think about my brother that way." Renea scrunched up her face and stuck her tongue out.

"Renea!" Her mother scolded. Renea, of course, didn't bat an eye.

"No, It's not like that." I took a deep breath. "Boy do we have some news to tell you."

❦ 23 ❧

The events of Obidias, the officers, and the unfortunate discovery of the plat gushed from Craig and I in about two minutes flat. He reassured me of our decision to not tell them more with stolen glances and nods. I too believed we made the right choice. It was obvious that what we *did* tell was more than enough to process. They sat, dumbstruck, while Craig and I finished making the last sandwiches.

Ada and Caroline broke the silence in unison with offers of help. Ada grabbed a pitcher of lemonade from the refrigerator, while Caroline wheeled into the pantry for paper plates.

"It's a lovely day! Let's sit at the picnic table!" Henry said, matter of fact.

"I don't think they have a picnic table, dad." Renea moved to his side, eager to grasp his moment of clarity.

"Sure they do, pumpkin!" Henry laid an arm over his daughter's shoulder, as if he had been intelligible all along. "It's right between the pond, and the drive way. You can see the shed there. We can watch and pretend we're just there to eat." He grinned at his own suggestion.

The rest of us were surprised.

"Y'all know we should, don't cha? Tell me we're not curious." Ada chirped.

She was right. Although I found it hard to believe I had somehow missed a picnic table, especially near the pond.

"Lydie, why don't you walk with me? I'll show you." Henry intuitively urged. Renea speared a glare at me, unwilling to share her father. "Wanna come kiddo?" He reached toward her and soothed her envy.

"I like that idea-uh. Why don't we pack everythin' up and head out there." Joe tossed a concerned glance Ada's way, it seemed he had his own protective streak.

"I'll get a table cloth." I offered and gave Henry the benefit of the doubt. When he was lucid he was bright, intelligent, and convincing.

Everyone gathered the sandwiches, some chips and a package of cookies. I found grandma's linen closet and plucked out a pretty white and rose bud cloth, then Craig held the door for us and we filed our way outside. Henry bopped down the hill and Renea trotted to keep up. He stopped before a large group of evergreens nestled between the driveway and the pond, their branches heavy and drooped. Sure enough, sheltered amongst them was a table. I had *no* idea how I could have missed it before. It was made of logs, robust, worn and inviting. It was magnificent.

I gawked, knocked to a teeter at the edge of my sanity. Ada motioned for me to spread the cloth. I did. She set the pitcher down, ice cubes clinking, and I was brought back. Everyone unloaded and scooted into the seats.

Except Craig. He stood, his eyes unmoving from the shed door. I peeked over to see if he had noticed anything out of the ordinary, but there was nothing. At least not that I could tell.

Henry studied the end of a straw, trapped again in the world of his mind. Joe stood to pass a sandwich to Carolyn, then didn't sit back down. I knew if Ike was home he would do the same. Actually, he'd probably be knocking the door down trying to scare the intruder away, whether he had a right to or not.

The shed door creaked. Our eyes snapped toward the sound, and Obidias stepped out. He hobbled around to the back, not noticing us, or if he had he didn't pay any attention.

"Oh my *God*! You guys were telling the truth." Renea made half an attempt to conceal her voice but was too shocked to do a very good job of it.

"Renea!" Craig shushed.

"That's it. I'm gonna sort this out." Joe balled his fists and started for the shed. "You comin' Craig?"

"Joe!" I caught him off guard. "We can't, remember? The plat..."

"Rhmph." He stomped back to the table.

Obidias peeked around the corner. My eyes locked with his, and words left my mouth before I gave them any thought. "We're about to have lunch, if you'd like to join us."

Renea dug her foot into my shin, but I continued. "It's just peanut butter and jelly. Or maybe you'd like a glass of juice?"

WHAT am I doing? I pushed from the table to make room for Obidias. *Giving us a chance to examine what's going on.* I assured myself, but contradiction frazzled me. My leg bumped the table, and I stumbled. My body contorted and rushed to the ground. I braced myself for the awkward fall, but it never came. Hands clasped around me, inches from the ground and I was standing before I had time to gasp. I blinked and turned.

Obidias hobbled back a few steps. His crooked gait and disheveled impression concealed an impossible strength. I swear, I thought I saw him wink.

"Th-tha-thank you." I stuttered and brushed at myself.

Craig hurried to my side. "Yes. Thank you. Please, join us?"

Joe crossed his arms.

"Oh yes, yes, have a seat." Ada squeezed next to Renea and Henry to make room.

Obidias grunted, and eyed us warily. Perhaps he sensed we were uncertain of him. On the other hand, perhaps he was just as uncertain of us. After a moment he shuffled toward the table.

"Dat's offly kind a yer Miss Lydie." He remained standing, but picked up a plastic cup. "I's has gots to be doin' lots yet." He held it toward the pitcher. "But yes, I'll accept yer offer for a refreshment. Iffin it's no trouble."

"No trouble." Caroline said and reached to pour his cup.

"Obidias!" Henry flashed him an absurd smile.

"Ello der!" Obidias greeted him. "Been a long time, ain't it?"

"Sure has!" Henry said and reached his arms in an offer of embrace. Obidias obliged. "Good to see you." Henry continued. "You been doin' alright with them nasty Etahs? Something must be goin' on around here eh?" He let go of the strange man and resumed fidgeting with the straw.

"Ah, yer knows me. Only do what I can do."

My jaw slacked at their unexpected exchange, and I wasn't the only one to stare in awe.

Obidias rolled along with Henry's nonsense so well it sounded believable, even if it didn't make sense.

"So I'll stay long 'nough to wet ma throat, den back to work for me. Didn't realize what a state I left it."

"It's a potting shed, it's not going to stay clean, is it?" Renea snickered.

"Potting shed? Nah. You'd be mistaken." He took a long swallow of lemonade.

"Obidias, forgive me for asking, but…" I felt hesitant to acknowledge what we were all wondering. "Are you moving in?"

He wiped his face with a tattered sleeve, then gave me a knowing smile. "Course I is. Why else would I be carryin' and a haulin' all my stuffs. Not just fer y'alls 'musements." He chuckled.

"You can't live in a *shed*." Renea countered.

His brow wrinkled and his jaw set. "Like I said, miss, you're mistaken 'bout dat." His voice dropped so low it was almost a growl.

Then, as quickly as he had hardened, his expression loosed and he set his empty cup down.

"Well, best be gittin back to work." He bent toward me, his wrinkled features melting to a buttery smile. "Tanks again Miss Lydie. It was sure nice o' ya." He offered me his hand. I was surprised to see it tremble. With reservation I placed my own in his.

Despite his filthy, rugged appearance, his hand was warm. And soft. It engulfed mine. He shook it once, then twice, dropped it, and tottered off behind the shed.

He didn't come back.

He was just... gone. Craig circled the shed, but found no trace of him.

"He must have disappeared into the woods." Ada tried to reason.

We didn't move. Nobody ate. We sat in silence.

Except Henry, who chattered away about Obidias, and more gibberish words. He kept repeating that he couldn't understand why we were all so sullen.

"Listen to you, Etahs, and Tirips- You're making up words ain't none of us heard of." Carolyn dismissed in hopes of breaking the tension. "I guess we shouldn't let this food go to waste." She tried to smile and doled out the rest of the sandwiches.

"This is *not* okay." Craig accepted his and absently set it down. "Lydie, I *really* don't think you should stay here alone. I should stay, or one of us at least, until Ike gets back."

Everyone nodded and mmhmm'd their agreement.

"I'll need to rearrange my night shifts, or better yet, get time off until he's here."

"Craig... that's too much." I reasoned, although I was glad for his offer.

"It's not. It's the least I can do. Did you see how he talked to Renea? And how he flipped a complete one-eighty when he talked to you? Something's not right." He thumped a fist on the table. "The police! We'll call them again! It's gotta be illegal to live in a potting shed, there isn't even a bathroom in there."

"You're on to somethin' kid." Joe wriggled his phone from his pocket.

"I've got to check this out." Renea started for the shed.

"Renea!" Her mother tried to stop her. "For goodness sakes! It's not your place!" And added when she didn't seem to get through to her, "What if he comes back?!"

Renea ignored her.

"Yeah, this is Joe Perelli, we need someone to Chrysalis drive, *now*. House numba 5876, right Lydie?" I nodded to him. "We got a crazy man tryin' to move into a potting shed."

"My God!" Renea shrieked.

"What!? What is it!?" Caroline pushed hard to move her chair through the grass. Even Henry was alerted by Renea's cry.

"There's nothing in there. Except the old gardening junk."

"Stop messin' around, Renea. That's impossible." Craig scolded, but jogged toward her none the less.

"He's carried tons in there!" I said in disbelief.

Craig peered in. "Joe! Hold up!" He wiped at the window, refusing to believe his eyes. "There's nothing here. She's right!" He reached for the door, and disappeared inside. "Nothing! Nothing more than what's always been here." He called out.

"Uh, hold on. Maybe we don'ts need ya. I might have to get back to ya." Joe hung up. "What you talkin' 'bout Ken?"

Craig staggered out of the shed, shaking his head. "There's nothing there man. See for yourself." He held the door for Joe, and stared at me. "I don't get it. I just don't get it."

His eyes didn't leave mine on the way back to the table, as if I was the only one there. "Please. Let me stay until Ike gets home." He circled his arms around me with a strength I recognized as pure protection, and drew me close.

I nodded my head. But I knew I didn't need to. He already knew my answer.

Everyone erupted over the mystery of Obidias and his shed. We dissected the information we knew, and more so, everything we didn't.

Our appetites finally surfaced after a torrent of debate, and the sandwiches disappeared one by one.

Still, Obidias didn't return.

Ada was the first to leave, the shop's duties calling her. Joe stayed until Craig had made sure his work schedule was rearranged, and eventually Carolyn took Henry home.

Then it was only Renea, Craig and myself.

"We need to talk you guys." I confronted them.

"Do we *have* toooooooo?" Renea whined as we brought the remnants of our picnic to the house. "My brain hurts from all of this, and over nothing! We have *nothing*." She groaned.

"Don't I know it." I muttered as I closed up a garbage bag.

Craig pointed a shoulder and nodded his head toward his sister, an eyebrow poised in question. I nodded back to him.

"We need to talk, whether we want to or not. There is something Craig and I need to tell you."

Renea flopped onto the couch. "Really? More drama?" She snapped her gum. "I don't think I can take any more."

But I had her figured out. I recognized her feigned boredom and sarcasm. It was her tool. The one she used most to cover an insecurity, or fear even.

Here we go, I thought, *welcome to our new reality*.

I took a deep breath. "This is real guys, we've all seen the lights."

❧ 24 ❧

"You?" Renea questioned her brother, like I was making it up. "You saw them too? Why didn't you tell me?!" She sounded jealous, and hurt.

"We just saw them this morning." Craig explained.

"*We?*" She squeaked at me.

"We saw them this morning, everything happened all at once. This is the first chance we've been able to talk to you." I turned toward Craig. "This is *not* our imaginations. Which I'm glad that it means I'm not crazy, and if I am, at least I'm not alone. But, it's insane! It scares me!"

"Mine was... beautiful." Renea's tough chick act broke. "Is that how it was for you?" The question wasn't directed at either of us in particular.

"Yeah, actually." Craig sat next to her on the couch.

"I wish Ike was here." She said, and leaned her head against her brother's shoulder.

"Me too." I sighed, and sat across from them. Angelina was quick to claim my lap, and curled herself into a fuzzy, purring ball.

Despite the extensive speculation over Obidias and the shed, more ensued as we discussed and devoured every detail of our experiences with the lights. Each of us glad for the company to share the absurdity with.

Hours passed in what felt like moments, and soon evening had colored the day.

We baked a frozen pizza and tried, rather unsuccessfully, to distract ourselves with a movie. Renea fell asleep curled into the corner of the couch, with one leg dangling, her arms tucked tight into a self-embrace. Craig covered her in one of Grandma's plush throws while I fished a pillow from the linen closet. We didn't want to wake her only to send her off to spend the night in her apartment alone. We were fairly certain she would agree.

Craig and I snuggled into the love seat, our legs stretched over the arm, and drifted in our warm haze of comfort. As thankful as I was to have him there, like Renea, I wished my brother was home, or that we could talk at the very least.

He would figure out what to do. It was his nature.

Even if he'd be more than upset.

My phone rang and flashed Ike's number like he had heard my thoughts.

"Ike!" I answered, anxious to tell him everything. I moved to the kitchen so I wouldn't wake the others.

"Well, today was a long one, but tomorrow's the day Lyd!" He didn't bother with a greeting. He sounded exhausted, with an edge of determination. "We've got tomorrow off while the bosses meet. The rest of the guys are headed out to raid the bars, but I'm long on my way to Portland." He announced.

"Ike." I tried to cut in, but he plowed on.

"I've decided I *am* going to propose! TOMORROW'S THE DAY Lyd! I'll be engaged!" His enthusiasm grew forced, like he was still trying to convince himself. Still, it made me dread to tell him about Obidias even more. Ike's plans with Brit, selfishly, were the least of my concerns, but I didn't want to rain on his parade.

"That's great Ike." I willed my voice to steady, but it betrayed me, and cracked.

"What's wrong?" He demanded. There was no deceiving my brother. As much as we could get on each other's nerves, he loved me, and protected me with everything he had.

"It's, complicated." I struggled over the lump in my throat. "It doesn't really make sense, and I don't think there's anything we can do about it."

"What is it, Lyd?" He tried to be patient, but I could hear the worry in his breath. "Is it Craig? Did he hurt you?"

"No, he'd never...."

"Is it the shed? I'm not there, you *have* to tell me."

"The shed lives in a... I mean, a *man* lives in the, the shed, and he's *supposed* to be there." I fumbled.

"What are you talking about?!" He interrupted. "I hope to God you're joking."

"He has a deed to the shed." I told him.

"WHAT?" He snapped, "No! Not while I'm away. This can't happen! There is no way I can make it home right now!"

"I know it sounds crazy. It IS crazy. Everyone was here. We all saw him, and talked to him even. He has a deed to our land, well, his land. Just a piece of it. The shed and a little bit around it."

"*Just* a piece of it?! It's *our* property!"

"Craig and I called the police, but then I saw our plat. It says it doesn't belong to us. There's nothing that any of us can do." I took a gulp of air before I continued. "On our copy there is a circle in our property, and inside it reads- 'This area is not to be transferred. It belongs to another deed holder.'"

"*WHAT?*" Unease rocketed through my brother.

"He left this afternoon. We haven't seen him since." I spared him the details of the missing items, and the lights. "Craig rearranged his schedule to make sure I won't have to be alone until you get home." I tried to put my brother's mind at ease. "Obidias seemed polite, enough." I left out his severe shift in moods. "He comes and goes quietly." I left out that he shows up out of nowhere, and vanishes just the same. "He has a thick, strange accent." But what I wanted to say was the way he speaks is as if he's stepped out from another time, or even, another dimension. "All in all, I think I'll be okay." I continued. "Craig will be here, even while I'm at work, and we've got dad's gun, and our dogs." Again, I spared him the details of Obidias's own dogs, and realized they were nowhere to be seen all day.

"Okay, okay." Ike said. It had been enough to soothe him, however little. "I'll try to make it home as soon as possible, but I don't know how I'll get out of this early. I'll keep you posted."

I shifted the focus back to my brother, and asked him exactly what it was that he was doing.

He explained that he planned to show up unannounced and surprise Brit, then take her to the Japanese Gardens to propose.

"Do you think I'm doing the right thing, sis?" He asked me.

"Only you can know Ike."

"That means you don't."

"I never said that. That's your interpretation." I wished he'd recognize his own hesitance.

"How's Renea?" He changed the subject.

"Asleep on the couch."

"Really?" He perked. To me this only proved his uncertainty about his decision. I hoped he recognized it, but he didn't say anymore, one way or another.

Soon we hung up, then the front door squeaked.

I froze and listened.

Nothing.

"Craig?" I darted to the living room. He wasn't there.

My heart shuttered.

Renea remained curled on the couch, sleep had finally relaxed her body. I eyed the door. It was left cracked... Something shuffled and bumped against it.

"Re-" My throat closed. *Renea wake up!* I wanted to scream. Another thunk knocked the door open,

and Craig's head peeked in, followed by all of him.
Princeton waddled through behind him with Addie
close at foot. One last scuffle outside produced
Jake's big red nose.

"Craig!" I croaked, and tried to keep myself
from shrieking.

"Thought they might want to go out." He gave
me a sheepish smile. "Mind if Jake comes in too?"

"No." I cleared my throat. "Not at all. I'm so
glad that it's you."

"I'm sorry. I tried to get your attention before
we went out, but you sounded like you really
needed to talk with Ike. I didn't think I should wake
her." He nodded to his sister.

"You were right. Just, man, when I heard the
door squeak I had no idea what it was… Some crazy
old man? Lights? Here, feel." I pulled his hand to
my chest. He laid his fingers still over my heart,
then softly pulled them way when he saw my blush.
"It's *still* racing." I concluded.

"I'm so sorry. Everything is okay. I'm here." He
smiled, and it was reassuring, not condescending.

I smiled back. "Good." Addie licked my leg,
and I bent to pick her up. "I assume they helped you
check the shed again, too?"

"Of course. What can I say? They're good
dogs." He pulled a pistol from his pocket, and set it
on the end table.

My breath caught.

"What? What is it??" He looked for what had
startled me.

"It's… just," I set Addie back down and rolled
my head back on my shoulders. "Ahg! I've *never*
cared for the idea of guns, *at all*. I knew dad had

one, but he always kept it put away. He only had it for emergency protection, and I never had to be around it. He had asked me a couple of times if I wanted to learn how to use it, but I told him if I could help it, I wouldn't ever touch it. Then, when 'The Dent' happened, not only were we left with it, but it's meant more to Ike than just a gun, it was dad's."

"I didn't know it made you uncomfortable. Please know that I *never* want to make you feel that way." He searched my eyes.

"I do." I assured him.

"Living in the country, a gun has some practicality to it. It can take the cops thirty minutes to get out here, as you know."

"I know, and I never thought I would find myself saying this, but I appreciate their purpose a little more now. Kinda makes me feel like I was being naive."

"No, your life was in a different place then. That's all." He leaned toward me. "I'm sorry Lyd." He whispered.

"You don't have to be, really." I leaned into him too. "I'm just not quite used to seeing them so... casually. It seems like every time I turn around now..." I stuck my arms out like James Bond.

Craig laughed and let go of me. He moved his gun into the drawer.

"You don't have to do that." I felt embarrassed.

"I know, but I want to."

"Thank you for checking on the shed." I ruffled Jakes hair as he nosed my hand. "Did you guys find anything?"

"Nothing but a potting shed." He nudged his dog out of the way and reached to gather me in his arms. "But the dogs thought it was more than interesting. Had to practically drag them back up the hill."

"I'm glad you're here." I leaned my head onto his shoulder and breathed in deep.

"Me too." He drew me as close as our bodies would allow. "I promise, I'm not going anywhere."

❧ 25 ❧

"Lydie!" Renea screeched. Her voice confused me, until the previous day's events slammed to the front of my memory, tailed by a heavy dose of dread. "Lydie! We overslept! We have to get to work!"

I lifted my head, and registered a severe kink in my neck. I squinted at Renea. "What time is it?" I wriggled from beneath Craig's arm, and somehow stopped from landing face down on the floor. I couldn't believe he and I had spent the whole night squished onto the loveseat.

"8:45, we have to open in fifteen minutes! It takes ten to get there!" She darted into the bathroom. "Throw on some clothes, I'll meet you at my car!" She shouted over the sound of toiletries being swooshed into her bag.

"Must be morning." Craig muffled through a cushion.

"Gotta run, you sure you don't mind staying?" I jabbed a kiss onto the top of his head, then stumbled toward my room before he had a chance to answer.

"Course not!" He called. "Especially if it means I get to sleep a little longer!"

I pulled on a long-sleeved tee, a sundress over it, slid into some leggings, then my leather pixie boots.

"Thank you Craig!" I hollered. "Help yourself to anything you need!" I dashed back down the hall to meet Renea. His hands tugged at my waist as I opened the door, he kissed me quickly, then Renea and I were off down the driveway.

We eyed the shed as we passed. The windows were dark. Nothing seemed amiss, nothing was unusual. It was just a plain old potting shed.

"Holy-eeee!" Renea shrieked.

My body flew toward her as she narrowly dodged the mailbox.

"Renea!" I gasped to catch my breath. "You scared me!"

"I scared me!" She panted, then giggled. Then I giggled, and soon we were gut rolling.

It felt relieving. It felt good.

We made it to Unicorn Books, and between the two of us managed to open the shop with two minutes to spare. The day stayed a nice level of comfortable busy. Enough to keep us distracted, but not enough to feel stressed. The boys came back, with their vendetta to pick on poor Renea. This time she found them with their fishing poles in hand, jeans rolled high, and feet dangling in the waterfall fountain. She shouted and scolded them until they high tailed it out of the shop, trailing wet footprints the entire way. When I found fake dog poo on my seat at the counter I knew I had made the cut as their newest victim.

Craig stopped by around lunch to inform us absolutely nothing was out of the ordinary at the house. Obidias was still nowhere to be found, nor his dogs. Then as we began our closing chores I invited Renea to dinner with Craig and I. She seemed surprised, and with an exaggerated reluctance decided to join us.

Princeton, Addie, and Jake were waiting for us at the top of Chrysalis Drive when we turned down our road, and ushered us to the house. As soon as we stepped through the front door a peculiar aroma wound itself around us.

"Welcome home, ladies." Craig greeted, covered in smears of powder, and two of Grandma's wine glasses filled with something sparkly and fruity. Judging by the unique scent, and the evidence on his clothes, Craig had been at work in the kitchen. He proudly escorted us to the table to present his feast.

Sprigs of celery were punched into the side of a bowl of mac'n cheese and sat alongside a tray of chicken nuggets. A couple of sliced apples were fanned onto a plate, and on another some crackers were spread in a similar manner.

Renea nudged me with her elbow. "I hope you weren't expecting him to be a fantastic cook." She said with a sly smile then sipped from her glass.

"What are you talking about? This looks delicious. He cooks just like I do!" I chuckled and defended him.

"Must be meant to be then." Craig winked.

"I have to ask though, how did this happen exactly?" I waved to his soiled shirt as we sat at Grandma's old table.

"Mr. Mac and Miss Cheese needed some couples therapy before they decided to get married. They're golden now." Craig burst out with a laugh. "Ha! Get it?!" He laughed again at himself, so much he began sputtering. "I.. I.. ma-ma-ma" He gasped. "I made a cheesy joke!" He guffawed.

Then we laughed too, we all cracked up! We couldn't help ourselves! It set the tone for the rest of the evening, light hearted, and fun. We truly enjoyed ourselves. By the time Renea said goodbye her reluctance was genuine. Craig and I waved to her until her tail lights were gone, then he pulled me close and we looked out into the night. I eyed the shed. I was sure he was as well. Still there was nothing. No Obidias. No dogs. No lights. Angelina weaved herself between our legs. She didn't hiss, or seem alarmed. She only purred. Everything appeared to be just fine.

"Are we insane?" I turned toward him.

"I'm beginning to wonder if we are, or if I am anyway." He said.

"That's how I've felt this whole time, until all of us saw him. And then you and I saw… whatever those were, together."

"I almost miss them, even as disturbing as they were…" He trailed off.

"Something about them felt," I thought for a moment, searching for the right word to use, "comforting?"

"Yes, exactly." He braided our fingers together, pulled my hand, and led me into the living room. "I know that everything seems fine out there now, but it feels safer in here, away from the window."

"It does to me too." I agreed. "Do you think it's just the unknown? Or do you think Obidias would actually do something to hurt us?"

"That's part of the unknown isn't it?"

I nodded and my eyes locked with his. He tilted my chin, and positioned his lips above mine. He brought them to me slowly, and when they touched he moved no further, but held them, and let them linger. A simple kiss. No extraordinary gestures. Ease swept through me. It was tantalizing, more than- it, it blew me away. It transported me to a place where very reality was invalid. There was only the kiss. The moment. Our moment.

I floated back when his lips parted from mine. With effort I opened my eyes and was pleased to see it had affected him too. His eyelids fluttered as he focused.

"Lydie..." He breathed.

"Yeah." I acknowledged and leaned my head on his chest. My arms wrapped naturally around him.

"We sure can kiss, you and I."

"That's the truth."

"It's getting late." He noted. "Are you about ready for sleep?"

I nodded against him.

Then my ease was replaced with apprehension.

How would the night come to pass? Since we had grown closer, would he expect anything from me? Did I expect anything? Curiosity steeped in our chemistry registered throughout me. Intellectually, emotionally, and, without a doubt, physically.

But it was too soon. Or was it? Did Craig feel this way too?

I recognized that my uncertainty probably meant I, at least, wasn't ready for more. Would he understand? Would he pressure me?

His right hand slid lower, and he kissed the top of my head. My anxiousness heightened.

"May I use your brothers room to change?" He asked.

My worry dissipated.

"Of course. I can't believe you're asking."

"Hey, I don't ever want to take you, or your family for granted. Got it?"

"Sounds fair." I smiled.

I slipped into my room and hurried into my most beloved pj's. They weren't the prettiest, but they made me feel good. I grabbed my toothbrush and flung open my door to signal I was done.

And there he was, leaned against the wall James Dean style, in faded sweats, and a tee. His eyes panned me and a smirk skipped onto the corner of his mouth.

"Pink polka dot, eh?" He observed.

I looked down at my flannels. The prevalent excitement I felt about our relationship was accompanied by an innate acceptance. Even in my most snuggly jammies. I pulled my toothbrush from my mouth, "Yeah? So?" I said through a mouthful of froth. I didn't feel nearly as defensive as I tried to sound.

"My favorite." He said, matter of fact.

"Oh dey are, are dey?"

"You could wear a garbage bag and it'd be my favorite." His smile broadened.

"You hab to admit, they're coot."

"Yeah, they are, but nowhere near as cute as you." He kissed me on top of my nose. "May I tuck you in?"

I hesitated. "Oo may," My voice waivered.

"What is it?" He followed me into the bathroom and leaned against the door frame as I finished scrubbing my teeth.

I mustered the courage to ask what should have been simple, "Where are you planning to sleep, anyway?" I rinsed, then spit.

"I wasn't."

"You have to sleep!" I cried through a towel as I dried my face.

"Oh, I'll sleep, I meant I wasn't planning."

"Ah. Well, there is, of course, my brothers bed, or the couch, or with me," The last words tumbled from my mouth before I could catch them.

"Or your floor?" He suggested.

"Craig, that won't be comfortable."

"No, not the most, but I feel protective over you right now, not that I wouldn't anyway." He followed me into my room. "But especially after everything that's been going on."

"You didn't jump at the chance to sleep with me!" I poked my bottom lip out playfully.

He gawked a second, then his features knotted with seriousness.

"Dear God Lydie, you *have* to know I would love to…" He backed me against the bedroom door, his palms flat against it, encasing me. "Dear *God*, would I love to." His voice was low, and his eyes locked with mine. His jaw set, he leaned toward me, hovered for a second, then rushed at me with something so deep, so primal, it was anything *but* simple.

Our kiss erupted.

Power threatened to unleash between us, vigorous and pure. My hands crawled under his shirt, making themselves at home against his waist. I willed him toward me. He stepped forward and I pulled him closer still. His body pressed into mine. He grasped the side of my neck, lifted my chin, and grazed his lips, tracing my jaw and nibbled toward my ear. "Lydie..." He exhaled. He kissed my forehead, then brought his mouth to mine again. His lips slowed, and then stilled.

After a moment he lifted his head and pulled in a long, deep breath.

"I'd better take the floor."

❧ 26 ❧

"Is Renea here?" Ike burst through the front door.

"Ike!" I jumped up from the game of chess I was battling Craig over. "She'll be here soon." I reached my arms out to him.

"Heya sis." Ike dropped his suitcase and threw an eager hug around me, picking me up from the ground. "You doin' alright Ken-doll?" He dropped me and clapped a half hug around Craig before nearly being pushed over by a barreling Princeton and a busily licking Addie.

"You betcha." Craig said.

"Anything funny going on?" Ike got straight to the point.

"Not since I talked to you, nothing at all." I scooped Addie up to let her give Ike a kiss.

"No funny business between you two either, I hope?" Ike crossed his arms, much to Princeton's disapproval, and pretended to scowl at us both.

"Like it's any of your business, but no." I wrinkled my face back at him.

"Renea's visiting mom, everything okay?" Craig patted Princeton to cheer him up.

"Yeah. Just, well…"

"Ike??" Something was going on with my brother, and I couldn't put my finger on it.

"I'm not engaged." He said.

"She'll be glad to hear that." Craig smiled.

I winced for my brother, but felt relief in my heart. "Man Ike… Is everything okay?? Are you okay?? I figured you didn't call because you were caught up in all the excitement." I moved to my brother's side, but he candidly brushed off my concern.

"Actually, I'm more than okay. Don't get me wrong. I was disturbed when I showed up to her parents' house to learn she was out with Shane, whoever the hell Shane is. They were kind enough to let me in while I waited. When she showed up, I got an eyeful of them wrapped around each other. She boo hooed when she realized I was there, for about five minutes, then we both agreed it should have been over long before." Ike reached down and gave in to Princeton's pleas for an ear scratching. "I did take the pleasure of showing her the ring she wouldn't get. Thought Shane might like a glimpse of how shallow she can be." He chuckled. "Man, when she saw the ring…"

Ike's tale was interrupted. Renea cracked the door and poked her head in, her eyes pierced my brother.

"You're home. Congrats." She spat with disdain, then turned and slammed the door behind her.

"Renea!" Ike leapt for the door.

A rush blew it open in his face. Angelina hissed and darted from the room. Addie whined and Princeton tried to climb into my arms. The burst was followed close by that same, awful, soul curdling sound I had heard before. But this time we all heard it. I know, because we all dropped to the floor and covered our heads. Craig threw his body over me. Renea pummeled into us, her eyes wide with terror.

"It's out there! Coming for me!" She screamed and dove into Ike.

"What the heck is that!?" Ike cried as the noise subsided slightly.

"I didn't see it, but I know it was there!" Her voice cracked.

Craig kicked the door shut, then ushered me toward Ike and Renea where we huddled into a lump, too scared to move. I watched Ike gather Renea in closer. The noise subsided more. She nestled her head into his chest, and closed her eyes. As she did the sound subdued to nothing more than a low roar.

"Renea... he's not engaged." A theory tugged at my thoughts.

"You're not?" She looked at my brother, tears threatening to spill. The noise ceased.

"No. Geesh, didn't even give me a chance to tell you." He hugged her. "I guess you weren't too keen on the idea, huh?"

She blushed and shrugged. Princeton nosed her hand.

"What *was* that??" Ike asked.

"I think it had something to do with Renea." I offered my observation.

"Why?!" She said defensively, and sure enough, in the far distance the rumble opened, supporting my theory.

"Hear that?" I asked. Renea glowered and the sound increased. "I am *not* causing it!" She ended with a shout. The windows trembled in their frames as the sound thundered around the house.

"Renea!" I screamed above the roar. "Hear me out! Take a deep breath, I don't think *you* caused it, but I do think that whatever it is, is reacting to you." My brother seemed to follow what I was saying and caressed her. The sound lowered.

Then he kissed her.

The sound died immediately.

"You're right." Craig kissed me too. He gave me a smug smile when he pulled away. "Wanted to see if anything else would happen."

"That doesn't make sense." Renea breathed and shook her head. "Why me?"

"I don't think it's *just* you, I heard it too, when I was upset, remember? Although this is the first we've heard it so loudly together, at the same time... Strange." I said.

"And I thought everything had been smooth going the last couple of days." Ike said. "I come home and *WHAM*. Maybe it's reacting to me."

"No, Lydie and I saw those strange lights at the same time while you were gone." Craig reminded him.

"Oh- Yeah." Ike bit his lip and dropped his head.

We sat in silence for a moment. None of us sure about what to think, or do, about any of it.

"So, if it was reacting to Renea while she was upset, and Craig and I saw the lights when we were both, well… happy…" I hypothesized.

"I was feeling good too when I saw mine too." Renea chimed in, blush tinting her cheeks. "I had just left from spending time with you." She glanced at Ike from under her lashes. "I was really happy."

"Why didn't you tell me how you felt?" He asked. "Especially when you knew I was going to propose."

"That's exactly why!" Exasperation strangled her voice. "If you had felt it too, you wouldn't. And you left anyway!" She shrieked. The wind gusted against the house, and with it a remnant of growl. Addie's ears pricked and she sounded a sharp bark, her eyes wide and waiting. Princeton went on guard too.

The back door burst open.

"Stop!" Obidias's deep voice boomed into the room.

"Wha-?" Ike jumped up.

"Just stop right der! All aw yous!" Addie darted toward Obidias then sat attentively at his feet. Princeton didn't move, but stared at him. Their behavior puzzled me. Obidias reached behind him to shut the door and Ike started for the kitchen. The grumble under the wind groaned louder. Tree branches clawed at the house. "Listen to me! Ya hears? Now jus stop!"

Ike stood still. Craig sheathed Renea under his other arm.

"You hears dat der?!" Obidias roared. "Yous be creatin' dat. All o' yous. That be the Etah!"

"We're not creating anything!" Ike snapped. "Get out of our house!" He yelled and reached for the knife block. The sounds intensified. The vibrations grew deeper, and violent.

"Son!" Obidias pointed a crooked finger at Ike. "I ain't here to hurts you!"

"Don't you DARE call me son!" Ike whipped the largest knife out and waved it at Obidias.

The raucous thundered around us.

"STOP IT I TELL YOU!" Obidias was impossibly loud as he commanded above the noise. None of us moved.

None of us *breathed*.

The wind whipped and the doors beat within their frames. "I's be yours Llewrenni. I's is here to help. Now please, jus stop yer panic, 'fore it's too late." The soul disrupting sound battered on. "None of dat's goin' to let up till you quiet yourselfs. Quiet your worries. Yer fears."

Ike inched his knife down. Craig loosened his grip on us. I breathed deep. Renea followed my lead and did too. The sound softened.

"Thar. You sees?" Obidias said calmly.

"What is all of this, who are you?" Craig asked and stood. Renea and I followed.

"Like I's said. I's is your Llewrenni. I's is here, cause the truth is near. That's why the Etahs be here too." Obidias explained.

"Can you lay off the cryptic speak?" Ike demanded. The vibrations increased in response.

"Son, Like I's been telling yous, I's here to help. I's here to protect yous."

"From *what*? How do we know we can trust you? What *is* that out there?" Ike darted questions at the gnarled man.

"What dat is, is what yous feelin here." Obidias thumped his chest with a fist. "Anytime da truths are nears, the realizations start bringing forth The Etahs, and alsos, like's yous seen, your Tirips."

"Our whatty waddys?" Renea tried to cover her anxiety with sarcasm.

"I can't be splainin now. I's gots to go. Keeps your heads up. You see how infectious the Etah be."

Knock knock knock.

I looked to the front door, then back to Obidias. He was gone.

"Where'd he go?" Ike swiveled his head back and forth, looking for the strange man.

"I didn't see." Craig accepted the knife Ike handed him.

"Me either." I said.

"Or me." Renea watched Ike disappear down the hallway.

Knock knock knock.

Ike emerged with dad's pistol and nodded to Craig, who held the knife behind his back, and cracked the door.

"Ken! Hi hon! These fellas were up by our house. We saw Norma's address on their collars. Didn't know if someone had moved into the ole place or not." A woman's voice greeted.

I peeked around Craig's shoulder to see a salt and pepper, soft around the edges lady, with a sharp nosed, thin man at her side.

"Hi, I'm Lydie." I said. They looked friendly enough. I looked down to see who they had brought to our door. A round black dog sat, tongue bobbing merrily, next to a scrawny little brown one.

Obidias's dogs.

ᕰ 27 ᕭ

The lady gasped. "Lydie! Why, you're Kara's girl, ain'tcha? Boy, I can tell! Why, you look just like her!" I nodded as more sing songy words flew from her. "Well I'll be. Welcome to Nepenthe! We're your neighbors, well, your other neighbors aside from the Craig's, that is. We're in the blue house out on the main road. Closest one. I'm sure you've seen it? Anywho, I'm Gail, this here's my husband, Grant. Williams. These dogs belong to ya'll?"

"Well, no, I mean yes, I mean, they belong here, kind of." I heaved a sigh.

"The shed belongs to someone else. These are his dogs, is what she is trying to say." Craig came to my rescue.

"The shed?" Gail's eyebrows hoisted.

"Don't sound right." Grant disapproved.

"No, we didn't think so either. But it seems to be. We found out a couple of days ago." Craig shifted so that I could stand in the door way.

"Oooo, Norma's *got* to be rolling in her grave! Right 'long 'side Bill, I'm sure." It was strange to hear her speak of my grandparents. Strange, but good. Cozy, like home.

"He says his name is Obidias. Have either of you heard of him? Do you know him by chance?" Craig asked.

"Don't sound one bit familiar to me." Gail was quick to answer, Grant on the other hand, fingered his chin and searched his memory.

"Nah, me neither." He concluded. The dogs squirmed with impatience. "Want me to take 'em to the shed?" Grant asked.

"I'll take them." Ike opened the door all the way and stepped onto the porch. "I'm Ike, Lydie's brother."

"Why! Of course you are dear, you look just like your father. It sure is a pity what happened to your parents. Poor Kara and Eric." Gail tsk'd.

"It is, thank you for your sympathy." My brother switched to auto pilot as he took the leads from Grant. We'd thanked people for their condolences so much in the last months.

"I forgot my manners," I stepped back and made room through the entryway, "would you like to come in?"

"That's awfully sweet o' you darlin', and yes, we would, some other time perhaps? Right now we gotta be goin'. Dinner is waitin'." Gail's eyes brightened. "Would ya'll like to join us? We'd surely love to have you."

"We're okay, thank you."

Gail raised an eyebrow at Ike's quick decline, then brushed it off with a smile. "Well okay, ya'll will have to come on over soon though. It'll be nice to have Norma and Bill's grandkids 'round, won't it Grant?"

"'Course it will. Anytime you'd like ya'll are more than welcome." Grant patted her shoulder. "Now let's let them get back to their evening dear."

"Alrighty then." Gail let Grant guide her from the porch. "Welcome to Nepenthe!" She called again over her shoulder. "We'll be seein' you!"

We watched as he opened the door to their sedan for her, shuffled to his side and wiggled in, then they disappeared out of Chrysalis Drive.

"Great. Freakin' great. What are we supposed to do with these guys?" Ike knelt to rub both of the dogs.

"I guess we should try and take them to the shed, see if he's there." Craig suggested and joined Ike on the porch. "I'll go with you."

"What about you guys? I can't believe he just walked into our house!" His frustration picked up, and in response a light breeze whipped.

"Ike!" I looked to the top of the trees. "The wind. What if there's truth to what Obidias said?"

"How can any of his nonsense be truth?" It was natural for Ike to deny what he didn't understand.

"Ike, there's gotta be." Renea surprised me as she confronted my brother. "You *have* to admit that was a lot more than just coincidence. Besides, even though *you* haven't see them, each of us have seen the lights. Trust me, there's nothing normal, or rational about them."

He groaned.

"We'll come with you." I stepped out to join them. Renea stayed inside, her eyes wide.

"Come on Renea." Craig motioned for her to join us.

She shook her head.

"Renea? Please?" Ike offered his hand. She contemplated, then slid her own into his. Princeton and Addie bounced out to greet the new comers. Ike struggled to keep them by his side, then gave up and let them loose to play.

The sky had slipped into dusk and whispered in ominous tones. The shed sat, hunched in shadow. We saw no sign of life, no sign of Obidias. My brother reached it first, and held Renea's hand as he rapped on the door. She crouched behind him.

Obidias's dogs inhaled in large puffs as they scratched at the door. Addie led Princeton in an inspection where it's walls met the ground.

No one came to the door.

Craig crept to the window and peered in. "He's not in there."

Ike joined him, then opened the door. He disappeared inside and Craig followed. At the sound of their shuffles and clunks I peeked in to find them both searching the place. I touched the floor. It was cold.

"Whatever. I don't get it." Ike dismissed and stomped out. The black dog happily placed herself on his feet, unfazed by his foul mood. "What are we supposed to do with these guys?" He bent to inspect her tag. "Molly."

Renea lifted the smaller one and checked his too. "Cooper." He licked her face in response.

"They could stay with us. They get along with ours." I suggested.

"No. I don't want *him* on our property," Ike jerked his head toward the shed, "let alone his dogs in our house. Besides, we don't know anything about them. They might destroy the place."

"*Come on* Ike, have a heart." I rubbed my arms. "The nights are still too cold to make them stay out."

"Plenty of dogs stay outside." He argued.

"Awe Ike, let 'um. I would take them to my apartment if I could." Renea rubbed her cheek against Coopers soft fur.

That won my brother over.

"Alright, but only if they stay in the laundry room." He conceded.

The new dogs settled into the living room the moment they entered the house, much to my brother's chagrin, and they didn't even destroy anything.

Once again, we were flabbergasted, without a thing we could do about any of the strangeness, and no evidence aside from two panting guests to prove there was anything amiss at all.

Craig soon had to leave for a night shift. I walked him to his Jeep, and his reluctance to leave was evident as his kiss goodbye lingered.

We had grown very accustomed, and comfortable with each other's company.

He waved me back into the safety of the house before he drove away. Once I was inside Renea and Ike barely acknowledged me as they were wrapped deep into their own conversations.

To afford both of them their privacy, I grabbed my novel from Unicorn Books and set out for the bathroom to indulge in some pampering. I lit some of the scented candles Grandma had tucked in with her bath treasures and as the tub's faucet gushed I generously poured other goodies in.

The bubbles grew thick, and deep. I swooshed my toes to test the water then carefully lowered myself in and escaped inside the whimsical world of my book.

Pages, along with puckered fingers and toes later, I finally pulled myself from my sanctuary. The uncertainty of the afternoon felt worlds away, leaving me relaxed and refreshed. Still, Ike and Renea's continuous chitchat carried down the hall to me, so I continued my pampering. I picked out a happy polish and brushed it on my toes. My fingers were next, with a barely-there blush tipped with iridescent glitter. Their voices softened. I flipped on my new favorite station and Nat King Cole crackled to life crooning, "Unforgettable". Pleased with my luxuriating I sashayed around my room, feet apart and fingers spread as I waved my hands to the melody and sang along with him.

I passed myself in Grandma's vanity mirror and couldn't help but laugh. Then I scrunched my face into a ridiculous pose. What would Craig think if he could see me now? *How did I get so lucky?* I wondered. Thinking of him made me smile. I missed him. How was I so attached already? The glitter from my paint glinted, and I smiled at it too. Would Craig think my glitter was silly? Would he like it? Because it was me, and he wouldn't expect anything less? I liked that I felt free to be me with him. I couldn't imagine trying to pretend to be someone I wasn't.

A violin soloist soared from the speakers next, and then an overture from 'Oklahoma!'. I cracked my door open to listen. All four dogs nosed their way in, and a miffed Angelina darted down the hall.

The talking had ceased and the sound of the front door was the only thing I heard. I waddled down the hall and peeked from the bay window.

Renea was leaned against her car, and Ike rested himself over her.

I knew it wasn't polite to watch, but I couldn't help it.

It was worth it as he bent to give her their first *real* kiss.

"Oooooo! I saw you!" I teased when Ike crept in. His mouth hung, searching for something clever. "Holy! You're, blushing!" I chided. The pink on his cheeks rivaled a sunburn.

"Like you have room to talk!" He crowed.

My phone interrupted our banter.

"How's it going? Anything else happen? I miss you." Craig's voice exhaled. "It's strange to not be there, you know, in case, um, in case you need me." He sounded bashful.

I turned my back to Ike and dropped my voice.

"I always need you." I felt a bit bashful as well. "And for what it's worth, I miss you too."

"HA!" Ike shouted in triumph.

"What was that? Is everything okay?! Did something happen?" Craig sounded startled.

"Just Ike." I laughed. "I was teasing him about kissing your sister."

"Really!?" He chuckled.

I confirmed, then reassured him everything was okay so far.

"Alright, well, be sure to call if you guys need *anything*. Or, just because." He hinted.

Ike picked on me for a moment after I got off the phone, and I picked right back. Even though our twinship brought us close, we were still brother and sister, entitled to harass each other every once in a while.

After our banter I tried to bring up Obidias, and the wind, and the noise. It was no use. Ike cursed Obidias for barging into our house, then flipped on the TV to signal he was done with the discussion. It was his escape, just as Renea did with her catty behavior, and I did with my books. My brother had stonewalled himself into a state of denial.

With resignation I told him goodnight and headed to my room. I snuggled deep under one of grandma's quilts and read some more of my book. Truth be told, I welcomed the distraction too.

❦ 28 ❧

"Lydie…" My name sighed around me. "Isn't it amazing?"

That voice… It was the same, and although it registered astoundingly familiar, I still couldn't place it.

"Whoooo- are- *you*?" My words were slow, and heavy, like molasses. "Where, are, we? What, are we- doinghere?" I pushed out the last in a rush. I tried to open my eyes, but I wasn't strong enough. They wouldn't budge.

A seducing warmth drifted along my body. I gave my struggle up and let the delightful waves wash me into peace.

"We're here, where we've always been. I'm so thankful. Thankful we're here, that we're with each other. We're here where we belong."

I heard, no- *felt* the voice inhale.

"Life is grand, isn't it? Isn't it amazing?" It asked.

Steeped in calm I was reluctant to answer. I didn't want to break the spell.

I didn't say anything.

I think it understood. Although my eye lids were still too heavy, light broke beneath them. The glow parted and gave way to a silhouette. Someone, or something, joined my space. It didn't feel invasive though. Not at all what so ever. In fact, I found myself willing it's warmth closer. The light around us variegated in an array of color.

"Isn't it amazing?" It whispered, incredibly close.

"Yes," I brought myself to answer. "I don't want to leave… ever." I exhaled. My statement surprised me, yet, realizing I meant it, I allowed myself to slip deeper into the profound peace.

Something cold, and fleshy pushed at my face.

I cringed.

The colors evaporated and cold dark replaced their splendor.

"Are you still here?" I whispered.

There was no answer.

The cool moist prodded my face again, this time with vigor, accompanied by an abrasive smell, then a slurp fringed in recognition.

I forced an eye open.

"Princeton! *Ugh*." He happily slurped again and his drool slid down my cheek. "Why couldn't you have woken Ike?"

His tail thumped against my bed.

It was only a dream. I thought.

But it had felt *so* vivid- *so* real.

With another smack of his tongue Princeton insisted I get up. I shook my head, wriggled into my slippers and stumbled down the hall as he led the way. Addie clicked from Ike's room to join us. I opened the door, let them out, and the doorframe drew my head to it like a magnet.

The cool night air whisked around my legs as Addie pranced through the inkiness. Princeton's muted bulk ambled out and nosed the terrain. Then Addie stopped, and pricked her ears. Princeton's coat doubled in size as his fur raised. I scanned the night before my eyes instinctively landed on the shed.

There was nothing.

A growl started from deep inside them both and rolled up through their throats.

A ray of light darted from underneath the shed door.

My heart dropped.

A red globe drifted slowly from around the shed's corner.

Fear, and a foreign twinge of excitement rushed through my veins. I closed my eyes, and willed the light away. Maybe I was still dreaming. I opened them again- no such luck. I scrubbed my eyes with my hands, and tried again.

Nope, it was still there.

It was fascinating, and alluring, just like the ones Craig and I had seen. *Maybe I am still dreaming, and I just can't wake myself up.* I tried to rationalize again. At least this made sense. I coaxed my eyes to pull away from the orb to examine everything else. The shadows of the trees were too defined. The noises that belonged to the night rang through the air, too clear. *It's all too vivid,* I thought. The moist scent of earth carried on the night breeze. Angelina brushed against me, her fur soft, and real. She watched the light as well, her eyes stretched in feline intrigue.

Worry inched over my back and wrapped its icy fingers around my throat. It was all *much* too vivid.

The ball of light twirled and a brilliant blue one floated to join it. Princeton and Addie still sat alert, but their growls had ceased. They too were mesmerized. The lights radiated brighter as they drew near one another, then they began a slow dance of orbiting and drifting.

Maybe Ike can wake me. I turned and started in a daze down the hall. *And if I'm not dreaming? I* need *to wake him.* Plain and simple.

I cracked his door and peeked my head in at my brother. A rainbow of light trickled through his window.

"Ike." My voice quivered. He didn't budge. I stumbled to the edge of his bed and shook his shoulder. "Ike!"

"Lydie?" He croaked. "What is it?"

"Am I dreaming?"

"What do you mean?" He sat himself up, groggy.

"I think, Obidias's shed... I thought,"

"Lyd, *what* is it?" He prompted again, his guard beginning to wake.

"The lights," I pointed to the colors drifting into his room. "They're here. Floating around Obidias's shed."

He shot out of bed and into the hall, turned, ran to his dresser, pulled out dad's gun, and bolted toward the hall again, colliding with my foot on his way.

It hurt. Bad.

Enough to confirm I was awake. For sure.

I chased after him. He had stopped in the front door by the time I reached him and he flinched as I sidled up next to him. His eyes were locked straight ahead, his body tensed. He held his arms out in a subconscious effort to guard me, the gun drooped in a way that told me he was no longer aware of it.

"My God." He breathed. "What *are* they?" He asked. I don't think he had believed me, and had just been alerted at the mention of Obidias.

"I thought… I was dreaming."

"I wish you were, I don't… understand…" He started out the door. "Stay here!"

"What are you doing?!" I called after him.

"I'm going to see if he's ther-" A horrific, deep sound pulsated the air. The wind kicked in response. Ike stopped long enough to make sure I was alright, then started down the hill again.

"Ike!" I shouted. "I don't think this is a good idea! Maybe we should get in the basement!"

Princeton charged past me into the house. Addie, on the other hand, ran to Ike's heel. My brother ignored me. He had remembered Dad's gun, and darted it out in front of him. I felt helpless and torn. *Do I run after him? Should I call 911? Craig? Should I lock myself in the basement with Princeton and Angelina?*

But I was too stunned, and didn't do any of it.

The blue light changed its pattern of circling and weaving and drifted toward Ike as he got closer.

I broke away to snatch my phone, and nearly fell as I fumbled to dial and make it back to the door at the same time. In the few seconds I was gone, the orb had grown incredibly large. Its edges radiated in a deep plum purple. It hovered in front of Ike and he didn't move. He just stood, staring.

I watched, horrified, as it slid across his feet and slowly twirled up his ankles. His head lolled, and his arms fell limp at his sides.

"Ike!" My legs felt useless as I tried to run to him. They were heavy, like dead weight. Like I was stuck in a bad dream, one in which I couldn't move fast enough, only this nightmare was *real*.

It felt like an eternity, but eventually I made it to my brother. I dove for the pistol dangling from his hand, not sure what good it would do, and landed face down in the earth, my effort was successful though. I rolled over and pointed it at the blue haze as it wrapped itself around Ike's waist. The other glowing sphere ducked behind them, and was next to me before I could blink.

It grew huge, it's deep red burning orange at its edges.

I squeezed my eyes, and pulled the trigger.

It didn't work. No click. No bang.

I tried again, quickly, repeatedly.

Nothing.

I scrambled up.

But it was too late, it's luminescent red-orange melded to my feet. I couldn't move. I opened my mouth to scream, but it never came out.

It didn't need to.

My body filled with something... *good.*

I was swept over with the most beautiful sensation I had ever experienced.

Any worry I had ever known was lapped away by a soothing phenomenon. It washed over me, infiltrating its way into my core. Enveloping me. My legs went limp and the rest of me followed. The ground cradled me as I dropped and my eyelids closed.

I wasn't greeted by dark though. Instead, it was as if I had opened them to a whole other world, similar to my dream.

Everything was hazy and blurry. An array of colors accompanied obscured shapes as they dissolved into one another. I worked to focus, but the harder I tried, the fuzzier everything became, so I stopped. I exhaled, and forced myself to relax. It worked, I began to see.

Abundant beauty surrounded me. There were bright, vibrantly colored plants perfumed in pleasing aromas, and creatures of all sizes, unlike any I had ever seen. I didn't seem to frighten them, they barely acknowledged I was there at all.

They didn't frighten me, either.

In fact, any trace of fear about anything left. It was just gone. I felt only calm, and peace. An exhilaration even.

A deep vibration rolled beneath us. The beings darted away. That same soul rattling scrunch rippled the world around me then shattered it and everything vanished. I was alone, and cold, greeted again by only dark. I blinked to focus. I was sprawled on the grass in front of our house.

The dazzling sphere was gone without so much of a trace of its magnificence left.

I remembered Ike, and squinted and searched the night around me. I found him with Addie licking his arm as he tried to prop himself up. A fusion of bliss and bewilderment splayed across his face as he smiled at me.

"Lydie!" He crawled to me. "Are you okay?"

"Yeah, I... think so." I brushed myself off and looked around as he helped me up. There was nothing mysterious flying through the air, no light coming from the shed. I took a deep breath.

I felt *great*. I felt rejuvenated, and rested.

"I feel magnificent." Ike stretched his arms over his head. "I don't get it. What happened? Last thing I remember was heading toward the shed," He fumbled through his memory, "to see... Obidias? Then... I don't know... amazing..." He sounded giddy, until his face fell and he pointed at my hand. "You have Dad's gun."

I lifted it in front of me. Memories marched through my brain, knocking serenity out of their way. I was reluctant to confront all of our unknowns. "Do you remember the lights?"

"Li- Oh... yeah..."

The shed door creaked.

"You's shouldn't be 'ere." Obidias's gruff voice barked.

"Obidias!" Ike snatched Dad's pistol and whipped around. "What *were* those?! What's happening to us?!"

"This 'eres my land, like I been tellin' yous. You shouldn't be messin 'round with things that don't be concernin' yous." Obidias retorted.

"We were ambushed by them! They attacked us! That very much concerns us! You said you would tell us more later. IT'S LATER! "The soul shaking sound interrupted Ike's defensive onslaught. This time it was excruciating, and sounded much, much closer. Addie unleashed her barking rage and Ike motioned for me to duck behind him.

Obidias's mild annoyance morphed to genuine concern. "Quick! Quick yous! Gits inside!"

The sound blasted again, shaking the ground beneath us. We didn't hesitate, and rushed to follow Obidias. Even Addie darted inside, with her ears flat and her tail tucked.

∽ 29 ∾

Ike gasped when he entered.

Mine followed.

Intricate, earthy scents grazed my nose.

I stared, dumbfounded.

This wasn't our shed. And I don't just mean Grandma's pots were replaced with Obidias's belongings.

No.

This was something else entirely.

It was impossible.

The walls had expanded to form a small cabin and were covered with raw logs accented by crude floral sconces. Strange odds and ends were strewn throughout, along with curios cluttered onto shelves and hanging from rafters. Scars that spoke of age saturated old floor boards, and gave way at the back to a mantel crowned in brightly colored river rock. Obidias's dogs basked in the glow of the fire, and brought their heads up long enough to acknowledge us, then dropped them again, cradled in coziness.

They had been in our house when we went to sleep, I remembered.

"Come in, sits yerselves." Obidias instructed.

Ike moved, wide eyed and mouth hanging to a pitted table nestled beside a tiny kitchen.

"Looks like yous boths deeper than I thoughts." Obidias fingered his unruly beard while his matching brow wrinkled.

"Deeper into what?" I asked.

"What... is... going... on...?" Ike struggled to maintain his composure. His hand shook as he set it full of Dad's weapon on the table.

"Hmph." Obidias grumbled.

"Obidias?" I prompted.

"Well, yous sees here..." He delved back into his thoughts.

"Obidias." Ike switched to offense.

"Well, dat dere," He started again, "dat sounds you heard, dat was an Etah. You ain't should be round one o' those. *Not at alls*, if yous can helps it."

"More." Ike demanded.

"Like I said, yous in deeper than I thoughts. I'm your Llewrenni. I knew you be deep, or I wouldn't be 'round here, but yous *much* deeper than I thoughts."

"You're *what*?" Ike interrupted. "What the heck is an Etah?!"

"Ike, let him talk. Please." I said and sat next to him.

"Exactly as I told yous. I'm your Llewrenni. Yer guardian. Somes calls us protectors, somes calls us dream keepers, somes even be callin' us angels."

Obidias stopped and sniffed the air- I noticed it too, an enticing aroma drifted from the stove. He turned and plucked a battered kettle from the range, then poured its creamy contents into a couple of funky mugs and set them before us. "Other folks thinks we's nothin' more than ghosts, or less even… just passersby's here on their small-minded journeys. They the ones that be stuck thinkin' life's just happenin' to them. When theys think like that they lose sight of the parts of life that *are* important!" He waved the pot through the air for emphasis. "O' life itself, in all forms! Of family, o' love, n' laughter. Hopes n' dreams!" he burst then squinted and leaned in close. "They lose sight o' da *magic*." A gust rustled his ragged clothes. Ike nudged my knee under the table. I ignored it. "There be hidden magic in everyday, yous sees, and yous gots to find it. Everybody must. Find the hidden magic in every day. Yous twos have been. See? Despite hurtin' from losin' yer parents, yous boths still choosin' to *really* live. To live, and choose happy, see?"

I squinted, and tried to understand. Ike remained incredulous.

Obidias's voice stooped into a slow hush. "Yous is openin' yer eyes. Openin' to all da possibilities, of what can happen, what can *be*. Openin' to the truths o' life. N' once yous dos that, well, life… Life is your *canvas*." He stopped to pour a mug for himself, then motioned for us to drink as he joined the table.

I tentatively sipped. Something exquisite slid along my lips. Not quite chocolate, not quite cinnamon, the flavor unlike anything I had ever tasted. It tickled my insides and sent a shiver along my skin. It tingled through my fingers and toes. I nodded to Ike. He didn't budge.

Obidias continued. "Once yous realize happiness not be somethin' that be happenin' to you, but that it's *yer* choice, yous starts seein' more good, effortlessly. Yer favorite dreams start making their ways to yous. Yous begin openin' the gates." Obidias's eyes spread wide in earnest. "The gates to the truth. When dat happens the Enivid keeps sendin' more good out yer way." Obidias took another sip from his mug. I followed suit. Ike nudged my knee under the table again, this time harder. I ignored him still, too intrigued to feel paranoid. "Most folks… they not be understandin' yous sees. Theys think life's just happenin' to them. They don't understand that *yous* is a happenin' to *life*. That within their hearts, and 'maginations, is the key to *anythin'* you'd have ever wanted. Choosin' those, regardless o' yer hurts, learnin' to smile through it," A shimmer of light glinted around the room. Obidias didn't seem to notice, or if he did, he didn't pay attention. Ike grasped my arm as Obidias went on, "seein da bright sides, started the process of yours realizations. That's why I's is here you see. I's been sent to guard yous, *and* yer Tirips. For once yer open to just how much *is* possible, realizin' the beauty and magics of all is real, all your dreams, *all* the *good* you can dreams up, yous also opened the door…" He glanced over his shoulder then whispered, "to their balance. Da opposites. That's the Etah. The opposites. Dat's why they be needin' us."

"Etah? This is messed up. And doesn't make sense. And what's a Tirips, or Enivid anyway? Who the heck are *They?!*" Ike demanded.

"*Ike.*" I nudged him with my elbow.

"Oh… yous knows." Obidias's voice filled with reverence. "Yous always been knowin' who *they* are. Yous feels 'em any time the sun be remindin' you yous alive. Any time serendipity grasps you by da hand to leads the way. Any time da wind whispers its song through yer soul, or love traces over yer heart. *They.* Da Universe. Divine. Deities. Gods. Goddesses, whatever a body be choosin' to call dem. The Enivid. Dat's who '*They*' be. 'They' be the very thread runnin' through all o' us. They be there when yer head be too heavy to lift. When yer spirit be too weak for another step. When tears fall over yous like a *thousand* needles, blindin' da way. Theys why we be believin'. Why all o' us be believin'. Every bein'. *Every* culture. Oh, bodies might be havin' different names for the Enivid. But names don't be no matter. It's *feelin'*." Obidias thumped his chest. "And bein' close. But yous, yous must be closer than most folks does get, cause you've seen yours Tirips, and yous hearin' the Etah- the Tirips opposites, the Tirips' balance. Everything needs be havin' balance."

Obidias threw a stern look at Ike and motioned again for him to drink. "Yous is gonna have to drink some o dats 'fore I'll go on furthers." Ike didn't respond, but did however bring his cup to his lips, then set it down again.

"DRINK." Obidias commanded. Ike lifted his mug, and this time truly swallowed some of the concoction. I knew, because I watched his tension melt, and the hand that gripped my arm relaxed.

Obidias continued, "The Etah also been havin' many names over da ages. Despair, havoc, hatred, destruction, monsters, death, demons, evil… They be the opposites of the Tirips and the Enivid. The thing is, they's meant to just keep balance, provide and keeps it. Most peoples float somewhere betweens you sees, not meetin' their Tirips, driftin' just outta reach of the Etah. Theys dance somewhere between their heavens and their hells. Livin' in the tides o' balance. Deys tries to stay above water, like. Most treadin', sometimes gettin' a breath of air, a break for happiness, then dips into some miseries other times. But *somes* gives up. When somes believin' there be nothin' more than miseries, and goes to start believin' there never will be, deys givin' up their Tirips to the Etah. Dat's the horrible awful sounds yous been hearin. Etahs comes when balance be needed, but Etah *also* comes to those that gives all in to angers and hatreds. Those dat believes their lifes be nothing more than to be endured, at best. They givin' up on their dreams. Givin' up on their souls. The Etah, well, dey take hold o' those souls, take hold o' their Tirips, and… well… it's not purdy to think about, let alone hear, or see…"

"What are Tirips?" I asked. Everything Obidias spoke of fascinated me, and truth be told, frightened me too.

"Dat's what yous twos met, out there. Dat's what yous saids 'attacked' yous." Obidias scowled at Ike, then pulled a long drink from his own mug.

"We both know that's not the case." He shook his head.

Ike lowered his eyes.

"I'm your Llewrenni. I know." Obidias's gaze drifted to a place far beyond his little cabin. "Once one meet's their Tirips, well, dat there, dat be one o' the most beautiful things a bein' can 'sperience." He sighed and gave a little smile at the thought. "Insurmountable, *overwhelmin'* peace. They's a manifestation of *harmony* with all dat you are. The whole o' da universe in harmony with *itself*. Tirips, well, they's a slice o' *Heaven*." His voice surged with emotion and sent goose bumps to dance over my body. "The Enivid be for birth, growth. *Creation.* Creations of ideas, o' life, of, of... *love*. Your Tirips be yer own manifestation of their support, their gifts to life, to *your* life. But the Enivid also support lettin' go of things no longer be servin' purpose, so that's be the job o' the Etah. That's how the balance keeps. Life n' death, see? Ain't no right nor wrong. Just truth. Tirips be possibilities, creativity, hopes, pure love, yer spirit, yer *Heaven*."

A blush snuck along my cheeks. His fervent outline described what I had experienced- *perfectly.*

"We met our Tirips? Out there?" I asked.

"Dat be right." He answered.

"Because anything is possible? Because we continue to choose good instead of misery? Because we didn't give up? Even when we lost our parents?" I saw Ike fidget from the corner of my eye, uncomfortable with the new ideas, new information. It didn't surprise me. Most things that didn't have a black and white explanation tended to make him uncomfortable.

"Yous been hearin' me correct 'nuff Miss Lydie." The old man's eyes brightened. "Bys the ways, yous ain't bein' without yer Ma and Pa. And theys not bein' without yous. Theys just different from when they be havin' bodies. Yer encounters with dem be different, too." Obidias eyed me knowingly.

What does he mean? I wondered. My dreams? Is that what he meant? Did he know? Or how sometimes when I was awake, I thought I felt them near?

"Lydie." Ike stood. "We need to go."

"I'm not sure dat's a good idea." Obidias warned. "Yous already heard the Etah out there. Ifn' they near 'nuff like that, they're near 'nuff to get wrapped up in- no matter how much goodness yous be havin'- findin', feelin' *or* creatin'. Even though they be necessary, Etahs be infectious, *nasty* things. You only be 'round someone's Etah for a *moments*, and you feels the effect. I'm sure yous knowd what I'm talkin' 'bout long before yous ever got to be seein' me." He waited for us to agree. I wasn't sure what he suggested and when Ike wrinkled his face in confusion, Obidias continued.

"Yous knows... when you hangin' round some despairin' persons. All deys does is make themselves, and those 'round them miserables! Only ever focusin' on depressin' hurtful things. Choosin' those things!" He thumped his fist on the table this time, then breathed in deep, calming himself. He pointed to each of us. "I don't mean da upsets we alls feels on occasions. I'm talking 'bout those peoples who forgo *all* sorts o' glimmers o' beauty, hope, happiness, magic, n' *love*. No matters if it danglin' right thar in front o' der faces."

He paused again. Sadness seeped onto his crooked face. "Emotional Vampires I's hears somes callin' 'em. They's be right. They leave you *drained*." Then his face morphed with seriousness. "When a person chooses always negatives like dat, theys justa beckonin' to the Etah. Those Etahs hear woefulness from *thousands* o' miles away. Yous be's assured the Etah be near 'nuff, waitin' for somebodies to gives up- gives in to sadness, or hatred. Dat soul screechin', resonatin' sound is the Etah tryin' to get near a body's Tirips. Or, worser…" Obidias leaned in close, his voice dampened to a harsh whisper. "Destroyin' it. Riddin' the universe of da empty vessel. An Etah is near 'nuff Mr. Ike if yous can hear it. I not be recccomendin' headin' out right now." Obidias finished with authority.

"Enough of this bull! Come on Lydie!" Ike snatched my hand and pulled me stumbling from my chair.

"Be carefuls if you go!" Obidias boomed "Don't yous be forgettin' the thruths!"

"Truths? Truths??! What truths? What exactly are they, Obidias?!" Ike countered. "All we've heard from you is nonsense!"

"The truth… the truth is," Obidias's gruff voice smoothed, it's harshness diminished. It became soothing, and rich. It resonated like- like our fathers. Gauging by Ike's expression he thought so too.

"The truth is, that everything is connected, and that you're in charge of your own reality. That you may choose to follow the life-giving force of your spirit, or you can choose to follow the destruction of hatred. It's as simple as that. If you look deep, deep inside of you, you will find your inner well. The place inside you where you will always be able to reach your truth, your strength, your love. It will help you find, and follow the path that is right for you. Your inner well will be your guardian."

"Dad?" Ike's voice waivered.

"Remember though,"

"Dad?" I asked too. Ike grasped my arm.

"Remember, to be careful with who, and *what's* around you. They're contagious you see, both for the good, or unfortunately, the devastating..." His voice cracked.

"Dad!?" Ike shook Obidias's shoulders. "Dad??! Are you in there?"

"Whoa now!" Obidias pulled from Ike. "You said I ain't to be callin' you son. I 'spect you ain't should be callin' me yer papa." His voice drew haggard and hoarse again. "Though eithers be fine by me."

"HOW DO YOU KNOW MY DAD'S VOICE? WHO ARE YOU?! WHAT THE HECK IS GOING ON?!" Ike shouted.

"Be careful out there, son." Obidias urged.

"DON'T YOU EVER, *EVER*, CALL ME SON AGAIN! I WANT NOTHING TO DO WITH YOU! Stay away from my sister, and you sure as hell better stay away from me!" Ike roared.

"Don't you be lettin' yourself gets wrapped up in yer own Etah. Lord knows one's already stirred up n' kickin'. Dat's what we been hearin." Obidias reminded Ike again, calm, and steady.

Ike yanked my arm.

"Ike!" I protested. "*Ike!*" I repeated as he resolutely pulled me to the door. "You heard Obidias! It could be dangerous!"

"Lydie!" He snapped and turned to me, his face stern. "It's bull shit! ALL BULL SHIT! We've never heard of any of this before. I don't know *what* this guy thinks he's trying to accomplish, except scaring you. I'm sick of it! We're getting out of here. *Now.*"

Ike had never treated me this way. Even in all of our childhood bickering and picking on one another, he had never attempted to control me.

Picking up on Ike's anger, Addie darted to the door. Obidias mumbled something apologetic as Ike pulled me outside.

"You be takin' real good care now Miss Lydie. Don't be givin' up the truths. They're in yer heart. You almost there Mr. Ike. Almost there..."

Ike yanked me into the night and charged up our hill dragging me behind. Obidias's mumbling carried after us the further away we got.

I swear, I thought I heard him cry.

ɜ 30 ɞ

"*Ike*! Let go of me!" I demanded. He dropped my wrist and stormed toward the house. The porch boards protested with a hollow echo as he stomped over them. "Ike!"

A deep rumble groaned in the distance. My heart lurched to my throat. It swept over the hill with a rage, distorted and squelching.

The Etah.

Ike turned, blood draining from his face.

"LYDIE!" He hurtled toward me. I urged my legs to move as fast as they could. We nearly collided, falling through the door together. An explosion of fury buffeted the house. Wind and leaves rushed over us. We untangled and scrambled to shut the door. Ike froze. I followed his gaze and saw it too.

It rolled, and twisted, writhing up and down our drive, jerking then dissipating, only to reappear in another spot all together. A *nothingness*. The only word close enough to describe it. A blackness so deep it blinded.

I lunged to shut the door and saw a diminishing light escape from the shed. Obidias had watched to make sure we'd made it safely inside.

I huddled on the floor next to my brother. "See!" I hissed. "Do you believe him now?!" Fear and anger whipped away the enchantment of the cabin.

Cabin? How did he do that?

Remembering its magic cooled my temper, then it licked and flared again when my brother inched closer. *How could Ike treat me that way! How dare he lead me like a puppy.* We've always regarded each other as equals, since, well, forever. It was our unsaid pact. I'd always been thankful for that.

"Lydie, I was trying to protect you. Shhhh…." He prompted as my breath grew jagged. "We need to stay calm… the Etah…" A hint of tremble infected his whisper.

He was right, my frustration was a screaming invitation to the nothingness. Obidias had said if it's close enough to hear, it's close enough to get wrapped up in, I can't imagine what it meant if it was close enough to *see*. Besides, it agonized me to see Ike feel vulnerable. He hadn't wanted to believe, but had been forced to. I rubbed my wrist absently.

"I'm so sorry." He pulled a throw blanket from the couch and draped it around me.

A great wind smashed against the house again, accompanied by a long horrific, groaning, moan.

"Let's keep our thoughts light." I urged my brother.

He nodded, but worry wouldn't budge from his face. It poisoned his body into rigidity.

"Ike, I bet mom and dad are with us, or, at least watching, from wherever they are." His shoulders let go of his ears and lowered. "And Renea wants to be with you, although I can't see why." That got him to crack a smile.

"I'm awesome, of course." He puffed his chest. "We've got it pretty good here, eh? Well, aside from the mad man living in our shed, and evil incarnate beating on our door. Who does it think it is, anyway?" He gave an exaggerated cackle. The wind slowed and wept through the chimney. It was working.

"I really do like it here." I agreed. I missed my parents terribly that instant. I wondered if Obidias had been right, if they really were near, even though we couldn't see them.

I missed Craig too, but realized in that moment he was only *one* of the reasons I loved our life in Nepenthe. Ultimately, I loved it because it felt like *home*. It felt like we belonged. Everything from Grandma's glorious house, to Unicorn Books, to the Craig family, my brother's genuine happiness, and, of course, my own. I *was* happy. And Craig was a large part of that. Craig was a part of my home.

A whiff of vanilla tickled my nose. Mom's perfume. "Ike! She's here! Isn't she? Can you smell her?"

He dropped his head onto my shoulder and breathed in deep. The scent clung to the throw he had draped over me. I took it as a sign that she was near. It had been her favorite to cuddle with in the evenings. I couldn't bring myself to wash it since 'The Dent'. The comforting warmth of the vanilla reminded me of the drink from Obidias's, and at the thought, the tingle it had given me trickled over me again.

"It really is magic here, isn't it Ike?"

Addie and Princeton paced as the wind continued its howl. They emitted the occasional growl and warning bark in response. Finally, the raucous slowed, then vanished as quick as it had begun.

Ike took the dogs with him and ventured outside to investigate. I watched, peeking from the bay window, phone in hand, not that I knew who to call. Whom was one to call when the whole world as you know it has gone awry. *Craig I suppose.* I told myself. And perhaps 911 again, although I didn't think they would be prepared to handle a black writhing mass of decimation. Angelina sat alongside me, attentive. She didn't hiss. When Ike returned he reported that not one thing seemed to be out of place. He couldn't see, nor hear the Etah, nor were there any floating Tirips.

"I even checked the shed. It was gone Lydie. Everything. Are we insane?" He asked as he checked that he had locked the door, for the third time.

"If we are, I'm right there with you. And so are Renea, and Craig. Remember?"

"Yeah," He eyed grandma's old clock. "I can't believe it's already four in the morning."

"I know. And we both have to work soon."

We bunked on the couch and loveseat for the rest of the night. Though my proud brother wouldn't admit it, I knew he didn't want to sleep alone just as much as I didn't.

Of course sleep wouldn't come easily. And from the sound of my brother as he flipped, and flopped, it didn't for him either. But eventually I did drift, I know because I dreamt of my Tirips, surrounded in it's beautiful splendor, but I also felt the dark tug of nothingness gnawing at the edge of my comfort.

A sound pierced my ears, the sound of the Etah? No... the sound of, barking.

Ike jumped up, disorientated. "Wha? Who?"

I registered Addie's familiar repetitive torrent. "The door, Ike."

"Addie, shh." He scrubbed his hair as he stumbled to open it.

"Don't you look like hell." Question hung in Craig's statement.

"Man, you would too if you had the night we had." Ike motioned him in.

"What? What happened? What's going on? Are you okay? Lydie?" Craig joined me on the couch. "Was it Obidias? You slept on the couch? Are you sick?" He placed his palm against my forehead as he shot more questions at us.

"No, I'm okay." I pulled his hand down to mine. His concern moved me. Gratefulness coupled with residual exhaustion and confusion welled tears into my eyes. *Oh no, not again.* I berated myself.

Ike excused himself and before I could explain anything to Craig the tears came, hot and heavy. The events of the night spilled from my mouth among them. He drew me into his lap, and listened. Listened as I cried for the unknowns. For the utter horror of the Etah. Balance as it might be, it was the root of destruction, and devastation. It was the scariest thing I had ever seen or experienced. And I cried for missing my parents, and how I wished they were there. To guide me, to hold me. I cried for the joy that was my Tirips, and that I was lucky enough to lay in the arms of someone so wonderful. Someone I loved. Craig stroked my hair and my breathing slowed to a soft hitch above normal.

"You could have called, guys." He addressed both of us as Ike flopped onto the loveseat, pop tart in hand.

"And said what?" My brother questioned. "We didn't even know what the heck was going on. *Still* don't."

"You know more than you want to admit, Obidias explained a lot." I said.

"That heaven is a flying ball of light? That hell can be called forth if you don't keep your bad attitude in check? The choice is yours, unless someone else makes it for you? Yeah Lyd. Makes a whole lotta sense."

"Heaven? That's what those flying balls are?? Yeah, not sure if I follow any of that either." Craig said, though he sounded curious, not dismissive.

I pushed myself to sit, and rested my head on Craig. "It made more sense to me when Obidias explained it. Maybe you can hear it from him yourself. Those floating balls of lights we saw are our Tirips. The experience when they come over you..." I closed my eyes and searched for a way to possibly explain it. When nothing came close I shook my head. "It was so astounding and amazing that it's unlike anything I can describe."

"It did something to you?" Craig started inspecting me.

"She's right man." Ike admitted. "It was… unimaginable. It didn't hurt us. I think she's okay." His openness surprised me.

Craig reluctantly stopped combing his hands over me. Then cracked that half smirk of his. "Can I still check to make sure?"

Ike cleared his throat. "I'm still here you know."

"Geesh guys." Craig exhaled and flumped against the back of the couch. "And I thought my night was crazy."

A rap at the door sent Addie barking again, more outraged than her normal alarm. The disruptions in the night had obviously upset her.

"You look like crap!" Renea pushed past Ike into the house.

"Yeah, so I've been told." He caught her by the waist and piled her onto the loveseat.

She threw a nod at Craig and I. "Hey."

"Craig was just about to tell us about the adventures he had last night." I informed her, welcoming the distraction, even if for just a moment.

"What happened now?" She snapped at her brother.

"Nothing compared to what happened to Ike and Lyd. But, yeah, it was crazy, Jen showed up at work with Candy."

"Did you save some for me?" Ike asked.

"Candy's her friend, fool." Renea chided.

"Candy, seriously? That's her name, her real name?" Ike asked in disbelief.

"Yeah, I know, I don't get it either." Renea agreed.

"Jen's here?" My voice shook. What did that mean?

"Yeah, they showed up looking for me at two in the morning. Had been driving for hours apparently."

"Were you glad to see her?" Uncertainty raised my question an octave.

"Well, sure." Craig answered, and although he squeezed his arm around me my heart dropped, then vanished. I couldn't feel it, only a huge gaping hole where it had been. A rush of sound flooded my ears.

"I *did* care about her you know, and I still do."

The decibels flew higher. I understood it now, my psyches call to the Etah.

"As a person. But we're done Lydie, long over. We're through." Craig continued. "I've told you that, although that's not what she had in mind. She was pretty upset when I told her about you last night."

The rush ceased.

"It was *her* Etah!" Ike exclaimed.

"Her whaddy?" Renea hoisted an eyebrow, then pointed her shoulder to the door. "And before we get too far into it, Lyd, you better get ready, we gotta get to work."

"Oh yeah, and oh yeah! You're right! You're both right!" I called as I headed to my room. "Ike fill Renea in!

My shower was quick. The kind with barely time to make sure the necessaries are scrubbed, although I would have preferred to stay under the water much, much longer, but Renea and I needed to get to the book store. Even though life was more than crazy at the moment, there was no way I wanted to let Ada down. Besides, a bit of normalcy, no matter how small, felt inviting.

If only Craig could hang out with me at work.

I was astonished at how much I had missed him. And what about *Jen?* I wanted to hear more. So much had happened to both of us, in such a small space of time, it felt like we had been apart for ages.

I toweled off and pulled a flowy tunic on over some comfy capris, then coerced my hair, strays included, into a messy bun.

"Good morning beautiful." Craig tapped at my bedroom door.

"Morning handsome." I smiled. He always made me smile. I met him on my toes and kissed his nose. He pulled my lips down until they found his. They swept me away into our own little world and the one around us fell away.

"Are you really okay? You don't have to go to work, you know." He pulled away and kissed my cheek, then my forehead as he waited for me to answer.

"I am, last night shook me up, but I am." I shrugged, the absurdity seemed a million miles away in the morning light. "Besides, maybe work will distract me from it." My eyebrows cinched. "*And* from your *fiancé* haunting you."

"Ex. Please, don't worry about her, Lyd."

I bit my lip and shook my head to keep from spouting- *Don't worry about her. Don't worry about her?!*

How could I not?

A fresh tear threatened to spill. He saw it, and kissed it away. I drew in a deep breath, determined to maintain a semblance of composure.

"She's not the one I love." He assured. "You are. I love *you* Lydie. Dear *God* do I love you." He wrapped himself around me.

Another tear reached my eye, one born of elation.

"I- I love you too." I stammered. "I really do." I let my eyes close as our lips met again, and I reveled in his arms as they pulled me tighter against his chest. My heart tingled with the sensations of he and I. Within moments I was sure I was floating. His lips quickened with hunger then softened and filled with extraordinary tenderness and love.

Bright, vibrant color leaked through my eyelids.

"Lydie!" Craig spun me so that my back was against the wall, then he held his body out to protect me.

There they were, both of them, our Tirips.

"They won't hurt us. I think." Their radiance vanquished any residual stress from the night. Or Jen for that matter.

"Still, stay behind me, just in case." He urged.

"You can't stop them, trust me," A giggle skipped over my lips. "I tried to shoot one!"

Tentative, Craig outstretched his arm, bringing his fingers within inches from the fiery light. Just as they had last night, it expanded, it's glow intensifying. "It feels... I feel... Extraordinary."

"Lyd! You ready? Your brother's spinning a mighty big tale out ther-" Renea marched into my room. "WHOA."

Our Tirips darted sporadically, then flew out through my bedroom window.

"IKE!" She shrieked.

His footsteps hammered down the hall.

"Part of me hoped it was all a story still! That everything from before was just a dream. I didn't want *any* of it to be real." Renea deflated.

"What happened?" Ike barged in.

"Our Tirips. They were here." I explained.

"Damn." Ike held Renea at arm's length and examined her, then skimmed a glance over me. "Everyone's okay?"

"Yeah. They, were... Amazing." Craig shook his head with disbelief, then nodded to Renea. "You alright sis?"

"Heck if I know!" She screeched.

"Obidias said those- our- Tirips, aren't anything to worry about. That it's a good thing when they're near. It's that horrible sound that means trouble. The Etah." Ike grasped at an explanation for Renea. I was so proud of my brother to have the nerve to try and explain the unexplainable.

Grandma's coo-coo clock sounded. "Renea, we need to go!" I side stepped from around Craig and grabbed a sweater.

"Argh. I don't get any of this." She complained. "I *never* thought I'd say this, but, I can't wait to get to work. Where the only scary thing we have to face are the nutsos coming in declaring that anyone who works in a store like Unicorn books must be devil worshipers."

"I need to get home and check on mom and dad." Craig sighed. He sounded exhausted.

"I need to get to work too." Ike scrubbed his hair again, eager to shower away the stress of the night away, no doubt.

"Wanna ride with me, Lyd?" Renea offered.

"Sure." I agreed.

Instinctively I looked to the shed once we were out of the house. Princeton and Addie bolted down the hill, but it turns out they were merely chasing a poor rabbit. They were joined, however, by Jake, and tagging behind Jake was a mound of dark fur, Molly, and skipping merrily after her was Cooper.

The guys hugged us and bid us farewell. I followed Renea to her car. Craig climbed into his jeep and continued further down Chrysalis Drive. Ike disappeared into the house, but not without giving the shed a good stare first.

I looked again too. So did Renea. Jake sniffed around the pond, and Princeton and Addie cajoled on their way to join him.

Just as we crested to leave our road, a glimmer caught my eye. There, above the shed, were two tiny lights, one red one, one orange, danced in an enchanted ballet. If I didn't know better I would have thought they were nothing more than dragonflies caught in the early morning sun. I wouldn't have recognized our Tirips.

Two more, purple and blue, frolicked nearby, then they all joined in a whirring escapade.

I didn't tell Renea, I didn't want to alarm her further. Instead I watched their merriment until I couldn't see them any longer.

Oh… they were *glorious*.

✃ 31 ✄

The bells announced our arrival to the empty shop as Renea unlocked the door, then locked it again behind us.

"Hey girls!" Ada's cheerful voice greeted us from behind some shelves.

"Ada? You're here?" Renea called.

"Just doin' some inventory." Her voice carried closer. "*And* we got these in. Couldn't wait to put 'em out, and I knew I just had to show you girls." She emerged from around a corner with her hands behind her back.

Renea and I watched, waiting for her to present whatever it was, when something glinted and caught my attention. I nudged Renea, and pointed to Ada's shoulder.

It's eyes glistened. An iridescent rainbow bounced from its wings.

"What the-" She squinted.

Ada chuckled and leaned closer. The artistic detail was stunning. A gorgeous dragon, with carefully etched scales, and real fur trims. The lifelike craftsmanship was marvelous. I stopped my finger just short of stroking it.

It turned its head and looked at me.

"WHAT THE?!" Renea shrieked then dove behind the counter. "I can't take it anymore! What the hell is going on! GET ME OUT OF HERE!"

Ada belted a hearty chuckle. I stood, dumbfounded. I was with Renea on this one. I didn't think my poor psyche was capable of handling anymore unknowns.

"Renea!" Ada managed through her belly laugh. "I thought you would like these most! It's a puppet!"

Renea peeked her head up. Her hair covered her face and she made no attempt to move it.

"Promise?" She asked.

"Promise." Ada assured, then brought her hands out from behind her back, exposing the wire that manipulated the puppet. She maneuvered a knob at the end and the dragon nodded it's head at Renea.

"It's... neat." Renea stood, interested. If only Ada had known everything we had been through.

"We've got a whole shipment of them. Dragons, Fairies, Unicorns- all sorts of enchanted creatures. I've been puttin' them throughout the shelves. I thought it would be fun to add a couple to our bird cages too. Whadda ya ladies think?"

Renea was tentative as she made her way toward Ada, and soon was stroking the puppet on her shoulder.

"Ada? Do you believe in magic?" Renea's voice was small.

"'Course I do, dear." Ada didn't miss a beat, but her expression spoke of surprise. "There's magic all around us. Every day. Magic, miracles, coincidence, call it whatever you want, but it's there." She nodded toward me to be sure I was included. "Each of us have it, each of us share in it."

"I know Ada, but I mean *real* magic." Renea prodded.

"Sure, sugar." Ada smiled, and waved her arms open. "Just look around. Stories, thousands of them, transported through space and time. Over great distances, and *many* centuries." She took the dragon off her shoulder and nestled it on top of some books. "What else could explain it? Or how a caterpillar can turn into a butterfly? How every day new life is brought into this world? How the stars twinkle? How we exist?" A very matter of fact expression crossed her face. "Science will have its say. Religion will have its say too. But it's all magic darlin'." She leaned close, "And that's just the stuff they *think* they can explain. But what about the ones that can't be? Like when we know a spirit is near." The hair on my arms pricked at her words. "Or when our thoughts travel to each other without havin' to use words." She straightened up again. "We all know what I'm talkin' about. Everyone experiences it, some just a little, and some of us a whole lot."

Renea crossed her arms.

Ada nodded at her. "You and I've done it here in the store. Like the day when that bully was getting too personal, and I just happened to feel the need to come up front."

Renea nodded reluctantly.

Ada continued. "It's all grander than any one of us can ever know in these earthly bodies. But we're here now. This is where we're meant to be in existence. You can either choose to be a part of the magic of the world, or not. The choice is yours." Ada reached for another puppet out of the box. "Believe, and you'll see."

Renea groaned and stomped off to get the money for the register. I don't think Ada's answer was quite the one she was looking for, but everything Ada had said made sense. At least to me. It was all so familiar too, similar to what Obidias had told us.

"You've really had an effect on her." Ada stated. I couldn't tell if she was scolding, or praising.

"I don't think I can take all the credit." I helped her unwrap another enchanted creature. "Some strange things have been going on," I hinted, "*and she and Ike are getting pretty close, too.*"

Ada flashed me a knowing smile. "I saw that coming from a mile away. And I'm glad. She needs a level-headed guy like your brother." She didn't seem to notice my clue. "She wasn't hanging out with very nice people before ya'll came along. She was drifting away fast."

"Away?"

"Yeah, she started becoming one of those-," Ada pointed to a jeweled mirror on the shelf in front of us.

Large, bold, red letters blazed in its reflection. 'ETAH'.

I whipped around to find a book title glaring back at me- 'PRISONERS OF HATE'.

The blood drained from the top of my head and pooled somewhere near my feet.

"How- Did you- Wha-?"

"Prisoner of hate. Always angry with the world. Victimizing herself to all the negatives she could imagine, but since you two have come to town, well, it's like she's a whole other person. Strange things happen. I know." I swear there was a twinkle in her eye when she smiled. She turned and continued unpacking.

"Lyd? Wanna open? I'm almost done with the money!" Renea called from the counter.

Ada nodded to me. "Go on, I'll get the rest of this up, then Joe and I are off on an adventure for the day. Some surprise he's got up his sleeve."

For fear that I would sound out of my mind I didn't say anything else as she walked away, but I wanted to.

I wanted to ask if she knew Obidias, or about Etahs, or Tirips, it seemed like she might, or did. But her nonchalance and bubble-liness made it impossible to tell.

Mortimer wound through my legs as I turned the key and jingled the bells. We were open for business.

Please, let the work day begin, and the distractions take over, I sent up the silent prayer.

✧ 32 ✧

The day held the perfect balance of customers. Enough to keep us busy, but pleasantly not overwhelmed.

Our other neighbors, Gail and Grant Williams, stopped in. They smiled when they saw me.

"The owner of them dogs ever show back up?" Grant squinted his eyes at me.

"You know, he did…" I stuttered, not knowing how to answer exactly. "But he was gone before we could make sure he took them with him, so they're still at our house." I finished, true enough.

"That still doesn't sound right." Gail tsk'd. "We know you have the Craigs a hair closer than we are, but you be sure to call if we can help!" She insisted, then they left to saunter through the shelves, being sure to wish upon a penny and into the fountain before they left.

Renea and I developed an easy rhythm of working the register and managing the shop. We took turns policing the snack table and corralling strewn books that congregated near loveseats and oversized armchairs. She fed the goldfish, then took the register over as I left to sweet talk the birds and freshen their seed.

A women's voice pierced the tranquility of Unicorn books.

"I *know* she's here." The demanding voice carried through the store. "Last night your brother told me she worked with you. Where is she?"

Jen. It had to be.

I closed the heart shaped door to the canaries, stepped from the stool, lifted my chin, and squared my shoulders. I guess I had figured I would have to meet his ex one day, I just hoped it would be later rather than sooner.

I was curious though.

I rounded the corner and saw her. My ego cowered. She was beautiful. Her flame hair was luxurious with a sheen that elicited envy when she swung it over her shoulder, turned, and looked at me. Or sized me up rather.

"Lydie." Her voice was cool and collected. The way her eyes analyzed contrasted with her forced smile. "The," she cleared her throat, "woman, with whom I share someone in common. Apparently." She took a step forward and jutted her hand out.

I accepted.

And felt stupid.

Young, boring, and stupid. How could I compete? She was the perfect age where there was nothing girlish left about her, and anything thicker was distributed in exactly the right places. Her curve hugging top dipped to display her feminine charm yet remain classy, and was accented by fitted slacks. She looked stunning. Powerful. Like the little country bumpkin town of Nepenthe was the last place she wanted to be.

She was here for a purpose.

Craig.

And he wanted me? Plain little me instead? *Psh.* Yeah right. I winced inside, but made a feeble attempt to maintain a brave face.

"Jen, I heard you were in town. Nice to meet you." I greeted. Dammit her hand was soft. I shook it twice, then let it drop. I'm sure she shared the sentiment.

"You heard? Already? But we just got in- *Oh.* You've talked with him already. I suppose he *is* serious about you."

The door jingled. In came another stunning woman. She joined Jen's side with a lollipop in her mouth, and long dark hair pulled into messy braids. Her olive skin, too tanned to be from the spring sun, shot from a pair of cut offs, mostly covered by a crocheted top.

She sure didn't look like a Candy. She was an intricate mesh between girl next door and exotic. Surely something like Jasmine, or Nikolette would have suited her better.

"You must be Candy. Craig mentioned you were with Jen." I kept my voice light as I shook her hand as well.

Candy's smile seemed genuine. She opened her mouth to confirm, but Jen cut her off.

"She is. I underestimated you." Jen had tried to sound sarcastic but her reserve had faltered, if only slightly. "I could barely get him to call first thing in the morning." She drug her fingers through her sea of waves. "This is going to be more difficult than I thought."

"Oh, he didn't call." A smug smile snuck onto my lips. "He stopped by." I reveled in the little triumph.

She looked confused for a second, then flipped her hair again.

"Whatever." She dismissed. "I mean- I see the appeal. You're young. You're cute. And obviously much too sweet for your own good. You *do* know who I am in his life. Don't you?" She arched a brow, high. "His *fiancé*." The word rolled off her tongue in a hiss.

"I do, actually. And I believe that's *ex*? Isn't it?" I prodded.

Or is it? Did he lie to me? My thoughts questioned. *No.* Renea, or Officer Luttel, or *someone* would have said otherwise I assured myself.

She pursed her lips.

"Back off Jen. I knew you wanted to get your ex back, but I didn't know it would turn you into such a jerk." Candy draped her long legs over a stool at the front counter and popped her sweet back in her mouth. She showed every sign she was carefree despite her choice of friend.

I kinda liked her.

"Candy, you're supposed to be on my side." Jen complained.

"Side? Who said anything about sides? I get that he's cute and you want him back, but it's been years. Let's get on with our trip. The coast is calling our name, I can hear it. *Spring break here we come!*" Candy broadcasted to the store. A couple of curious customers turned to look, and two of the men didn't turn back to their books.

Freaking gorgeous women.

"I know you think you want him back," Candy winked at me as she continued. "But there's plenty more out there. Let's go."

"Yeah, Jen." Renea piped. "He's over you. You made it clear long ago that he wasn't what you wanted. He's happy now. Go back to Chicago, or whatever city you scuttled out from."

"No." Jen said with resolve. "I get what I want."

And even though she was responding to both of them, her eyes never left mine.

"Can you believe her?" Renea guffawed after the blaze that was Jen tore from the store dragging her companion behind her. "I'm glad they broke up."

"Was she always such a…?"

"Bitch?" Renea finished for me. "She wasn't too bad, to be honest. But she wasn't too good either. Not like you."

"Me?" I balked. "You know I'm not. And *holy…* she's gorgeous. Do you think she really wants him back? How can I compete?"

"You don't have to Lyd, besides, you're gorgeous too, in a softer, prettier way." She smiled. "And my brother likes you, I mean *really* likes you. I've never seen him look at Jen the way he looks at you. You know that part about getting him to call her in the morning? She wasn't joking. Jen was an accessory in his life. They both took each other for granted. But you, I've never seen my brother care for *anyone* the way he cares for you." She scrunched her face up. "I think he loves you Lyd."

Saying the word seemed to make her uncomfortable. She tapped her nails on the counter as a result. Mortimer took it as an invitation for play and batted at them.

Maybe he really did love me.

"I'm pretty sure my brother really cares about you too." I divulged.

"Do you really think so?" In rare form Renea sounded giddy.

"I do." I assured her. It was obvious to me that the two of them shared an affinity for one another. *Much* more than I had seen him have with Brit. I told her that I was happy my brother had chosen to try things out with her, and that I could see how much he genuinely cared for her.

I meant it. All of it.

The girly reverie was nice. By the time our work day drew to its end Jen, Obidias, the Tirips, and the Etah, had escaped our minds. Just what we had wanted.

We began to close up shop.

I grabbed the keys from the register and felt a pinch that almost dropped me to the floor. I spun my head. Renea's hand shook on my shoulder. She pointed to the front window. Bright yellow rays of glow danced in through it, and was joined by a swiftly spanning green light. They were enormous. Then, out on the sidewalk enveloped inside of each I saw Ada, accompanied by Joe.

"Their," I pushed out a whisper, "Tirips?"

"D-d-d-d-do you th-th-th-think they can s-s-ee them?" Renea's lip trembled as she worked to form words.

I watched as close as I could from behind the counter. They stopped and hugged. Ada laughed. Joe tilted his head toward her then grabbed her waist and pulled her close. His lips met hers. The vibrations of light swirled and danced around them.

Neither of them showed any sign they were enveloped inside of spectacular colors.

"I don't think so, or we'd probably know it." I whispered back to her.

"Oh." Was all she replied.

The bells slammed and the shop door flew open.

"GIRLS!" Ada trumpeted a summons. "GIRLS, come see!" She shouted.

"You can see them?!?" I blurted, hoping we weren't alone in our madness.

"See what honey?" Ada questioned through a bright smile. "Come here, come close! I have something I want you girls to see."

My relief deflated. She was unaware she had been swallowed by a yellow mass of light.

"Is everything okay?" My voice waivered as I made my way to her, unsure if I should stop as if nothing was happening, or run as fast as I could.

Renea clung to the back of my shirt as she huffed behind me, and whipped her head from side to side.

"Oh boy is it!" Ada beamed and stuck an arm out in front of her, it's hand bent straight down. "Look!" She coaxed.

Renea searched her over. She squinted, her eyes bouncing from Ada to the colorful sphere. She wouldn't stop tapping her heel, like she was ready to dart at any moment too.

"What's wrong girl? Do you see a ghost? You lookin' for another puppet?" Ada laughed. "I promise I don't have one. Do you need to pee?" Ada continued to ask, then snapped her fingers at Renea to gain her attention. "Just look, look for one minute before you go."

I grasped Renea's arm in an effort to keep her still.

It seemed we were safe, and that Ada truly was clueless about what perplexed us.

Then I saw the sparkle.

"Joe proposed?!" I squeaked through my uncertainty.

"FINALLY." Renea's voice shook as she pretended to roll her eyes and sound sarcastic.

"I know!" Ada shrieked. "He wouldn't tell me where we were going, and when he finally stopped the car we were at the Crater of Diamonds! So much fun! Of course I suspected, but he didn't mention a thing as we went traipsing through the dirt, searching for our own diamond."

"Did you find one?" Renea was too distracted to pay much attention to Ada's story.

"THIS ONE!" Ada chirped. "He slipped it into our tray when I wasn't looking. I almost dumped it too!" Ada burst into giggles. "But he screamed 'NO! Just check one more time for me, baby, please?'" She chuckled at herself. "Can you imagine?!"

"Wow Ada, it's wonderful." My eyes slipped to her Tirips, mingling over her, as if it was ordinary for bright colors to follow people. It's beautiful gold flashed with hues of green. It didn't reach for me, or Renea. It didn't seem to do anything except hover over her. Almost like it was stroking her. I remembered how Craig's had interacted with us. Both of ours had, together at the same time.

I couldn't help but indulge in a fleeting day dream about Ada's afternoon, but with Craig and myself in the leading roles.

Would our Tirips be there? Were our Tirips always near? We just hadn't known?

My thoughts, all of them, were interrupted by another jangling of the bells.

"You showin' off beautiful?" Joe puffed his chest and sidled up to his new fiancé. His dazzling green sphere entangled with hers as he did. "Did good, didn't I girls?"

I gasped as both of their Tirips exploded in a majestic fusion of light. It was Renea's turn to nudge me to keep me focused.

"Yah Joe, didn't think you had it in you." Renea settled into our surreal surroundings.

"Psh. Only the best for Mrs. Perelli." He retorted.

Renea and I struggled to concentrate while we finished closing. Joe followed Ada around the shop like a proud little puppy and the occasional coo or giggle made its way to us through the shelves. We knew exactly where they were thanks to the vibrant display that continued to emit from them both, brighter and brighter as the moments passed.

"Let's go." I nudged Renea after she and I had finished, and found ourselves just starring at the magnificent show. Perhaps making a sort of peace with the Tirips being a reality, at least for us.

"It's usually special when those things come out, isn't it?" Renea observed.

I thought for a moment. She was right. I remembered Obidias's explanation. What if it really all was real? It looked like it really might be. Indeed, every time we had seen ours, things had been going very well, for each of us.

"From my very limited experience, I'd say so." I said and unlocked the door. I held it open for Renea. "We're off guys!" I yelled to be sure the elated couple heard us. "Congratulations!"

"Already? Where did the time go?" Ada giggled. "Good night girls! I'll get the door behind you! Thank you sooooo much for covering today." She shouted in happy sing song. "You can both take the weekend off!" She added.

She was definitely in high spirits.

I smiled, and turned to Renea. She was smiling too. It wasn't just because we had the weekend off, either. Ada's joy, and Ada's Tirips had been infectious. Just like Obidias had said they could be.

↭ 33 ↫

Ike was home when Renea and I strode through the door.

"Ike!" I called for my brother. "You'll never believe-"

"Ladies! Welcome home!" He stepped from around the corner and passed each of us a drink.

Drinks of the adult kind. And while my brother and I were adults, we weren't quite of the *legal* age, yet.

I was thrown off, again.

"Where did you get these?" I raised an eyebrow at my brother.

"One of the guys at work. We're going to a bonfire. Whadda ya think? Wanna go?" He nodded as he asked.

Renea was quick to grab one from him and take a gulp. "Yes!" She exclaimed, "Lyd and I definitely need it after today. We have the weekend off, too!"

Hesitant, I took a sip, a delicious one, to my surprise. I wasn't a big fan of drinking. I had tried it before, back home with a couple of friends. But not since 'The Dent.'

"Don't worry Lyd, we only have a couple." Ike soothed my unspoken anxiety. I took another sip.

"Oh, this is good." Renea pulled another long drink. She nearly drained half of her bottle.

"Woah pretty lady." Ike inserted himself under her arm. "No need to rush."

"I'm not. It's just, well. Lyd and I really did have a wild day." She explained.

"Yeah we.." My phone dinged in my purse and interrupted me again. Renea shot a glance and little shake of her head that conveyed she'd rather not discuss it further, so I let it go. I reached for my phone as if I was too distracted to finish.

"You home? Miss you." My face lit up at Craig's message. Then I remembered Jen. The day truly had been unbelievable.

"Yeah. Just got here. Stop by??" I replied. Then I sent, "Miss you too, by the way :)" And then, "Wish you didn't have to work, we need to talk, a lot. About a lot." *Geesh Lyd, get a hold of yourself, my* thoughts scolded.

My phone was quick to chime in response. I smirked and opened his message.

"Already on my way. I don't have to work. ;)" Then another message chimed in. "We can talk as long as you want, about anything you want, always. You know that."

My smile turned big and goofy. He had a magic way of putting me at ease.

"Is that Ken-doll?" Ike asked as he retrieved a drink for himself. "And what were you going to tell me."

I should have known my brothers protective streak would insist that he know.

"Ike! How much did you get? And if you're drinking, who's driving?" I quizzed instead of answering. Like Renea, I realized I wasn't in the mood to dissect our strange afternoon. I took another sip.

"Ron's picking us up. The bonfire's in a field behind his house. He said we can crash at his place. Tell Kenny to get over here, we're headed to a party."

"Ron? That big guy you work with? Ugh, I don't want to stay at his house." Renea complained.

"Then stop drinking and you can drive." Ike countered. "Seriously you two, tell me what's up." He insisted.

Renea responded with another long pull.

"We..." Again I was interrupted, this time by a knock at the front door. Then it opened.

"A normal potting shed still?" Craig asked as he let himself in.

"You weren't kidding! That was fast!" I squeaked.

"Told you I was on the way." Craig grinned at me. His eyes simultaneously awoke butterflies, love, and gratitude throughout me. The hedge of doubt I felt about Jen and the impact she may have, vanished.

"Apparently, I checked it too. His dogs were gone as well." Ike informed us.

"No, they're at my house. They were playing with Jake when I left." Craig eyed our drinks with a hint of disapproval. "Renea?"

Renea pointed her bottle at Ike. "His idea. We're going to a bonfire."

Craig glared at my brother. "Dude, she likes you. No need to get her drunk."

Ike scowled back. "I can't believe you'd think that. I would never."

My heart dropped.

"We barely have enough for a drink each. *Literally.* I didn't think you'd be such a killjoy." Ike defended himself further.

The wind whipped outside, along with the low unmistakable rumble of the Etah.

Please. No.

Not only did I not want to deal with a supernatural destructive force, I certainly didn't want a confrontation between my two favorite men.

"Call it whatever you want. You forget I see all of the insane and senseless accidents that come through the hospital."

My throat tightened.

"Gah Ken. Chill." Renea grumbled.

He raised an eyebrow at her, but turned and headed to the kitchen. "Who's driving?" He asked.

"Big dumb, Ron Calloway." Renea moaned.

"Awe, sis, he's just a big teddy bear who's always thought you were cute." The tension had thawed from Craig's voice.

"That's the problem!" She barked back.

"I should have figured!" He called. "Carrie left him last week. It's just like him to throw a 'get over her' party. He'll use anything as an excuse." The fridge door opened and closed. "Anyway, I'm not against a drink or maybe two." Craig joined us with one of his own. "As long as no one gets out of control, and no one's drinking and driving." He cleared his throat at his sister. "I will *not* be left babysitting a bunch of plastered people."

The wind outside slowed.

"Lydie and I don't get plastered." Ike stated, firm. "And we'll *never* drink and drive."

"Good." Craig circled his arms around me from behind, and nuzzled his nose into my hair. "I love you." He whispered low, so that only I could hear.

"The Dent." My voice was meek. "It was a drunk driver." I divulged.

"Ours too." Renea shrugged like it meant nothing.

Which for Ike and I it obviously did. My throat tightened further.

The low growl roared to life.

Renea's eyes widened.

Ike jerked away from her. "Bull Renea! Why would you joke about that?!" He spat.

Craig spread his hands in front of Ike. "Unfortunately, she's not." Craig said. "And it sucks, for all of us. We know now that's the Etah we hear. Let's stay calm."

"You guys are serious?" Ike tentatively questioned.

I set my drink down, no longer interested.

The happiness of the afternoon, even if it was from a strange source, was swiftly diminishing. Renea drained the rest of her beverage then flumped onto the couch.

"Why would I joke about something that killed your parents, and left my dad useless? My mom *broken?*" She tried her bitchy, defensive, sarcastic tone, but was too wilted to make it believable.

It was enough to break Ike from his anger.

My heart steeped in empathy for them, then shuddered a sob for Ike and I.

We sat in silence.

Renea fidgeted with her hair. Ike took a seat beside her, and stilled her hand as he took it into his own. Craig wrapped his arms around me and I let my head rest against his shoulder.

All at once words flew from each of us in a torrent of emotions. We expressed our anger about our tragedies, and we thoroughly scrutinized our devastation. From there our conversation roamed from how much Ike and I missed our parents, to how grateful we were that Carolyn and Henry were alive still, even if their lives had been altered. I divulged how deeply much it meant to me that the Craigs felt like family for Ike and I. All of them. And from there we unearthed, uncovered and shared our most favorite and treasured memories.

It was hard, and sad. But I believe it was healing. It brought relief and comfort. We felt understood. We were not alone, despite all that we had been through.

Then, although I knew it would make my brother uncomfortable, I decided it was time to reveal what I had been sensing.

"I think…" I inhaled, bolstering myself. "I think I feel mom and dad, I mean their spirit, or their ghost, or… or- whatever you want to call it, but I feel them sometimes." I looked to Ike from under my lashes, then shyly at Renea and Craig. "Like even now, I can feel them a little, maybe grandma too."

"I believe you." Renea sounded sincere, which caught me off guard. "I mean, I think, even if we didn't know about Etahs or Tirips, I can tell sometimes that things are more than we can know. Like with Dad. Even though it frustrates me that he doesn't remember who I am sometimes, I get the feeling that he really does know, even when his words say otherwise. At least I still have him." Her eyes flicked to Ike, then she dropped them. "Oh… sorry."

"Don't apologize." He reassured her. "It's good that you still have him. Lyd and I are glad you do." Ike nodded to me as he rubbed Renea's arms. "And to be fair Lyd, sometimes I think I feel them, too."

As if on cue, a stream of colored light trickled into Grandma's living room.

None of us panicked this time. We watched, curious and mesmerized. Soon more colors arrived, and in the midst of the rainbow of splendor the sphere's themselves drifted in to join us.

"Our Tirips." I whispered.

✄ 34 ☙

"Lydie,"

Warmth engulfed me, warmth, and… the unexplainable. The world I had experienced in front of Obidias's shed, and the one I had encountered in my dreams, melded into one. I could still see Craig, Renea, and Ike, hovering somewhere in the in-between. Ike smiled, then Craig and Renea too. We waved, slow, dreamlike gestures, acknowledging each other, along with the marvelous altered reality of our Tirips.

"Lydie," the voice coaxed again. I had heard a disembodied voice before. This was different, yet still familiar.

"Mom?" No one regarded my question, or, perhaps hadn't even heard.

"I'm here. I've always been here Lydie." Her airy voice affirmed. "I never left, I never will. Things are different for me now, but I'm still here, and will be, whenever you might need. Please trust-Please believe, and I'll be here."

"Dad too?"

"Oh yes. He's here. Visiting with Ike. Grandma is near too. We're all here, in some way or another. Our physical bodies change Lydie, but we never leave. The energy that makes us what we are, our spirit, of this world, of all worlds, it never dies. That's what Tirips are Lydie, a representation of our spirit. We just see things a little backwards sometimes in the reality you know now. That's all."

"It wasn't your voice I heard before, though, was it?" I asked in wonderment.

"Sometimes our spirits visit, sometimes your spirit mingles with others important to you, and the life journey that you are traveling. Sometimes your spirit- your Tirips- is important to their journey. We are each a part of the whole Lydie. Our journeys change and evolve, just as our physical bodies and worlds change and evolve as well. We live in this life, or others, but our constant exchange in experience never ceases. We are each different threads of the same Universe, the Divine." A smiling image of my mother fluttered just out of focus. "There is always a different way to see and understand *everything*." As impossible as it was to believe, her voice grew even more lovely.

Colors and silhouettes fluxed before me. I contemplated her words, and how they tied with the things Obidias spoke of.

Backwards? Divine - Enivid. Sometimes things were a little backwards, she had said. Or did Obidias have it backwards? It was so much to think about. Remarkably though, the peace that surrounded me did not allow for frustration.

Deep quiet blanketed us.

I still felt her near.

More understanding dawned on me. *I had seen Etah written in the mirror at the shop. Of course! Etah-Hate...*

Feathery sensations circled me, soothing and intimate. I saw Craig nearby. Our Tirips touched, then overlapped. Our Spirits. *I'm so glad I've found you again,* the voice had said before. Had it been him? Or had it been Obidias? My Llewrenni, as Obidias called it. Of course Craig and I would interact with each other, wouldn't we? Would Obidias and I visit in a sleepy other world? It *had* been Craig, hadn't it? Had our Tirips been interacting in our dreams? *Is anything really possible?* I felt more connected to Craig, to my mother, my brother, *the universe as a whole,* than ever in my entire life. *This life,* I clarified. And here we were, each of us, experiencing our Spirit, in ways we hadn't done so before in these bodies.

I scrubbed my eyes and glanced around. We were all still in Grandma's house. Everything faded, drifted back and forth, in and out, in an exchange with our familiar and the vibrantly colored world of our Spirit. A world of love, and peace.

Heaven.

A horrific pulse shocked through the brilliance of my Tirips. The ethereal colors wavered, and Grandma's cozy farm house solidified.

I heard my mother again. "Lydie, the Etah-don't let yourself get wrapped up in hate, or anger. It's only purpose is destruction and devastation. Things can be worked on, or stepped away from if need be. But senseless hate, *especially hers,* when she's so close, will not be of any benefit."

Hers? Who's? Renea's? I'm sure my mother would have mentioned protecting Ike. Or- Oh, the peace had slipped *her* memory away from me. *Jen.* Ah. I'm sure that's who she meant.

My mother's voice continued. "The Tirips, they radiate with so much good, that even people unrelated to the experience can feel them. They can affect everyone. A little good goes a long way. Unfortunately, the same is true of the Etah. The Etah survives on the stolen minutes of our life. Once they have them we can never get them back. We may suffer unpleasantness from time to time, worry, stress, anger or pain, it's part of our human experience. But if we don't give undo attention to these things, if we don't give our life over to the Etah, which thrive on these, they *cannot* survive."

The sound blasted again, and pulled me completely from the remnants of my Tirips. I looked around the room, and could see I wasn't the only one who had heard the soul jarring chaos.

"Etah?" Renea looked confused. "But how? Not while our Tirips were here?"

"Maybe it was someone else's? Maybe we were able to sense it while we were so in tune?" I suggested.

My mom's warning nagged at me. I wondered if I should tell them.

Renea leaned toward Ike and whispered in his ear. "I saw you in mine."

"I know." He winked back at her.

Such a happy haze had settled over us that true alarm hadn't sunk it's icy fingers in, yet. I decided to keep the warning to myself.

The unmistakable sound pulsed again, this time further, like a distant storm that had breathed it's last threat.

"I didn't see you, but I felt your peace. Are you okay?" Craig questioned into my hair.

"I saw my mom." The heat of tears threatened. I coaxed myself to take a calming breath, and relaxed my shoulders. "I felt your peace too." I lifted my chin and smiled at him.

He bent close, and let his lips linger just above mine.

Knock-Knock, Knockity, Knock-Knock.

Addie, who had been sound asleep on the floor, alerted and sounded her furious warning, while dear sweet Princeton did nothing but lift his head.

"Guess that's Ron." Ike lifted his bottle. "To drinking responsibly."

We raised ours as well.

"To friends, *true* friends, and to family," He continued, his voice ragged. He cleared his throat, "and to our parents, all of them." Despite the tears that welled in our eyes, we smiled and clinked our bottles against Ike's. "And enough of this sentimental crap, here's to a fun night!" He concluded. We cheered to his toast.

ॐ 35 ॐ

Renea was right. Ron *was* big, and burly too.
And apparently he adored her.

His affections, never inappropriate mind you,
could be where her distaste stemmed from. His
goofy laugh at anything she said, and his eagerness
to assist her with *everything* displayed just how bad
he had it for her. Within the few minutes of
introductions and polite conversation I caught Ron
eye my brother a handful of times. Ike stood, and
smiled, and never let go of Renea's hand.

We didn't mention what had happened
moments before. Ron hadn't seemed to notice any
of it. We did, however, slip smug smiles to each
other, confirming our secret, and the bond it had
created.

Outside Ron's old Bronco waited for us, it's
color a mystery cloaked beneath sheets of dust.
Craig and Ike piled into the back, and I, careful not
to rub against the grunge, wedged between them.
Which left Renea to sit in the front much to her
chagrin. Ike patted her shoulder from behind and

Craig blanketed his hand over my knee. It felt like it belonged there. I liked it.

The Bronco's tired suspension bucked us from side to side as we left Chrysalis Drive. Ike and Craig watched the shed until it disappeared. I too couldn't help but give a backward glance. There sat Grandma's house, *our* house, atop its hill, looking grand in the golden glow of the setting sun. If it wasn't for the strange happenings I would have thought it was the most beautiful and normal country setting I had ever seen.

It was still the most beautiful.

Dusk settled on Nepenthe as we made our way through its center and then continued out into the country again. We slowed for the occasional deer or rabbit crossing the road, on their way to the other side of their wilderness. After a while we bumped down a spit of gravel that brought us to an unkempt happy-mint green trailer surrounded by a halo of wonky pickets. A large oak tree reigned in the center of its scrappy lawn. Cars were strewn where ever they had landed and a jubilant glow met us as Ron continued around to the back of his house.

The fire leapt toward the sky contained in a prison ring. Several other vehicles were parked around it with tail gates down and hatchbacks open, making for impromptu seating and tables. In the corner of the field near the edge of the forest, an old chimney stood as a lonesome memorial of the homestead that had worked the land long ago. Where only crops of shrubs and wild grasses now grew in their place.

Ron parked, jumped out, then scurried to open Renea's door. Ike smirked, unthreatened. Craig held his hand out to help me down, chivalrous and sweet, then Renea began to thread through the crowd and motioned for me to follow. Boisterous partygoers were quick to greet us. I recognized a few of the faces from our shop, and Renea introduced me to the ones I didn't, or Craig did, even Ron made me feel welcome by acquainting me with a few of his guests.

"Oh, uh... Have you two met?" Ron stumbled with his words when we turned and found ourselves face to face with Jen.

"We have." She stated, an eyebrow raised, short and dismissive.

I was surprised to see her, but the evening had been too pleasant to let myself feel intimidated. No matter what her relationship with Craig had been. I felt sure that what he and I shared was far deeper than anything the two of them had reached.

"Jen." I coaxed myself to smile. "I suppose you know everyone here. Ron was just introducing me to his friends."

She stared for a second. I think my genuine politeness threw her off again.

"That's sweet." She tossed her hair and sent a preoccupied scan through the crowd. "And of course I know everyone." She pursed her lips and got straight to the point. "Is Craig here too?"

"He is." I loathed the waiver in my voice.

What if I was wrong?

What if their love had been like ours? They *had* been engaged at one point. What would they feel for each other, away from the analyzing fluorescents of the hospital? Tucked into the seductive privacy of the night? In a place where beverages flowed, and emotions followed?

"Good." She dismissed, then turned and sauntered away.

"Wow, I don't remember her being so rude." Ron sympathized.

"Ah. Guess she is now." I tried to laugh, and heard how fake it sounded, so I sipped my beverage instead.

"Don't let her bug you Lyd." Ron threw an arm over my shoulder and bumped his head against mine. "I know we just met, but I can tell you're more wonderful than she could ever be. Purttier too." He smiled a toothy grin at me, then waved to the next group of people for introductions.

After he felt certain he'd done his duty of good host, he pointed to some hay bales left from the season before. "I see your man there. Have lots of fun tonight. That's what this place is for."

"Thanks Ron." I said. He left me and called out a cheer to a group of guys as he joined them.

I squinted and tried to avoid tripping while I muddled through the dark, stopping just short of Craig.

How did I get so lucky? He was a genuinely good guy, and to top it off, impressively attractive.

And he *loved* me?

He sat with his elbows rested on his knees, his haphazard mop of hair particularly wild in the fire light. His eyes were intense as he watched the flames dance. He was alone and I couldn't wait to join him. I couldn't wait for a moment to ourselves to discuss *all* of our recent events.

And truthfully, just to be near the man that I loved was all I really wanted.

I stepped to approach him, but she beat me too it.

Jen.

I stopped.

He seemed pleased to see her as he patted the bale next to him, inviting her to sit.

A splinter nicked my heart.

This Jen was not the one I had met in Unicorn Books, nor moments before with Ron. This Jen seemed sweet, and caring. Joyful even. This Jen wore an amazing smile. She was beautiful. Scratch that- she was *stunning*.

To make matters worse, Craig's smile was genuine too. Then I couldn't see it anymore, he had turned to face her.

She was positively glowing.

It's the fire light, Lyd, that's all. I tried to convince myself. That's why they looked so warm, and happy. *He loves you.* Doesn't he? *She was his fiancé,* my subconscious countered.

He patted her knee, then his hand stayed there, the way he had held mine on the drive here. The way that felt so intimate, and good. A scowl slunk across my face, and the low howl of an Etah opened in the distance.

Her smile grew, if that was possible. I couldn't hear what she said as she became more animated. He sat and listened, his hand still on her knee, offering the occasional pat. She slid an arm seductively around him, then whispered in his ear.

My heart dropped, no longer deflating, but breaking.

She leaned closer.

He shook his head. Then pulled his hand from her. She leaned in again, and this time lingered. She leaned so close that I couldn't make out one from the other.

It wasn't just a whisper, was it?

He shot up.

"NO." He exclaimed. Then he was animated too. Differently though, irritated.

The Etah's scream growled and roared nearer.

I couldn't hear what Craig said, but her face crumbled. "*Lydie.*" He finished, the only discernible word I could make out.

Her face smoothed and she smiled. *Why was she smiling?* I had hoped he had just declared his love for me. Was it childish to want for that? What if he had told her he needed to get rid of me, so they could be together?

Yes, she was definitely smiling, this was different though, forced, like the ones she reserved for me.

Of course it was. It *was* for me. Her eyes bore into my own.

She stood, nodded to Craig, then stalked toward me.

"Don't *think* I'm ready to give up." She hissed under her fake smile as she passed by. The fire lit a glint of tear in her eye.

Oh yes, the Etah roared loud and clear. It's rumble fast approaching. The wind whipped at the fire and the flames jumped higher. The happy-go-lucky crowd cheered in response. No, this Etah was no longer mine. It was hers.

My mother was right- I needed to be careful of her.

"What was that about?" I sat next to Craig, right where he patted, right where she had been.

"She has different ideas about where our relationship should be." He said.

"Who's? 'Our', as in you and I? Or 'our' as in the two of you?" I asked.

"C. All of the above." He made a feeble attempt at a smile.

"And what's your opinion on the matter?" A teeny quiver bit my voice. I worried the answer might be something I didn't want to hear.

"Do you really have to ask?" His smile gathered strength and he leaned toward me, stopping just short of my lips in that seductive manner I was growing to love. "Haven't I made it clear how I feel about you Miss Lydie Baker?" His whisper brushed my lips. "In fact, I'm not sure about that last name of yours, maybe we should change it." His eyes searched my own, questioning if his statement had crossed a line.

My pulse beat its tempo through my head and my throat clenched.

Was he implying?

Did he feel so strongly?

Surely it was too soon? Did I even feel so confident about us? I knew I was smitten with him, but, oh, who was I kidding, of course I did. Even if I didn't want to admit it, yet. Was it possible he did too? I didn't know *what* to believe anymore.

But before we could have one more moment to ourselves, she made herself known again.

"I can't! Mmph! Oh! Help!" Jen called, tugging her leg. Her heel had caught in one of the old pallets waiting to be thrown on the fire. "Ken! Help!" Was she for real? Who wore heels to a bonfire anyway? Jen, that's who. "Can you come? Please?" Her request hedged on demand.

"Don't go anywhere, promise? I'll be right back." His eyes questioned mine still. I nodded.

He left to assist the damsel in distress, and I took a big satisfying gulp of my drink.

He had distracted me from the Etah. I listened to the subtle noises of the night beneath the roar of the party, searching for a trace of it. Sure enough, it was there. It's groan low and subdued. I was safe. From the look on Jen's face she was safe too, pleased with herself to have pulled Craig away from me.

He loves you, you know he does. Remember that. Everything will be amazing. I thought I heard my mother's voice, or was it only my own thoughts? I couldn't be sure, and from what I had discovered within my Tirips, and from Obidias, it was probably a bit of both.

"Hey sis, want me to beat her up?" Ike tapped my shoulder. I watched Jen coo at Craig as he helped her free and found a touch of gratification at the thought.

"No, but thanks for looking out for me." I smiled up at my brother.

"Alright, well let me know. You just say the word." He flexed a fist.

I knew he would never really hurt her, but it felt nice that he wanted to protect me regardless.

"Are you guys settling into the house alright?" A disembodied voice asked from the dark.

"Yeah?" My eyebrows knitted and Ike scanned the night behind us.

"It's me, Ethan." The voice stepped to where the firelight rendered recognition. "You'd be homeless without me, remember?" He teased.

"Oh! It's been great. We're starting to settle in. We were so lucky that Grandma left it for us. And I love Nepenthe too." I rambled.

"I'll say. Do you know how many people would love to be in a place like that? I know I would." Ethan agreed.

"Do you know anything about a man named Obidias?" My brother blurted.

"Hmm... Doesn't sound familiar. You'd think I'd remember a name like that. Know his last name?" Ethan asked.

Ike and I shook our heads. It hadn't even occurred to me to ask Obidias what it was.

"He says he owns the shed. Funny stuff seems to go on down there." Ike disclosed.

I jabbed my brother in the side.

"You know, I remember seeing that on your plat. A little circle near the pond, right? I thought it was odd. Is he causing problems? I could look into it if you'd like." Ethan offered.

"We had the cops check, they said it was legal." I was quick to answer, although unsure of why I felt a sudden protective streak for Obidias.

Perhaps I didn't want to lose the magic.

He brought magic into our lives. As scary as it was to have all of these new things happen, they felt integrally personal.

Exciting even.

And he's brought our parents back. My thoughts admitted.

Craig appeared by my side, leaving Jen with a freed foot and a glower as she tossed herself into the crowd.

"See, told you I'd be back."

"Good to see you Ken-doll." Ethan clapped Craig on the back.

"Ah, guess I don't get credit for the clever nick name?" My brother chided.

"Unfortunately no." Craig laughed. "How's it goin' Ethan? You know these two?"

"Signed their house over to them."

"'Course you did! Then I don't have to introduce you to my girlfriend." Craig wrapped an arm over my shoulder.

"Your girlfriend, huh? That's regrettable. Looks like I've missed my chance." Ethan winked at me.

I blushed, not knowing what to say. Luckily Craig spoke up instead.

"You did, and man am I glad." He laughed. "I believe I just might keep her." He winked at me as well. "If she'll have me." He corrected himself.

Craig and Ethan chatted away. It became apparent they had been in school together. Craig told my brother and I that all of them used to hang out a lot. Then we were interrupted by Renea. She tugged Ike's arm, and insisted he make s'mores with her. Ethan asked Craig about Jen's return to town. It felt awkward for me, and soon after he left to find her.

Craig and I were alone again.

"It was convenient that you were the one she called for, wasn't it? Even though there were plenty of people nearby?" I observed.

"Yeah. She's trying her hardest to get us together again. She's trying to convince me that you're too immature for me."

The Etahs roar rushed us, but Craig's back blocked it as he pulled me into his arms.

"But she's always been a little conceited, and foolish. She *obviously* doesn't know you." His words once again put me at ease. The sound of the Etah quieted. "It's crazy being this open to 'it', isn't it?" He asked.

"You heard it too?"

"Oh yeah. I have since we've been here." He ran his hand over my hair.

I nuzzled deeper into his chest.

"I don't want to be with her Lydie. She doesn't know you, and truthfully, she doesn't know me, she never has. Not the real me, the inside me, like you do." He bent his head down and rested it against mine, and inhaled deep.

I breathed in too.

"I love *you*. There is no reason for the Etah to have anything to do with you." He assured me.

I believed him. Wholeheartedly I believed him, and with that, the call of the Etah vanished. I couldn't hear it anymore, at all.

But from the distortion of Jens mouth as she eyed Craig and I cuddled by the fire, I knew where it had disappeared to. She stomped off, throwing her arms around Ethan when he approached her. Her exaggerated laugh whisked above the roar of the fire.

I didn't mind. Craig and I were wrapped up amidst it all, enjoying the warmth and each other.

In the corner near the forest, I swear I caught the dance of two teeny Tirips in the fire lit glow. I nudged Craig and lifted my hand silently to point at them.

"Fireflies." He informed me. "Now that spring's beginning to turn into summer, it's time for them to make their way into the world again."

They made me happier than I had been already. I had never seen them before; the magnificent little sprites weren't native to Portland.

Craig pulled me closer, his arms securing me tight against him. It was heaven. The rest of the party fell away and I floated in our own little world.

Then I saw *him* over Craig's shoulder. Obidias. He smiled, that big broad, wild eyed smile. I shook Craig's arm and pointed again, but by the time he looked, Obidias had turned, and ducked into the forests edge.

✂ 36 ✂

"What is it?" Craig sounded concerned.

"I, uh," But I wasn't sure I had seen what I thought I had seen. Maybe everything was just too much. "I thought I saw Obidias, but, he's gone now."

"You did?! Where?" Craig searched the crowd.

"No, over there," I pointed to the forest, "but, there's a stump where I thought I had seen him go into the forest. I think I'm just tired."

"Are you sure?" Craig scrutinized the tree line.

I sighed. "No, but, what could we do?"

"He may, or may not own property on Chrysalis Drive, but I'm pretty sure if he's out here, he's trespassing. Maybe I should look…"

"I think he means well, really. Besides, it's late, I've had a little to drink, the day has been, well, a lot, to say the least. Don't leave me, just stay here. Hold me?"

The night drew to a close with Craig's arms a soothing shield to the uncertainties. I didn't hear

any more from the Etah. I didn't see any more
Tirips, or fireflies, or even Obidias.

Craig noticed my head begin to bob as we
enjoyed the fire light, he insisted I stand and follow
him. We worked through the partiers and made our
way back to the house. Renea and Ike were curled
onto the couch playing cards at the coffee table with
a few other people, while more of Ron's company
were splayed over the floor, bed, armchair… awake,
or asleep, anywhere they could fit.

Craig finagled his way into a closet and found
some bedding tucked neatly away. Probably by
Ron's mother, or grandmother, or whomever had
once lived here. There were too many dated
feminine remnants mingled amidst Ron's
belongings to believe it was his choice. I imagined
this place had belonged to one of those prominent
ladies, or maybe both, until Ron moved in. But who
knew? Judging from those feminine touches, and
the overflowing baskets that dripped with blooms,
or the tended flower beds along the pickets, perhaps
they stole away here still. Maybe for an afternoon to
themselves, away from Nepenthe to breath in the
country air. While Ron was at work with my
brother, while no one paid attention. When they
could have the place to themselves. Perhaps they sat
in the dappled sun as it soaked the old oak tree.
Maybe they read a book, cozied upon the very
blanket that Craig held reserved for he and I. It was
beautiful, if not a touch shabby, quilt faded to
pastels with sun and love.

"You know, the night's mild enough, we *could*
sleep under the stars." Craig suggested as we

stepped back onto the porch. He wrapped the quilt over my shoulders, then kissed my nose. "There are more blankets where this came from. It's gotta be better than a bunch of smelly people draped everywhere." His eyebrows drew to a cute question, like he was asking to bring home a wriggling puppy. "Wanna?" He wrapped his arms around me. "I promise to keep you safe, and warm."

Inside I jumped at the idea. It had been years since I had slept under the night. Camping throughout our teenage years hadn't amounted to much, and when it did there were too many friends cramped inside too few tents. Not the peaceful elation I imagined Craig and I would share.

I smiled and nodded.

"Whew, because not only do I love sleeping under the stars, but I love you, and the two together?" Craig picked me up and whirled me, my feet nearly hitting the porch rail. "Besides, I think I caught a glimpse of Jen bouncing from Ron, to Ethan, to who knows next. I don't want it to be me." He set me down and held my face. "And more than anything, I'd love some quiet time, alone, with you."

My smile must have been enormous as I nodded again. Being far from Jen, her negativity, and hopefully her Etah, were definitely high on my list as well.

"I'll be right back." He opened the door to an eruption of noise and slipped inside. He popped back out a moment later with an arm load of bedding. "Where should we thet up campth?" His muffled voice broke through at least four stacked high in front of him. Apparently he *did* intend to keep us warm. "We could thleep oud here under the trees, or in da field under the sthars, or, by da fire, if there's space enoughth."

I nodded yet again, although he couldn't see it over the top of the quilted mountain. "I think by the fire." I raised my voice. We muddled our way to where the bon fire had dissolved itself into a pile of embers. The gathering had dwindled and quieted. Those left sat, discussing dreams, or memories, the universe, or physics, or the paranormal. I was beginning to believe such topics were really one in the same. A few random people lifted their fingers in a tired wave as we passed. Craig tried to peer around his cargo to find a spot when I was struck with inspiration.

"What about by the chimney?" I suggested. The idea felt sweet and somehow like our own little home, in our own little world.

"YESH." He agreed through the bedding.

The night had invaded the old ruin, and proved to be darker than I had expected when we arrived. Still, I was pleasantly surprised to see a corner of wall standing near the back. Craig handed me our nest bundle then pinpointed stones with a flashlight and kicked them away. We laid the blankets, one by one, flattening the grass, until it formed a cozy, makeshift mattress.

"You don't mind getting close, do you? Really close?" He asked.

I shook my head, appalled with the lack of conversation I offered, a result of excitement, nerves, and quiet awe of Craig.

"I thought we could fold the blankets with us sandwiched between. That'll give us optimum padding, and optimum coverage. I'll take the outside. What do you think?"

"Sounds good to me." I agreed.

He halved the blankets then held up a pile of corners and ushered me beneath. I wriggled from my shoes and crawled inside. He covered me, then instead of joining me reached into his back pockets.

"I've brought a surprise." He pulled out two flat circles and held them up.

"Ah, very thoughtful of you. Whatever would we have done without- jar lids?" I questioned with a tease.

"But wait! That's not all." He dug in his front pockets and pulled out two more objects, and a lighter. "See? Candles, and candle holders." He smirked, pleased with himself. "I wouldn't want you to be scared of the dark, you know." He set them on a rock then lit them. He scurried under the blankets and wrapped me in his arms. "I really don't want you to feel afraid, ever." His voice sounded delicious, and granulated, like caramel. "Not that I think you're not brave, I do. You're one of the bravest people I know, it's just… Things have been kinda…" He brushed a hair from my face as he searched for the right word. "Well- strange would be an understatement for what's been going on recently. Sometimes I'm scared you'll give up on Nepenthe with all of this weird stuff and run back to that beloved town of yours." A hint of worry tainted his sugary voice.

I ran my fingers through his fringe of blond mess.

"I loved Portland. It'll always have a special place in my heart, but here feels like home now.

Chrysalis Drive feels like home. *You* feel like home."
My eyes darted between his, hoping he felt the
same.

"You feel like home to me, too." His gaze held
mine, strong, and steadfast. In one fluid movement
all of his body was impossibly close to mine. He
brought his lips to within a breath widths of mine.

"I love you, Lydie." He hovered.

My pulse jumped and my lips parted. I inhaled
anticipation.

His eyes never left mine. His hand slid along
my waist and he pulled me tighter, willing me to
answer.

"I love you too." I barely heard my own raspy
reply.

Craig tucked my bottom lip between his, and
nibbled, slow, and lingering. Tantalizingly patient. I
sampled his in turn, savoring his taste. He pulled
back, then leaned toward me and stopped short.
This time his eyes searched mine, before he sunk
into a fierce and luxurious devour, only to slow
again to tenderness.

Deep inside I pulled alive. I willed him closer,
rocking against him. I could *feel* him, and it elicited
a primal desire inside of me.

"Lydie," He breathed my name and pulled
back, dazed.

"I'm here." My lips quirked.

"God." He exhaled. "What you do to me…" His
voice rolled in a mix of desire, and restraint.

"I feel safe with you." I confided. "I've never
truly felt with anyone before."

"You *are* safe." He confirmed. He wriggled down then laid his head on my chest. "I hear your life." He whispered.

"It beats for you." I answered. My seductive smile turned into a sheepish grin. I knew it must have sounded cheesy, but I couldn't help myself.

"Mine too." He didn't seem to notice.

He held me and we listened to our breath, accompanied by the orchestra of the night.

"I want to make love to you." He whispered. His eyelashes descended as he relished being nested by my heart.

If my smile wasn't goofy before, it was now.
"I know."

"Do you know that I would never?" His eyebrows raised, his gaze met mine. "Until I knew you were ready? *Really* ready?"

"I do." It was true, I knew it. I knew he meant it. That's part of why I felt such safety in his arms.

He settled onto my chest again and inhaled, letting all of him relax against me.

I slid my fingers through his hair. I felt free. Free to relax. Free to enjoy. Free to tell him exactly what I thought. How I felt.

"I've thought I was ready before, and fortunately was able to realize it wasn't real. So, I waited. I've always wanted to wait, you know, until I was *in* love. *Real* love."

He responded with a slight nod of his head against me.

My fingers toyed with the tip of his ear, then traced his brow down to his jaw, then pulled gently at his chin until he hovered over me again.

"I admire you. Your strength. And I honor it, and you." He didn't kiss me though, or wouldn't, I wasn't sure which.

With a rush I rolled him over, and slid so that my legs straddled along either side of him. I ran my lips over his, then his jaw, along the indentation of his neck, back to his lips again, and finished with a sweet kiss on his forehead.

His eyes fluttered open.

"I'm in love with you…" I whispered onto his lips.

He nodded, holding my stare, acknowledging the depth of the truth between us.

"I'm ready." I breathed.

He nodded again.

He embraced my face, and with a soft tug secured my lips to his. His fingers skimmed my neck and wove into my hair, then over my shoulders. They drifted along my ribs, tentatively exploring where his head had lain moments before. His thumbs found the hem of my top, and peeked beneath, then his hands followed until they discovered the crescent of my back. The tips of his fingers dipped into my leggings and he pressed me into him, letting a satisfying sigh escape his lips.

My body responded, and rocked against his again, full of craving, and want. Thirsty with need.

He whimpered, I released my own sigh of pleasure.

"God, Lydie. I love you." His hands were on my chest again, but this time they pushed me up, and away from him. He blinked to focus and collected himself. "I do, I *do* want you. But not like this. Not tonight, not when we've been drinking.

Not when there is a house full of passed out people in stumbling distance from us." His eyes closed, and he shook his head. "No, you deserve better than that." When they opened again they pleaded with me. "Please. Let me give you better than that?"

Disappointment came first, then dread that maybe I wasn't enough for him. My ego dropped and bruised. My chin followed. He lifted it and his expression told my heart I was right to trust him. This wasn't rejection. Not in the slightest.

"Okay." I whispered.

His hands slid just barely further into my leggings. "This isn't easy." He chuckled.

I smiled back at him, grateful for the wonderful person he was. All of his attempts to do what was right for me, only made me want to explore him that much more. I lost any care of drinks, or that he wanted to honor me. I had waited all of my life for this. I had waited all of my life, for *him*. I dipped my hips across him again and ran my teeth over his bottom lip. I nibbled the side of his neck. His palms slid onto my back, under my bra, where they circled until his hands were full of me. His thumbs slipped across the tips of my chest and a whole new jolt sparked in my depths.

"Gah! Come, lay against me." His hands flew out from my clothes and he pulled me close, with a barrier of cotton between us. He rolled us to our sides, facing one another. His arms pulled me so tightly against him.

"Please don't be upset Lydie. Please know that I want nothing more…but for you…" His eyes searched mine again, then grew stern with clarity. "I want everything for you." His voice deepened with conviction. "The first time we make love, I want it to be your choice, and not influenced by drinks. I want everything to be exquisite, not with rocks in your back. I want nothing short of *perfection* for you."

"Thank you." I said, my voice small and I nodded solemnly. "You're right." I conceded, despite the frustration I felt. I brushed my lips over his. "I appreciate you thinking of me. You *are* perfect for me." It was my turn to lay my head on his chest. "I love you."

His fingers wove into my hair again, cupped the back of my head, and he brought my lips to his once more, then nestled his chin on top of my head.

"*Lydie*." He said in an urgent hush and gestured above us.

The air was alive and pulsing in an interplay of exchange between red and orange. Our Tirips.

I reached my hand into their brilliance and gasped. Vibrant light streamed from my fingertips. "Our Tirips, are they coming from us?" I wondered out loud.

Craig wiggled his fingers in front of us too. Sure enough, an orange flow of color wavered from his as well. "They're inside of us. They really *are* connected with our spirits." He observed.

He chuckled at me as I beamed my own red light towards him. We watched the colors magically play and dance as we waved our hands, pointed in different directions, then finally watched them melt into each other as we intertwined our fingers and he brought them to his chest. He pulled the blankets tight around our shoulders and I nestled my chin between him and the night air. The glowing swirl of our Tirips tinted the stars, and we laid, quietly enjoying their splendor, mesmerized. Soon my eyes grew heavy, and I felt myself drift between peaceful waves of enchantment and love.

"Marry me Lydie." He whispered into my hair.

"My soul already has." I said through my contented, sleepy haze.

"Marry me, body, heart, and soul?" He whispered back.

My heart slammed and jerked awake.

Was he serious?

Nervous I had mistaken him, I lifted to meet his gaze.

His eyes were wide, awake, and watching me. It appeared he was.

"Are you for real?" My voice shook. I wondered if I was dreaming. The stars twinkled in their iridescent radiance behind him, cascading rainbows through our Tirips.

"Yes," He inhaled an anxious breath. "I mean it, I really do. Although perhaps you shouldn't answer quite yet, but, think it over, will you? Will you marry me Lydie Baker?"

I struggled to steady myself.

Marry him?

Of course I wanted to. I didn't care if it was rash or not. My heart threatened to rocket from my chest.

I bit my lip to keep from shouting. "I will. I don't need to wait to tell you. I've known from the moment I knew that I loved you."

A huge grin spread over his face. He stared at me a moment, that grin growing bigger and bigger until I was certain it might split his happy face in two. Finally, I tugged at his shirt, and brought his lips to mine.

To say our lips were heated would be an understatement.

Our Tirips blazed as our kisses were devoured and melted into one another.

To say our kiss erupted with the strength of volcanoes, still, would be an understatement.

The red and orange glow of our Tirips merged seamlessly.

To imagine a pristine sweet bloom, born of the wild mist of roaring falls as they descended from the grace of a lazy day to land in the sultry seduction of the night, then, and *only* then, could one imagine the way his lips felt against mine.

❦ 37 ❧

The merriment of birdsong filtered through my sleep to herald the morning. Sunlight traced my lashes and tickled the contours of my face. I shifted under its touch to find myself cradled in Craig's arms.

His eyes were closed. I watched his slow catch breath of sleep.

Did we? Were we, engaged?

Memories rushed my haze, filling me with exhilaration, followed swiftly by dread.

What if he didn't remember? What if he didn't mean it?

Or worse?

What if he... regretted it? What if he had been drunk? The proposal certainly hadn't seemed planned.

No ring.

"Good morning, future Mrs. Craig." He launched himself above me and covered my face in kisses. "Are you happy?"

I relaxed. "Uh, ye-ah." I gave a tentative smile.

"Uh?" He leaned on his elbow and examined me. "Is everything okay? Are you having second thoughts? I should have waited, but, I just couldn't help it. Last night, with you, was... perfect. I know I didn't have your ring. You'll get it soon- No time flat. I have big plans for it."

"You already have it?" I squeaked.

"That's for me to know, and yoooou to find out." He ran his fingers over my ribs to coax a chuckle. It worked and we rolled over each other in laughter.

Somewhere in the distance a rooster crowed. Bees and tiny things buzzed to life around us. Life reigned abundant. Craig grinned a wide, happy smile and mine opened to match.

"Where have you been?!" Ike grouched when we stepped through the door of Ron's trailer.

"I told you they were fine." Renea elbowed him.

"Hmpf." Ike sidled up next to me. "Did he take advantage of you?" He quizzed and casted Craig a scowl.

"What? No!" I admonished.

"Ike, one day you *will* learn that my only interest is to be there for your sister. I will *never* harm her." Craig's voice was even, and cool as he stared back at my brother. He slid an arm over my shoulder.

"Are you sure Lydie?" Ike searched my eyes, once again the protector.

"Gah Ike! Yes. I'm sure. This is a good morning, it's a BEAUTIFUL morning. I feel better than I ever have. *Don't* ruin it." I scolded my brother.

"Ah! You guys did *it*. Didn't you?!" Renea accused.

"No." Craig shook his head at his sister. "Besides, would it really be your business? Give us a break. Besides *Ike*, I could ask you the same thing." Craig defended and turned to face my brother square on.

"Hmph." Ike grumped again, and rolled his eyes. "Fine. Whatever."

"Hey, ready to roll?" Ron approached us with his shoes in hand. Despite his effort to sound jovial, he looked worse for the wear. The night may have been too much fun for him.

We piled into his Bronco. Craig and Ike silently made peace as we slipped back into our everyday casual comfort. Though Craig and I were more like two little kids, sneaking smiles at an inside confidence. Then I would giggle, which would make him laugh.

We crested Chrysalis drive to find Obidias sat in the grass outside of his little shed. He stood and waved, then turned and vanished inside to emerge a moment later alongside of Cooper and Molly.

Ike's eyebrows knitted. "I don't like it. At all."

"Who's that?" Ron mumbled.

"Just, one of grandma's old friends." I blurted. Again, my instinct to defend Obidias surprised me.

I flinched as Ike pinched me. "Friends?!" He mouthed.

"Ah." Ron lifted a weary nod, too tired to care much anyway.

Obidias waved once more then gave his attention to his dogs. He tossed a stick, and scratched behind their ears. I swear, when I shifted my attention away I caught him in a little dance, or a little jig from the corner of my eye. But the moment I looked back, he only picked up another stick to throw for Molly.

Obidias appeared positively gleeful.

Ron dropped us off then left again for home and rest. We watched him drive away, and realized Obidias was gone.

"That's it, I'm going down there." My brother stomped forward. "You wanna come?" He called.

"You know it." Craig said, already behind him.

I tugged on Renea's sweatshirt, motioning for us to join them.

"Oh… Not again." She complained.

The Earth fell silent around us. The breeze shifted, then stood still. The birds ceased to sing their song. I watched a butterfly land nearby, flap it's wings once, then stilled.

Ike reached the shed first. He pressed his face against a window.

"Nothing!?" He stormed away from the glass, alighting the butterfly to flight again. "You've GOT to be kidding me!" A robin twittered into the silence, instigating a jumble of sound from the other living creatures.

"What? What is it?" Renea ducked behind me.

"Nothing!" Ike whipped the door open and charged inside. "Like he was never here!" The sound of plastic gave an empty thud against a shed wall. "It's bullshit! Even Ron had seen him. Right?" He continued to search for any clue he could find. Any clue to declare that he wasn't insane. That none of us were crazy. "Not again!" He demanded, his plea futile.

"What can we do Ike? Every part of this has been outside the realm of what can be understood." I said. "It is what it is. Whatever it is."

I joined Craig at the door and watched my brother. He turned without a sound and squeezed between us to step outside.

"Ike, your hair." I lifted my hand above his head. "It's, full of static again."

"I don't care." He said in defeat.

We didn't say a thing as we made our way back to the house.

None of us mentioned it further. There wasn't anything left to say. We had exhausted all of the ideas and possibilities. We were left again to operate as if nothing had happened. We remained solemn, until Craig and I moved back into our giddy mood. Renea and Ike were annoyed by us, until finally enough of our cheer was able to rub off on them.

We didn't tell them why we were happy with ourselves. Renea insisted she knew, no matter how many times we assured her she did not. Craig asked if we could keep our engagement between ourselves. It was difficult, but he insisted. For a split second I feared again he hadn't meant it. But then he day dreamed aloud about the get-together he wanted to have to let everyone know at once. Also, he said, that he wanted to make up for not giving me a proper proposal. I tried to convince him what nonsense that was. That what we had shared had been real, and entirely enchanted on its own. Our Tirips alongside of it all had escalated our night to perfection. Our engagement, exactly as it had happened, was so precious to me.

Still he pleaded, so I gave in.

Back at work Renea and Ada helped me to make colorful invitations during lulls between customers and shop duties. For the life of them they couldn't figure out what the meaning of red, and orange could have to do with my secret, or why I wouldn't let them in on it. I told them the time would come for them to know, although they had guessed it fifty times over.

"Do I hear wedding bells?" Ada would ask.

"Yeah, why else would the party be at mom and dad's house?" Renea would chime in.

Or, with hushed voices they would corner me and ask if I was pregnant. That pretty much summed up their guesses. Repeatedly they bounced back and forth between the two, with strange little side guesses occasionally interjected. Though my non-traditional colors did keep them uncertain enough. I liked that. It was a secret meaning for only Craig and I. Or, anyone else who might see our Tirips together. Then perhaps they would understand, but until then, it was special. Reserved for just he and I.

Everyone I knew had been invited, to include so many that I didn't.

"Should we address one to Jen?" Renea eyed me with suspicion.

"My gut says no." I sealed an envelope and adorned it with an aqua rhinestone. "But maybe you should check with your brother. We'll let him say for sure."

"See Ada!" Renea shouted across the store. "We were right, it *is* one of those two!"

"You don't know anything." I attempted a lofty tone of authority. It didn't work very well.

Renea consulted with Craig, and he consulted with me. We *did* in fact decide to invite Jen. I didn't feel sure about her coming to *our* engagement party. The greedy side of me wanted to have him to myself and to never lay eyes on her again. The caring side of me wanted to save her embarrassment, while my naughty side wanted her very much to be there while he declared his love for me to the world.

The days crawled slower than the fat, indulgent caterpillars that readied for slumber in order that their lives may grow wings.

But they were good days. Happy days. *Ordinary* days. There was such little incident of Tirips, Etah, or Obidias, that it felt like our world may have returned to something manageable. Only Molly and Cooper as they frolicked with our dogs were left to remind us something much deeper was still going on.

Ike and Renea grew increasingly inseparable. I knew the same was true for Craig and I.

Every chance he was able, he would steal me on little surprise trips. One day we hiked to a hidden spring and waterfall, one of Nepenthe's favorite secrets nested deep inside the forest. Another, it was for a stroll through an abandoned orchard. We wandered through the trees, hand in hand, or with our arms about one another and dreamed that perhaps one day we might have our own fruit trees.

One evening, as the sun tucked into the blanket of trees around Nepenthe's town edge, Craig and I found ourselves on another impromptu date.

"You do know, don't you Lydie?" Craig said through a mouthful of sherbet. "That I need to stay near mom and dad." I had found him, with his foot on the bumper of my baby blue after Renea and I had closed up Unicorn Books. He had treated us to the cute ice cream shop on the square. After she left Craig and I continued to walk and window shop for the hour and a half before he had to begin his night shift.

"The thought had never crossed my mind that you would leave." I licked a drip threatening to escape.

"It didn't?" Disbelief hiked his voice. "You haven't been fantasizing about where we might live once we're man and wife?" He pulled my waist so that our bodies knocked side to side, nearly toppling my desert.

Of course I had. But no, I never imagined he would leave them. Although every time I did dream of our home together it was a home created in Grandma's house. Only Craig and I. I don't know where my mind displaced Ike, or Carolyn and Henry to.

"I have." I admitted out loud. "I guess I assumed we'd stay on Chrysalis drive." I blanketed an explanation over reality and daydream.

"That'd be nice." He bent to lick a drip I had missed from my cone. I pointed to his own streams of cream. Spring had definitely given way to summer. "I don't want to be too far away, in case they need me, but I would never expect you to want to live in the same house. I've actually talked to a contractor about building across from them."

"You did?" I stopped in my tracks, excitement that he had begun to plan volleyed with discouragement. I *would* be involved in my future, and included on decisions. *Not* have them made for me.

"I did. I don't want to live with my parents forever, you know." He winked. "And now that you're part of my forever picture, I have someone to make these plans with."

He had spoken with a contractor before, I realized. I scolded myself for assuming he would ever try to push me into something.

"I always imagine us in Grandma's house. I don't know where my imagination sends Ike." I confessed.

"Whoa." He spun toward me, his eyes serious. "I don't know if I'll ever get used to this… supernatural stuff, or spirit stuff or whatever it is, both I suppose, but, ever since we met, while you were still in the hospital, I have felt, a… pull… to that house. It was foreign, and undeniable. *Then*, when we started to become, well, close, recently especially, I keep imaging us there too."

A faint haze radiated around him.

"You're glowing Lydie." He whispered, then looked around us. It was strange for us to see things others less aware could not. "It feels good doesn't it? Imagining us living there, together?" He asked.

I held my arm up, and saw my own light emanating. "It really does. Who knows what we're going to do with my brother." I giggled. "And you're glowing too, you know. You match your sherbet." He held his cone up between our arms and smiled.

"It'll work itself out." He assured me. "It always does, one way or another. I'm just glad we have each other, no matter *where* we end up."

"Even if it's in a cardboard box?" I prodded.

"I'd never let that happen to you." He kissed me with, sugary orange flavored lips. "But yes. Even."

"Me too." I smiled.

Our Tirips blazed and met in a slow, fiery dance around us.

❧ 38 ❧

Finally, the day of the party arrived.

Craig was home with his parents to greet any early arrivals, while Renea and Ike helped me finish some preparations at Grandma's house. Renea artfully sculpted some deviled eggs as Ike helped me to finish a veggie tray.

"You know Lyd, we really could do all of this at moms." Renea scolded me.

"I do know. She has been good enough to open her house up for my party, it's the least I can do to get as much ready here to save her some of the mess." It had been Craig's idea to have the party there, he thought it would make his mom feel extra included, I had agreed.

"So we still don't get a hint?" Ike begged. "Come onnnnn." He whined. "Don't we get special family privileges?" He wink-winked at Renea.

"Argh." I huffed and started for the door with a cooler of condiments. "Like I've said a *hundred* times, you will know soon enough." My spirits were too high to let their badgering get to me.

I neared the front door and glanced through the bay window at the beautiful day blossoming outside.

The blood drained from my face. I barely caught the cooler before it crashed to the floor.

Obidias stood in front of his shed, staring straight at me. A twisted grimace distorted his unusual face. It was no smile. No, it was something much more frightening.

"Ike!" I cried. *Why today, of all days?* "Obi-" I didn't need to finish before my brother was by my side.

"Shit." Ike breathed.

"What's going on?" Renea joined us with her container full of yolk. "Oh. Damn."

"Stay here." Ike instructed and stepped onto the porch. "Mornin' Obidias, everything okay?" He called to the peculiar old man.

"Need Lydie." Obidias grunted up the hill. "Matter o' facts, why don'ts all y'all come down here." He beckoned with a wave. "We needs to talk."

"Oh, *no way.* Nah-uh. I don't want to go down there." Renea shook her head and back stepped toward the kitchen.

"Lyd," Ike hissed under his breath. "Go, get dad's…"

"On my way." I hated that Ike felt so reliant on dad's weapon, but like Ike, I felt safe knowing we had it. Especially when Obidias, Llewrenni or not, looked so worked up. Besides, it had been a while since we had seen or heard from him. His presence felt foreign, like a strange dream.

"You two don't have to come." Ike assured us as I handed him the gun. He tucked it into the small of his back. "I'll see what he wants."

"I needs *ALL* o' yous." Obidias boomed. Surely he couldn't have heard what Ike had said? But it seemed he had. I was reminded that anything, especially when it came to Obidias, was, in fact, possible.

"And if we don't?" Ike called back. His defiance made me nervous.

"Trust me. I not leadin' you to dangers." Obidias softened. "I needs yous, all o' yous, for your owns safetys."

"Let's go Ike. Remember, in his cabin? He said he was our guardian. Aside from that creepy frown he hasn't given us reason to think otherwise."

"Except he owns part of our land. And besides, that creepy frown is reason enough." Ike said indignant.

"It isn't ours Ike. Let's go." Princeton and Addie wormed between us and darted down the hill toward Obidias.

"Here, take my hand." Ike held it toward Renea and she grasped onto it. We made our way down the hill, past the picnic table, through the blue grass circle, until we were face to face with Obidias. Sunlight sprung from the pond and glimmered along the shed. My eyes flitted to our dock.

I sighed. I wished that Craig and I were sat in those rays, in our own little world, soaking in our heaven. I would much rather that than be confronting a bizarre man and a shed full of static. Magic or no magic. Without worry of Tirips or Etah.

I was ready to get on with an ordinary life.

A life with Craig.

"Sumfin' painful's comin'." Obidias started right in. "An Etahs been roarin' for days." He paused and studied each of us. "Wanted to makes sure yous all be doin' alright. It feels mighty wicked dis mornins." Obidias informed.

"What are you talking about? It's a beautiful day." Ike gestured around us. "Besides, we haven't heard or seen *any* Etah, or any sign of it." He dismissed.

Obidias lifted an incredulous brow at my brother. "No? Maybes you's gettin' comfortable. Not noticin' again. Side's it's not yers, but it be close. Close, close, *close*." Obidias's voice grew harsh and his body trembled. He clenched his hands, closed his eyes and sucked a deep breath in. Once he had composed himself he continued. "I need to give you guys some Evol." He huffed and shook out his hands.

"Evil?!" Renea screeched and peeked over Ike's shoulder.

"No! NO! By golly! Evol! Exacts opposits! It's what's gonna helps you keep evil aways, or least, makes you stronger, in case it does gets too close."

"Evol? Geesh, Obidias. You *know* all of this is new to us. Don't get yourself riled up." Renea confronted him.

"Oh's I just wish you *could* be knowin'." Obidias sighed. "I'm not angries. I just wanna protects yous as much as I can be doin'. It's my jobs." He looked sternly at Renea. "Lydie's had somes before. Yous sees it ain't done her no harms." He sounded calm. "Ike wouldn't be tryin' it though. Don't know why. Tastes purdy good, wouldn't ya say miss Lydie? Side's, I's afraid not havin' somes, is not an options this time." Obidias finished.

"Evol? That's what I had, in there?" I nodded to the wooden door. I wondered if it was a shed inside, full of static, or the magical cabin it had been before. "That's what it's called? Evol.. like.. Love? Backwards... you had said that before... that sometimes.. we just understand things a little backwards?"

I had heard people refer to alcohol as drinking 'courage'. Obidias's concoction had been *nothing* like that. It wasn't stupefying, or intoxicating. Everything about it had been so very, very much the opposite. Truly, like I *had* been filled with love. Invigorating, and empowering. It's taste more delicious than anything I knew to exist, and did in fact, leave me strong and fortified, emotionally and physically.

"Yups. Now y'alls come insides. Where's Ken? He be needin' a dose too. I's feel it."

"Wanna get him Lyd? We'll wait here." Ike urged. I translated it to mean- 'Get help, we'll keep an eye on Obidias.'

"I think dat be a great idea, firsts though, come in. Feels mighty importants you havin' some strength." Obidias opened the door, stooped inside, and held it for us. Ike led Renea. I followed her gasp in.

Once again, pots and soil were gone and Obidias's enchanted dominion sat cozy in front of us.

Molly and Cooper yipped, licked and wagged in greeting, then darted outside to play with Princeton and Addie. Ike took a seat at the worn table. Renea stumbled into his lap just as her legs threatened to give from underneath her.

"Drink." Obidias nudged one of his funky mugs to Renea. Ike reached to block it, but she snatched it and gulped it down before he had a chance.

Immediately the stress that had been cinched across her forehead melted. Her tentative smile gave way to a small 'o' as she took in the cabin and its bizarre intricacies.

"You too, Lydie." Obidias advised. "I fear you be needin' to get Ken *right* now. I feel it fierce."

"Then I'll go." I turned and ducked from the door, too impatient to stay for Obidias's potion. His emphasis on getting Craig spooked me. I wanted to make sure he was alright. Evol or no.

❧ 39 ❧

The early summer air filled my lungs with its sweet scent. The glitter of sun followed a breeze as it tripped over me. I relaxed. Things couldn't be as bad as Obidias had made them sound, could they? I hadn't felt, nor heard any Etah, let alone my own. Their exaggerated presence had been unmistakable before. I paused and listened. The sound of the dogs as they wrestled carried to my ears. A song bird belted it's chorus along with a few errant insects. Old Jake let out a woof as he joined the others. I heard a soft eruption of Renea's muffled giggles from inside the shed, then chuckles from my brother and Obidias joined her.

No, there didn't seem to be anything to worry about after all.

Besides, if there had been Obidias wouldn't be laughing, would he? Never the less, it still made sense to get Craig. Not only would it put Obidias, *and* the rest of us at ease, but it would be good to have him near in case anything crazier than a bewitched shed *did* occur.

And, it was a good excuse to see him before the day's events got under way.

The allayed excitement of our party made its way back to me.

"See? Nothing to worry about." I said out loud to myself. *You can't know that.* My subconscious was quick to scold. *The shed is real, the Tirips and the Etah are real. Something is happening. We've seen it before. All of this is real.*

I shook my head and continued down our road.

A pair of dragon flies danced around me as I met the bridge before the Craig's house. They flew down the creek and disappeared over the pretty yard adorned with weeping willows that trailed their branches through the stream.

Something long and creamy laid over the ground.

Is that a leg?

I stepped onto the bridge and squinted around the last pine between myself and full view. Yes, it was. A feminine one, wet and languid. Then I saw a man.

Craig?

Craig! He was wet too, and bent over her. A pile of clothes sat jumbled nearby. Whose? Hers? Must have been. There was a lot of skin accented by a red tangle of hair.

Jen.

My jaw clenched.

I watched in horror as he swooped from his bent position and placed his lips on hers.

"Craig?!" I shrieked. I couldn't believe what I saw. He jerked his head up, startled.

I didn't wait for his answer. I didn't want to give him the gratification. I took off full force back down Chrysalis drive.

"Lydie!" I barely heard him call behind me. There may have been more, but the rest was lost beneath the sound of my pounding feet, lurching heart, and rushing wind.

And Etah. Pure Etah. Charging straight toward me, and I didn't *care*.

HOW COULD HE?!

I screamed, loud and piercing. I was engulfed by hurt and frustration. I screamed at being had. At believing in my dreams. I screamed into the wind, at the sun that had only moments before assured me of peace. I screamed to the Etah as profanities spewed from my mouth.

I had loved him, and I had actually believed that he loved me too.

"HOW COULD HE?!" I continued my chaotic cry.

And on the day of our engagement party? Had he no shame?? Where had Carolyn been? Or Henry?

But it didn't matter, did it?

He chose *her*. No one else had known we were engaged.

The joke's on me.

I screamed again as the Etah broke from the forest. It's hot scorch of fury and pain licked at my ankles, it sent more anguish, and the image of my parents flashed before me. I was struck with the loss of them as well, again, hard and true.

I stumbled.

Why did I lose those I cared for the most?! They were gone. Would there ever be a time where traumatizing pain wasn't scorched onto my soul??

My eyes burned, and my breath heaved. The malevolent Etah jerked and wound its way over my body, pushing and forcing further despair through my veins. I stumbled again, and this time let myself fall. I didn't care. I had nothing left to lose.

The roaring of a thousand wildfires, obliterating everything in hungry destruction burned over my skin, and through my ears. I crouched, sobbing, trying to shield myself from the horrible onslaught. My personal pain and frustration fueled and whipped with the Etah's hatred. My throat closed in fierce constraint, the fire in my eyes spilling over into an unquenching ocean of tears.

Then it all stopped. Just stopped.

And it was *worse*.

Much, much worse.

A putrid chasm pierced through my heart, into the very center of my being, and split it wide, with a great gaping dark wretchedness. The blackness of pain and fury, a pure, empty nothingness reached its talons into my soul and slowly drug it from me, coursing and writhing, with a bellowing scream from which no sound came… for the vacuumed void had abolished it all.

How could I ever survive? How would I ever survive?

I cowered, and quaked. My lips chattering and stuttering against my teeth in that silence.

My body, starved of life, forced a gasp.

I opened my eyes, wide.

The sunlight pierced blurry and magnified through my tears. My body was forced a wretch of gasp again. It heaved the huge devastating pitch of soul racking sobs. I relented to them. The pain of them, their sear upon my heart a welcome retreat from the hollow nothingness evaporating my soul moments before.

The heat of my body reminded me I could be stronger than the Etah, that I could outsmart it with my psyche, but I hesitated, nothing had ever felt so real. Could I really crawl from beneath its bleak darkness as it consumed me?

My legs shook as I stood myself up.

I swiped at my tears, and breathed a last deep shutter. The Etah's icy tendrils squeezed my temples. I struggled to inhale again.

Craig was gone. My parents had been taken from me, but I was alive.

I breathed in deep. I was still full of life.

"I AM ALIVE!" I screamed at the top of my lungs. The black smear of Etah flinched. "I AM ALIVE!" I triumphed as it slipped down from my body further. I didn't care if anyone heard me. I didn't care if Jen and Craig laughed.

It was my truth, and I held on to it with all of my might.

Brief recognition of the Etah's sting burned. My heart knocked in painful thuds inside of me. I kicked my feet- hard, kicked its inkiness as fast as I could, and I ran.

As if nothing could ever stop me.

✌ 40 ✍

I reached the shed and tumbled inside, my breath failing to satiate my lungs. Grief seeped where strength had coursed moments before. I slumped onto Obidias's worn floorboards. My war with fear and fury held rational thought hostage.

Before Renea and Ike had time to react Obidias poured Evol down my throat, straight from his kettle.

"Lydie?!" Ike jumped up and nearly toppled Renea to the floor.

"I'sa knew it!" Obidias shouted. "I's knew it! How did I not realize that's what it'd be!" He fussed over me and continued to pour a never-ending stream. I coughed and sputtered, he wouldn't stop.

Branches whipped against the windows and my Etah's roar and rumble shook the walls. It had followed me. The enchantment of the cabin wavered. Glimpses of flower pots materialized where the couch should have been, bags of soil took over the colorful hearth, then it solidified again.

I couldn't bring myself to care though. I didn't try to slow the hate that birthed the monstrous destruction. I hurt too much. Its dark scourge satisfied the anger that quaked through my body.

Hate sliced a satisfying numbness into my pain.

"What's wrong with her?! What's happening?!" Ike yelled at Obidias.

"Lyd?" Renea quivered while she smoothed hair from my face.

"The Evol ought be havin' strengths an' love kickin' back in to hers. I knews I shoulda mades you had some 'fors you left, but that Etah wasn't bein' yours..." Obidias said to me, continuing to force me to drink. "I don't gets it." His brows screwed together in confusion.

"What the hell is happening?!" My brother demanded. He bent and ran his hands over my arms and legs, investigating my limbs. "Come back, Lyd." He made a raspy plea.

Finally, mercifully, Obidias set the kettle down.

"I..." Gasp, "I ccccc....." gasp, cough, "can't believe he'd do that to me!" I sputtered amidst my agony fueled tears.

"Oh- my- God." Renea stood. "Who? Ken? *What* did my brother do?!"

"Did he hurt you?" Ike stiffened. "Lyd! Hey!" He shook my shoulder. "Did he hurt YOU?!" Impatient rage disfigured his face.

The dark nothing of the Etah quieted outside.

But still, I heard it, and worse, I *felt* it. It's cold claws scrambled along my back, then slid a thousand needle pricks over my shoulders and down my arms. A frozen sear gaped where it grazed. Further and further. Reaching. Exploring.

Searching my inner most sacred parts of me. Seeking the heart of my soul. My Tirips. Deadened tendrils of my being laid in its wake.

It meant to destroy me. Destroy my very essence.

Still, I couldn't bring myself to care.

I dropped my head, and willed myself to succumb to its nothingness. Then, maybe then, the pain would dissipate.

My brother's hands twitched as they worked over me, then he snatched them back. A burn struck along my arm and the Etah's black haze reached from it to swipe at him. Horror swamped his face and a teeny blue light shot away from him. It hovered near a window, small and nearly obscure.

"Lydie! Don't give in!" Ike shook my shoulders. The blue spot bolted toward him, then weaved around us.

His Tirips, I recognized. My body jerked. Another, separate war struck hot like a match. Love for my brother made a meager attempt to push at the hatred consuming me. Confusion overwhelmed my consciousness. I dropped further onto the floor, sure that any given moment I'd sink into it.

"Why isn't the Evol helping?!" Ike yelled, desperate.

"It's gots to." Obidias mumbled. "I think it might be startin'."

"I... hate... him, I hate...." The Etah made me labor for breath. Short stagnant heaves were all I could draw. "Leave me alone! It's not worth... Your Tirips, your Spirit." I mustered. The ink lashed out at Ike again, then, turned and swiped for Renea.

"Gets back! Infectious!" Obidias charged between Renea and I, but it was too late for Ike, he was, after all, my good big brother.

"I'll kill him." Ike's eyes flashed.

The severity of his words, along with the fortifying Evol at work, gave me an edge over the Etah.

"Ike, no!" I pushed myself up. My legs shook as I climbed to my feet. "Don't! Oh-no- I'm sorry!"

"Lydie stop. Don't apologize." Ike snapped, his face hardened to an indiscernible mask. His eyes were dark. I could barely recognize the volatile man as my brother. He must have refused Obidias's drink again. "You didn't do anything." He sneered. "If that mother-UGH, if he hurt you in the slightest, I'll kill him!"

"Ike!" Renea and I shouted.

"Listen to what you're saying," I continued. "Craig's one of your closest friends…" My Etah snaked its way inside of him. It writhed through the air, connecting our bodies with its darkness. The faint red of my Tirips hazed from my skin. It pushed against the Etah, forcing it further into Ike. His threat toward Craig bore the frozen mark of the Etah. I was afraid it was more than idle, that under the hatred of the Etah anything was possible.

"*Was* my friend. But if he hurt you…" Ike stormed to the door.

"Ike! Wait! Come back. He didn't…" That caught his attention, he turned, and looked at me. "He didn't… *hurt* me… exactly." The Etah was losing its battle against Obidias's strength, concern for my brother, and my Tirips. But it's shadow still weighed in my heart where pain lingered. I knew, for at least the moment, I was safe. My brother was the Etah's focus. "I saw him kiss Jen." The Etah flexed in both of us as the words left my lips.

"*What*?!" Renea grabbed Ike's wrist and tugged him from the door. "You've got it wrong Lyd. He can't stand her. He told me yesterday how glad he was that he had found you. How it amazed him that he and Jen had ever been together, let alone lasted as long as they had. Hind sight's twenty-twenty."

"I *know* what I saw." The scene played in my memory and chilled the warmth of my Tirips. "She was sprawled by the creek. He leaned over her. His mouth was on hers. I saw it with my own *eyes*!" The cold swell of hate contorted and twisted inside of me again.

"No! No way." Renea refused. "Something's wrong. That's not right. It can't be..."

The smoky trail lunged from Ike toward me.

"Lydie! Don'ts give in again!" Obidias grabbed the kettle and drained it over me, making a huge mess until I begrudgingly opened my mouth. "Ike! Drinks some o' this. Quick!" He ordered.

The Etah grasped my ankles.

Awareness flicked through Ike's eyes. He grabbed the kettle himself and gulped as he pulled Renea until their bodies crowded over me, and shoved me to the ground.

"We're here Lydie. We love you." Ike pulled another long swallow, returning to his protective self. Renea, pinned next to him, nodded her head.

"We'll check it out, I just *know* something isn't right." She assured.

"Damn right it's not!" My ankles burned where the Etah scratched and pulled, dragging itself over me, seducing me with demise.

"Lydie, if he kissed her, then he doesn't deserve you. It doesn't make you any less of a person, we love you, you'll find someone better." Ike tried to soothe.

"There is no one better! I don't want anyone else. I loved him so much, I've never felt what I feel with him! I was going to marry him!" My face contorted as the reality struck me again. "I trusted him! I trusted him with every part of me, with all of me!" The nails of the Etah burned into my throat and my breath hitched.

"Lydie comes back." Obidias coaxed. Renea stroked my cheek and Ike rubbed my arms.

"Don't worry Lyd, I'll take care of it." Ike kept his voice calm, trying to distract me, bring me back from the dark.

It didn't work. I wasn't strong enough. The pain of seeing Craig over her burned through Obidias's Evol, or any of the love I held for my brother.

Then the idea of my brother not being enough to help, immediately brought my parents to mind. Not only were they gone, I knew it would disappoint them, that I put a boyfriend before my brother. I felt even worse about myself. I was weakened too far to defend myself. My breath heaved faster. Hot tears forged over my face.

"He's right Miss Lydie, you ought not worry. I's so sorry I let dis happen. I shouldn't hab never let you go witout strength." Obidias heaved a great sigh. "I'm your Llewrenni."

The Etah slid a tentative coil toward Obidias, then instantly jumped away.

"Do you hear that?" Renea brought her head up.

Her Tirips bopped and weaved with Ike's. Seeing it reminded me of my own, and of exactly who I was, regardless of what Craig meant in my life. I shook my head, trying to pry away from the nasty dark in my mind, I watched it shrink low around my body. My parents weren't truly gone. They were always near, somehow, some way. Even Obidias had said. Even *they* had said. They loved me, no matter what. Even if I couldn't see them, or hear them, I knew they were here for me, for us. The Etah's pull lessened.

"I don't hea-" Ike started.

"Shhhh! Listen!" Renea hissed. The sound was unmistakable.

A shrill wail in the distance. A siren.

It drew closer, it's scream increased. We listened. It didn't fade, instead it grew louder, it's screech drawing near.

Renea sprung to the window. Ike sat up, but didn't leave my side. My Tirips swooped back into the cabin and hovered above him, reassuring me. Waiting for me to realize everything, even if only eventually, would be okay.

"My God! Dad!" Panic grated Renea's voice. She ran out of the door, and bolted up the hill.

Ike darted out to follow her. "Come on Lyd!" He beckoned. Remarkably I somehow made my way outside. I swiveled my head, in search of the Etah, but all I could hear was the siren.

Obidias stood in his door way, his deep-set eyes shifted between sadness and fear.

"Keeps safes." He mumbled. "Keeps real safe. There's nothin' I cans do anymores." Then he dipped inside and shut the door.

"We'll get to the bottom of this. *All* of *this*." Ike pulled me behind him. Renea had jumped in her car and peeled by us down the driveway. We scrambled up the hill, Ike's strong arms righting me if my legs faltered. We clambered into dad's truck, then tore down the road to the Craig's house.

❦ 41 ❧

The sirens wailed closer as we pulled in front of Craig's home. Renea flung herself from her car and shouted in hysterics for her father.

Craig stood on the front stoop, still wet from the creek.

"Renea!" He called as she ran into the house. She didn't stop.

I hardened a resolve of indifference, until his eyes locked on mine. Tears burned, hot and heavy and turned the world into an underwater blur. Before either of us could say anything the ambulance pulled between us.

"Wait here, I'll see what's going on, what I can do. And Renea...." Ike stormed toward the house. I didn't have the gall or energy to argue.

Carolyn. I gasped. How could I stand there feeling sorry for myself? What if she was hurt? I needed to make sure she, and Henry for that matter, were okay. Both of them. Despite how much their son had hurt me. I shook my head, swiped my tears, and rounded the ambulance.

The EMT's maneuvered a gurney on their way out of the house. Man they were fast.

Red hair spilled over the stretcher. I gasped. "Jen?" I managed a harsh whisper.

"I tried to tell you." Craig moved to my side and pressed his damp arms around me.

"Wait. No." I shook my head. "What?" I didn't know what he meant. I stepped back. "I don't…"

"Ride with me." He ordered, then turned, grabbed my hand and pulled me toward his jeep.

"But Ike, Ren…" I felt confused and uncertain. What had *happened*? He had just kissed her, now she was on the way to the hospital? Had my Etah hurt her? A sliver of shame pricked me.

But he had been kissing her. My subconscious reminded me.

And he *demanded* I follow him? That wasn't like him.

"Wait!" I dug my heals into the gravel.

He turned, his eyelids heavy. "Lydie." His voice frayed and he jerked his head toward her. "We've got to go." He whipped back toward his car. "I'll explain on the way."

The shame of my reaction, and the love I saw for her in his teary eyes made me feel so small. And embarrassed. How could I stand to ride with him? No matter what had happened.

"Please?" He begged. His tears didn't just brim, they poured down his face. I shook my head to clear it again, then strode to the passenger door. I did care about him, and genuinely wanted to know what had happened.

Besides, he owed me an apology.

Truthfully, I suppose I owed Jen one, if my Etah had indeed injured her. Just because he had reconciled with her, didn't mean I wanted either of them to be hurt. Okay, maybe I imagined hurtful things, but not a trip to the emergency room.

Stupid Etahs. Stupid Jen. Stupid Craig. Why did I love him?

I took a deep breath, jerked the jeep open and climbed inside.

The moment my legs were in he tore down the road after the ambulance.

"I love you." He whispered.

When I didn't answer he said it louder. "I love you, Lydie Craig."

"Lydie Craig?! Yeah. Right." I blew him off.

He choked on a sniff.

I warred inside of myself. I wanted to comfort him. I wanted to tell him it was going to all be alright. But *I* didn't know if it would be alright, for me, *let alone* him, or his choice of girlfriend.

And he had been my fiancé!

I bit my lip and pressed my feet to the floor board to keep from stomping them. My frustration pinched my forehead. It was all I could do to keep from screaming every thought, rational or not, at him.

Jen was hurt. He was hers. It didn't matter anymore. I shook my head and resolved to ignore him.

The Etah's scream blared and squelched loud, competing with the siren. I didn't want to face it again, especially when Obidias's Evol wasn't near, nor the people that loved me, truly loved me.

"How can you say that?" My voice cracked.

"I wish you could have seen. I wish you could have been there. I wish Jen hadn't been so freaking foolish." He groaned with frustration, then clenched his jaw and pulled over to the side of the road.

The Etah was near. I could hear it's scourge wreak havoc on its way to us. I turned my head from Craig and stared out from the window, trying to silence the frustration that beckoned the hatred.

A tan cow stared back, chewing her cud, oblivious to the turmoil in the world around her.

I corrected myself. *My world.*

"Lydie," Craig reached for my hand. I flinched, but let him take it. *What am I doing?* "Lydie, *God.*" He heaved again, then paused. I slid my eyes to him. He dropped his head back on the seat, and inhaled a deep breath. He looked at me. His eyes pleaded with mine. It was hard to keep my gaze steady. But I tried. I wanted to get to the bottom of it all. "God I'm so thankful you're here." He lifted my hand to his lips and laid them softly on top of my knuckles.

"Please. Just tell me what's going on?" I had wanted to sound strong, and indifferent, but my voice shook.

"I'm trying." He kissed my hand again then reached toward my face. I pulled back, not ready for his intimacy. *Did he want to kiss me?* No matter what state Jen was in, how could he? She was on her way to the hospital for God knows what. *And he was on top of her.* My hardened resolve against the Etah weakened, it roared in response. A guttural hiss startled me from outside of my window. I turned to the peaceful bovine. There she still stood, peacefully chewing her cud, and there on the road between she and I sat a vulture. It stared straight at me with its wings fanned, clucked, then hissed again. It's feet carried it side to side in a disturbing little dance, it's eyes locked with mine.

Cold skittered over me. "Drive. Please? You can tell me on the way."

He pulled back like I had wounded him. His eyebrows crinkled and he plunged the pedal into a fierce jerk toward Nepenthe. We were going fast. His knuckles blanched on the steering wheel. We swooped into erratic wide swings through the bends in the country road.

He gave me a quick, earnest look, then turned to watch the road. "I know how it must have looked." He had regained his composure. "But you have to know it wasn't Lydie. *God* it wasn't." He cleared his throat, "Jen showed up drunk, *plastered* drunk, this morning. She bombarded me, going on and on about how she had never gotten over me. That I should be with her. She kept trying to convince me I was wasting my time with you. I told her she was wrong, and that I loved you with all of my heart. I reminded her that we were done a long time ago, and that everything happens for a reason. I tried to assure her that she will find the right person for her, just like I have found you." He looked at me again. My shoulders relaxed, and my skin regained warmth where I had felt the Etah's frozen sting from before.

Maybe it hadn't been how it appeared? Maybe he hadn't been kissing her? But, I know what I saw! Shame pierced me, along with fury. The Etah screamed. *The Etah. Oh God, my Etah* had *hurt her.* I realized. I swallowed hard and nodded, urging him to tell me more. He jerked the wheel and swerved to miss another vulture.

"She was drunk, and frantic." He shook his head. "She said she would do anything to make sure you knew you weren't for me. That she and I were meant to be. I told her that's just not possible. I told her that you were who I loved, and that we're getting married. She stormed outside. I followed her to try and calm her down. She threw herself at me, stripping her clothes off. I tried to stop her. When I realized it was no use, I turned to leave. She screamed when I didn't come back. She shouted, 'Fine! You're not worth it anyway! LIFE'S not worth it!' Then she dove into the creek. She was so drunk." He took a deep breath and clenched his jaw. "She slipped, and hit one of the rocks full on." He heaved once. Swallowed. Inhaled and held it. His jaw flexed again.

The color drained from my face, and my mouth hung open.

"By the time I reached her she was floating, face down, and limp." He looked to me again. The last piece of story clicked into place. "That's when you saw us."

Is this really what had happened? My thoughts questioned. It hadn't been my Etah after all? He was telling the truth. I was sure. Or at least I wanted to be.

He held my gaze. Tears betrayed me and I attempted to blink them away. When it didn't work, I looked ahead. Another stupid vulture was in the road.

In our lane.

"Craig!" I cried.

He swerved to miss it.

And then there was Obidias, standing in the middle of the road, staring straight at us.

Craig swerved again, but we were going too fast.

❧ 42 ❧

A deep familiar peace surrounded me. My eye lids felt heavy. I tried to open them, they refused. That felt familiar too. I gave in to the pulsing warmth. Serenity. I let my eyes rest.

"Lydie." My mom called in her good-morning sing song voice. "Lydie, wake up…"

"Mom?" Anxiously I tried to open them again. Something didn't feel right.

"Mom? I can't see, something's wrong."

A rush of confusion blurred my tranquility. I drifted between the sensations.

Finally, the calm prevailed once more.

"Lydie, I'll always be here." Her voice surrounded me. "Don't forget."

"She'll be gettin' here, just gives her a moments." A different voice encouraged, it's familiar caramel dialect tugged at my memory.

"Lydie, it's time to come back." Ike's voice this time.

"Lydie, we won't ever be far, all you have to do is remember." Now it was my father that reassured me.

What is going on? I tried again to open my eyes, sure that my effort would be in vain, but it wasn't. Drops of rainbow colored light infused familiar images.

My parents! They were here! And Craig, and Ike. Even Renea, and Ada. Obidias too, he stood, and nodded knowingly. I looked past him, confused. More figures were blurred in the distance. I could barely make out a couple of friends from school. And there was Caroline and Henry. Even Brit was there, and Jen.

The colors darkened and grayed, then my eyes fell on Craig. Their brilliance returned.

"Where are we? What are we doing here?" I asked, looking to everyone.

"You be realized truth, Miss Lydie." Obidias stated.

"Truth?" I stared at him.

"You realized *we* is happenin' to life. We not helpless victims that life be happenin' to. Once you realize that…" His broad grin morphed his wrinkles into folds like a comfortable well-loved blanket. "You find *truth*."

"Truth?" I asked again. I looked around to everyone, and realized their eyes were on me. Why weren't they asking questions too? What was this about?

"Truth Lydie." Obidias continued. "What somes be callin' peace. Somes calls enlightenments. Somes even call Heavens. At firsts, when yous awakenin', becomin' aware of possibilities, when yous first realize no matters what you can choose to be okays, yous start realizin' yous can be choosin' peace, or, feeling and being love. Happiness. We all gets down at times, we all feels happy at times, but when yous becomes aware it really be you that chooses how things effect yous for the mosts parts, it can be scary, downright frightenin' to know yous be such a major role of happenin' to life!" He watched me, and gave me a moment to let it sink in.

I was familiar with some of what he said, from when he had tried to explain it to Ike and I in the shed. I thought about how much it hurt when we lost our parents. About how Ike and I had found this little piece of Heaven, how good it was to feel well, despite the grief that had been so prevalent in our lives.

He cleared his throat, and continued. "The ways human bodies 'xperience things affects us. Leads us to believin' life is happenin' to us. But once yous gets in touch with yours true, spirit self, yous realize you not be a victim to yours life, you can realize you very much contributes the source yours life is created from. Do you see? You be in touch with the Divine, the very cloth we all be threads of. You touch Heaven."

Gently, Obidias lifted his hand, the same colored red heart glow of my Tirips poured from his palm. He held it over my chest. "It's all theres insides yous Miss Lydie. The yous that's part o' life, more than that, the yous that understands that there really not be anything that be separate all us. Once yous realize that, that's touchin' Heaven."

He concentrated, the Tirips glow growing warmer and brighter between us. He waved his hands over me, spreading the light in waves that enveloped my body.

He stepped back and his face pulled tight. A grimace replaced where his smile had been.

"And, then there be the opposites. The dark sides, where the Etah reign, where bodies be so fueled of anguish, and miseries, well, that's... not bein' able to realize sacredness be *within* yous. It's as somes be callin' it... damnation or Hell. It's lettin' yerself stay drownin' in painful places and wretchedness, lettin' it be a way of living. When a body perceives a hurt, or anger, or a fear, it be real. Even if it be only real in your head, or imaginations. For you it be real. Inside yous don't knows a difference. Same be true for peace, and loves, and joys. If you be full o' turbulence, but takes a moment to find peace, think a thankful thing, a grateful or lovin' thought, the light it be bringin' to your soul be real. Yous touch Spirit. Then delvin' deeper intos Heavens instead of Hells. Look into you, you'll see, it's all right there miss Lydie, all right there."

"Why are you here then? Why would I need a Llewrenni?" I questioned the strange little man, whose wisdom seeped deeper than all that he spoke of.

"Well it be like dis yous sees, when a body comes to be more and more harmonized with their truths, yous starts realizin' 'xactly how entwined every one of us be, and *everything* be. Then you start noticin' us, your helpers nearby. Most people don't be noticin' their Llewrenni be 'round, but us guardians, we always be every wheres all o' the times."

"What do you mean? How is all of this possible?" I asked.

"Lydie, there always be the Divine energy swirlin' constant around us. Heck! We be nothing but swirlin' bundles o' that energy ourselves. You." He tapped his finger on the center of my forehead. "Me." He tapped his own. "Just 'cause we can't be seein' it all o' the times with these human eyes, don't mean it not be there. Think o' the lil' ole earthworm. He ain't got no eyes, but does that mean there be no thing as sight? So very *much* o' life, so much of *existin'* be beyond understanin' while we be in human bodies. Iffin truths be told we all be weaved together by the Divine, the Enivid. That be the very thread that be runnin' through us all. It's thar, right thar insides yous." Obidias thumped his chest and I felt the reverberation inside of my own. "Your inner well, da spirit in which you draws yours very life, yours essence. We each be part o' the whole, not separates as these bodies sometimes be portryin'. Our energies all be one, we just each an expression fillin' different purposes, with these here bodies as tools. But it all be right inside each 'o us. All o' it, in all o' us." His words echoed and resounded around me.

Craig strode toward me, then wrapped his arms over me. He laid his lips to my head in that comforting manner of his. A rush of light enveloped us. Our Tirips. Everyone melted away except for he and I. We were left surrounded in the splendor of our whole. The warmth of our Tirips melded, lighting over my skin and into my soul. Our soul. I smiled at the thought. Is this how it could be? Is this how it was?

Our Heaven.

"Craig?" Other than our brilliant light, I couldn't see much of anything, although I could feel him against me.

"We're meant to be together, you know that, don't you?" Craig swaddled me against him. I returned an eager nod, though something nagged in the back of my mind. I couldn't remember what it was. How could everything feel so right while laced with confusion. He tilted my chin towards his.

When he looked into my eyes, I could see every future, and every past, that our souls had ever journeyed together.

"You won't forget me, will you?" He asked

"No... How could I?" I replied, dazed he would ask such a ridiculous question, especially now.

"Because, most people do. They get a glimpse, a taste of understanding, then give it up. They give up at the first sign of Etah. It's too much for them. So they wrap themselves up in their cocoon of numbness. Back to where they started from, only to try and understand all over again. Such a vicious cycle."

"I'm not most people. You know that."

"I know Lydie, but please... promise me you won't forget."

It had all been so much. There was no way I would ever lose this.

After all, I had found Heaven.

I nestled my head against his shoulder.

"What if we just never leave? What if we don't have to. Why should we ever go back to anywhere, this is perfect." I nuzzled into his neck. The pulse along his throat beat it's life dance against my cheek.

"Because I need you Lydie. You have to come back with me. We have to go back. We have life to fulfill. We haven't met this time Lydie. Please, come back to me?"

"What are you talking about, we're here now, I'm here now. You're beginning to sound like Obidias." Confusion set its icy teeth in me.

Craig jerked from me, my arms flailed and I squeezed them tighter, but it was too late. Grimy mist replaced the empty space where he had been.

Being ripped from part of my soul pierced my heart. I tried to reach out, but my arms refused my command. They wouldn't move. The red of my Tirips blazed one last beat, then I was engulfed in a void. Surrounded by utter dark, my severed heart stole my breath.

I must be dead, my thoughts whispered. Reality and consciousness eluded me.

I let myself drift, willing the nothingness to take away the devastation in my soul.

Excruciating agony perforated everywhere! The pain was *real*. It scorched through every part of me, my being, my spirit, *and my body*.

"Come back Lydie," His disembodied voice beckoned. "Don't forget. I'm here, waiting. I know you'll find me, you always have, we always will."

"Craig!" I screamed. "Noooooo! I can't do this!" He was gone.

They all were. I was left, alone in oblivion, with nothing but torment to cling to.

Kathryn Eli

ᥱ 43 ᥣ

The weight of my body tugged and pulled at me, magnifying my torture. It felt foreign, I'd been away too long. I tried once more to peer into the saturated black. It worked and muted light filtered through my eyelids.

Foreign, monotonous tones stung my ears. I didn't understand. Nothing made sense. I struggled against bright flashes with each attempt to open my eyes. I squinted until my lashes allowed a dim, unfocused blur, then slowly, carefully, I opened them. Bubbles of black splotches broke against white above me. A familiar pocked ceiling. Confusion worried my forehead, the movement breathed fresh pain over my body. I was in bed, but it wasn't my own. White sheets peeked from under a light blue blanket. Definitely not mine.

And there were rails… Oh, not again. This wasn't good.

My eyes abandoned tentative exploration and ricocheted around the room. Gadgets and machines greeted me with digital faces, wove between tubes and wires. Horrified, I realized I was entangled in their web. A wire was leached to my finger, a tube was bound to my arm.

My arms!

Violent abrasions were thrown over my skin, masking deep jewel colored bruises.

"Lydie!" Ike's voice broke into my disorientation. I tried to turn my head toward his voice but searing pain shot through my neck and down my back. "Careful, not too quickly." He urged.

Using my eyes, I searched for him again and found him next to me. Relief at seeing him was thwarted by a bandage taped to his forehead, accompanied by a large plum splotch that grazed the lower half of his jaw. Other tiny wounds had bit him in various places.

"Wha-" My words felt cemented inside of me. I never knew speaking could take such effort. "Wha-w-what happened?" My voice was husky and dry, my throat devoid of moisture.

"Lydie, we were in an accident,"

Accident.

A floodgate of memories released. We had been driving, moving here. They were in the front, Ike and I in the back. He sulked, and pouted, upset we were drug along. We were too old to be forced to move, he had argued with them. Really, he hadn't wanted to leave Brit. Brit, but, hadn't she hurt him? It was all muddled, I couldn't remember what was real, and what wasn't. Facts were quickly slipping from my grasp like sand set loose in the wind.

I remembered I hadn't minded the idea, the move. I thought change would be the perfect way to start my world as an adult. Just what I needed to try and sort out what I wanted to do with myself for the rest of my life.

That was then. 'The Dent'.

Then I remembered, we had found our Heaven. That happiness is a choice, we choose what we focus on. Right or wrong is usually just a matter of being different. And *Craig*, he was mine. I was his. Then the vultures, the weaving, and swerving, *my parents*.

"Where's Craig?! Is he okay? How could this happen again?" I protested.

"Craig??" Ike looked concerned. "Lydie listen, I'm here... We were in an accident."

"We? Is Renea okay? You weren't even with us?"

"Renea?? No one else was with us, Lyd. Just you, me, Mom, and Dad." Ike's voice broke.

"Where's Craig?!" Panic flipped in my stomach. I couldn't imagine what would cause my brother to say that. *Where was Craig!?*

"Lydie..." He put his hand to his mouth and tried to cover a sob with a cough. He ducked his head to hide his tears. But they fell, fast, and straight from his face. "I have to tell you something."

Dread came over me. I didn't want to hear it. A vicious sense of de-ja-vu tugged my memories.

"No! Ike! *Don't!* Where's Craig?! I need to know he's okay!"

Ike stared at me, straight through his tears. His eyebrows worked furiously. "Please Lydie, you need to listen, I have to tell you something. Please-"

"Ike!" It hurt to raise my voice, but I managed. Why was this happening again? I looked away. A bedraggled man with tufts of dirty snow hair drifted by on a stretcher. The comforting familiarity pulled at my heart. "Obidias!" I shouted. The realization that I needed him as well struck me fierce. He would help. He would explain this to me. He would know what to say, he would know how to take this pain away, take me away, back to my heaven.

The man didn't move, but I was sure it was him. One of the nurses held his stocking cap clenched in her hand.

I pushed against the bed rails, trying to lift myself. Fresh pain shot throughout me.

"Lydie! You have to stay here! You're hurt!" My brother commanded. "Who's Obidias? Or Craig? I'll get a nurse. I'll get your doctor. But first I need to tell you- "

I went limp in defeat. I closed my eyes. "I don't know why you're acting like you don't remember." I cringed with pain and frustration.

"Remember? Can you remember? We were in an accident Lydie, and… Mom and Dad," he sucked in a deep breath, "they didn't make it, they're gone." He blurted. More tears betrayed his attempt to remain steady and collected.

They filled my eyes too. Why would he do this to me? "Of course I remember! How could I forget, Ike?! It changed our whole lives. So much has happened, can't you remember? I miss them so much too, but I need you here now, I need you to tell me where Craig is." *Maybe his accident had affected his memory? Why else would he do this? Why couldn't he remember??*

"Nothing's happened since then Lydie, except me sitting here night and day worrying that you might leave me too." He croaked in a harsh whisper.

I shook my head. "No..."

He continued, "You've been in a coma Lydie. You couldn't have known they were gone. You've been unconscious." He dropped his chin. "Maybe they were wrong." He wondered under his breath. He arched his eyebrows when he looked at me again. "You're my sister Lydie, and as much as we get on each other's nerves, you're my best friend. I need you." A fluent slip of tears poured over his face again.

Commotion in the hall distracted us both. The nurses stopped alongside of the old man and yelled for help, calling for doctors. A couple of them bent over him and began CPR.

"Obidias, No!" I pushed myself further this time. Pain clawed at me, but I sat up through it. I swung my legs from the bed and pulled at the tubes and wires. I managed one step before Ike's arms encircled me.

But one step was all I needed.

It was him. *Obidias.*

Horrified, I watched the commotion stop as they stepped back in nodded confirmation to one another.

He was gone?

"You've got to get back in bed." My brother said with gentle force. "He was homeless and suffered from Hypothermia. I overheard them when they brought him in."

"Hypothermia?? It's the middle of summer!" I felt close to Hysteria. My world was completely upside down. Nothing made sense anymore.

Obidias, my Llewrenni.

What kind of cruel trick was my brother playing at?

I sobbed, hard, racking sobs. Each threw agony across my body. But I couldn't help it. They kept coming. Ike laid me back in bed, then stayed, with his arms around me. I hugged him back, my hot tears drenching his shirt.

"It's February, Lyd." He sat, and pulled his chair as close to me as he could. He took a deep breath. Words tumbled from his mouth, explaining everything I didn't want to hear. "Can you remember? We were moving to Grandma's, we were almost all the way here when we hit the ice. They went quickly Lydie."

It was true.

I knew it. I felt it.

I remembered now. But it felt like so long ago, why didn't he remember everything else? Everything that had happened since we had moved here? How could this happen again? It had been such a long while since then, hadn't it?

Am I wrong? I questioned myself.

What about Obidias? My heart broke for him again. He was gone.

My parents are gone. Fresh pain fueled my racking sobs.

My Llewrenni, he must have known, he must have known that my parents had died, and that I would need help, that I would need him, that I would need Craig.

Craig... His memory came to me again, so real, and authentic. But according to my brother none of it was real? How could that be? I hadn't met him? Or had I? *Find me,* he had said. I remembered our last touch before he had been ripped away. But it was growing hazy, all of it, like a dream stolen within moments of waking. I clung to the ghost of it. It had felt so real. He had meant so much to me, didn't he? Something nagged in my memory.

But I'm here now. I'm here now and my parents are gone. Or are they? I remember dreaming of them too. *They're not gone, none of them are.* Isn't that what Obidias had tried to show me? It's only different. What we focus on is what we see.

They're with me now. Feel them. I instructed myself.

Peace washed over me in waves, growing larger and larger. I wondered if Ike could feel it too. I laid back. My pain eased a bit. Ike stroked my head, like mom used to. "We'll make it Lyd, somehow. We've got to." He sighed. "I'll get a job. I'll take care of you. At least we have Grandma's house. We'll start over."

Cold, and lonely, the morning exhaled its first breath along the hospital window. I thought I saw Obidias, his white familiar tuft of hair, then realized how impossible that was. It was only a cloud. Ike's hands were warm, one on my face, the other on my hand.

Grandma's house, yes. We had Grandma's house. And life. We still had our lives, and each other, and Heaven, if we would choose, we'd have Heaven.

"I see she's decided to join us." A familiar drawl rolled into the room.

"Doc!" Ike shot from his chair and jumped up to greet him. "She's awake! You did it! You didn't let her leave."

In an uncommon show of gratitude Ike slung his arms around the man. I maneuvered my head to try to see. But it was no use, my body was too weak. Finally Ike stepped back, and gestured toward me.

"Lyd, this is Dr. Kendall, he saved your life."

My heart trembled.

"Good morning Lydie." Golden hair moved into view above me.

"C-cc-Craig?" I asked.

"Sorry Doc, she keeps asking for somebody named Craig."

"Hmm... Interesting." His voice neared. "Who's this Craig you've been asking for Lydie?" He questioned. "If things worked a little backwards you would both know me by Craig. It's my first name. I'm Craig Kendall, at your service."

A forehead, wrinkled with questioning moved further into my view, followed by a familiar dimple that ushered a smile across his face.

"Your name is Craig?" My brother asked.

A liquid pool set of eyes met mine, then flicked to my brother.

"That's right." He nodded then looked to me again. Those crystalline blues squinted a little, with something akin to recognition.

"Hello, Lydie." He breathed, his voice dropped soft. "It's good to see you, I've waited a long time to look into these eyes of yours."

About the Author

Kathryn Eli is a Northwest transplant to Georgia, where she found her own little world in the middle of nowhere. Her husband, their two dogs, and three cats keep her in good and amusing company when she's not paddle boarding, playing her harp, or dancing with the muses of creation.

Made in the USA
Middletown, DE
05 September 2021